THE D

AS **I WAS** reaching for the p
up and before I even spo
neck. I don't know what it was, but there was a hollow, creepy electronic hum on the line . . .

"Peachtree Investigations," I said.

"I want to talk to Gunnar." It was that Darth Vader voice again.

"He's not here. But he got your message. The problem is—"

"Eight o'clock. I'm only dealing with Gunnar," the voice said. "No cops, no flunkies. If I don't see a big white mustache, there's no deal."

"Listen! Gunnar's not—"

The line went dead.

I hung up the phone, cursed, took a deep breath, and called the homicide unit . . .

"It's Sunny Childs," I said. "We need to talk."

ATLANTA GRAVES

IN THE TRADITION OF KINSEY MILLHONE AND V.I. WARSHAWSKI . . . A SMART NEW MYSTERY SERIES STARRING SHARP-TONGUED PI SUNNY CHILDS!

"Sunny Childs is an unwilling liar, but she's also a wham-bam thank you ma'am great read."
—J.A. Jance, author of NAME WITHHELD

"Ruth Birmingham has established herself as the Queen of Atlanta crime fiction. Read and enjoy."
—Fred Willard, author of DOWN ON PONCE

MORE MYSTERIES FROM THE
BERKLEY PUBLISHING GROUP...

CAT CALIBAN MYSTERIES: She was married for thirty-eight years. Raised three kids. Compared to that, tracking down killers is easy . . .

by D. B. Borton

ONE FOR THE MONEY	TWO POINTS FOR MURDER
THREE IS A CROWD	FOUR ELEMENTS OF MURDER
FIVE ALARM FIRE	SIX FEET UNDER

ELENA JARVIS MYSTERIES: There are some pretty bizarre crimes deep in the heart of Texas—and a pretty gutsy police detective who rounds up the unusual suspects . . .

by Nancy Herndon

ACID BATH	WIDOWS' WATCH
LETHAL STATUES	HUNTING GAME
TIME BOMBS	C.O.P. OUT

FREDDIE O'NEAL, P.I., MYSTERIES: You can bet that this appealing Reno private investigator will get her man . . . "A winner."—Linda Grant

by Catherine Dain

LAY IT ON THE LINE	SING A SONG OF DEATH
WALK A CROOKED MILE	LAMENT FOR A DEAD COWBOY
BET AGAINST THE HOUSE	THE LUCK OF THE DRAW
DEAD MAN'S HAND	

BENNI HARPER MYSTERIES: Meet Benni Harper—a quilter and folk-art expert with an eye for murderous designs . . .

by Earlene Fowler

FOOL'S PUZZLE	IRISH CHAIN
KANSAS TROUBLES	GOOSE IN THE POND

HANNAH BARLOW MYSTERIES: For ex-cop and law student Hannah Barlow, justice isn't just a word in a textbook. Sometimes, it's a matter of life and death . . .

by Carroll Lachnit

MURDER IN BRIEF	A BLESSED DEATH

PEACHES DANN MYSTERIES: Peaches has never had a very good memory. But she's learned to cope with it over the years . . . Fortunately, though, when it comes to murder, this absentminded amateur sleuth doesn't forgive and forget!

by Elizabeth Daniels Squire

WHO KILLED WHAT'S-HER-NAME?	REMEMBER THE ALIBI
MEMORY CAN BE MURDER	WHOSE DEATH IS IT ANYWAY?
IS THERE A DEAD MAN IN THE HOUSE?	

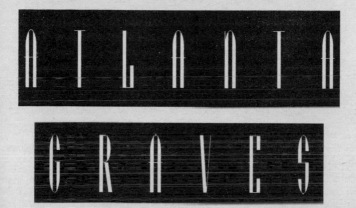

ATLANTA GRAVES

RUTH BIRMINGHAM

BERKLEY PRIME CRIME, NEW YORK

ATLANTA GRAVES

A Berkley Prime Crime Book / published by arrangement with the author

PRINTING HISTORY
Berkley Prime Crime mass-market edition / April 1998

The Penguin Putnam Inc. World Wide Web site address is
http://www.penguinputnam.com

ISBN: 0-425-16267-2

Berkley Prime Crime Books are published
by The Berkley Publishing Group,
a member of Penguin Putnam Inc.,
200 Madison Avenue, New York, NY 10016.
The name BERKLEY PRIME CRIME and the BERKLEY PRIME CRIME
design are trademarks belonging to Berkley Publishing Corporation.

PRINTED IN THE UNITED STATES OF AMERICA

10 9 8 7 6 5 4 3 2 1

CHAPTER 1

FOR YEARS **I** have deluded myself that there's nothing I hate worse than artifice and deception. No lie, man.

I tell myself: you are Sunny Childs, a plain person. You are Sunny Childs, all cross-training shoes and sweatshirts—no lipstick, no eye shadow, no matching handbag. You are Sunny Childs, the chick who tells it like it is.

I'm coming to realize what a bunch of crap this is. I love a white lie and a silver lamé dress as much as the next girl. Maybe more. I am, after all, my mother's daughter. It's in the blood and there's no sweating it out.

You could say this whole thing came about because of a lie. You could say that Leslie-Anne Gilmartin would still be alive if she had just played it straight, lived her life without artifice or deception.

But you could probably argue the reverse, too. There's deception and then there's deception, right? If Leslie-Anne had been willing to go along to get along, had been willing to put up with a certain amount of the quotidian fraudulence that we all live with day in and day out, she wouldn't have gotten into this mess in the first place.

I'm coming to the conclusion that honesty has its limits; deception and artifice, their uses. So maybe I'm finally growing up. Then again maybe something in me has gone sour.

Here, you judge.

CHAPTER 2

WHEN THE CALL finally came in, I was sitting behind Gunnar Brushwood's grandly fatuous desk forging Gunnar's signature on a bunch of payroll checks.

"It's him!" my assistant Keesha yelled to me through the open door.

Payton Link sat in one of the green leather wing chairs, looking at me through his rimless glasses and waiting patiently. Gunnar's office is our client showplace: walnut paneling, floor-to-ceiling windows, lots of framed photographs on the wall: the legendary Gunnar shaking hands with John Wayne and Ronald Reagan; the legendary Gunnar with his legendary white handlebar mustache, picturesquely stained with nicotine; the legendary Gunnar with his legendary Aussie hat and bush jacket; the legendary Gunnar with his legendary elephant gun. And so on, ad nauseam. I know, I know; I'm probably too hard on Gunnar. But I can't help it.

I picked up the phone. "Do you have it with you right now?" I said.

"Yes," the thief said. They were using one of those voice distortion boxes you buy for twenty-nine ninety-five at the Spy Store. The electronic thingamajig had dropped the thief's voice to a Darth Vader basso profundo. But there was something about the voice that sounded like a woman, something in the vowels or the inflection.

"I want you to look at the back of the painting," I said. "Down in the bottom left corner. What do you see?"

"Hey, look dude—" the thief said indignantly.

I interrupted: "Do you want to do this or not?"

"Yeah, but—"

"Then act like a professional. The bottom left corner— not of the picture but of the stretcher that it's mounted on. What do you see?"

"There's a collector's mark stamped on the wood," the thief said. "Two interlocking circles in red ink with the letter P inside one circle and the letter S inside the other."

"Ah," I said. Then I looked over at Payton Link and nodded.

Payton, as usual, was impassive as stone. "Do it," he said.

"Okay," I said into the phone. "My client has given approval to your figure. Your move."

"Okay. Um. There's this Popeye's Fried Chicken down at the corner of Ralph David Abernathy and Pryor," the thief said. "Go in and tell the white guy at the register that you left a leather coat in the bathroom. He'll give you something."

"That's kind of a crummy neighborhood," I said. Since I'm five feet nothing and weigh about ninety-five pounds, I try to stay out of the bad parts of Atlanta.

"Yeah, well stand up real straight and act like a professional," the thief said with electronic sarcasm. "I'm sure you'll be fine." Then the line went dead.

After I put the phone down, I turned to Payton and said, "I guess you better give it to me."

Payton shook his head lugubriously. He was a former military officer and even when he was being lugubrious he looked like someone was counting off double time inside his head. "Nothing personal, Sunny, but I'd feel a whale of a lot more comfortable if Gunnar were handling this himself."

"He's on an extremely delicate and important assignment right now."

That was the first lie.

Looking back on it I realize that once I'd slithered over that hurdle, I never really turned back. All the bad things that happened after that probably would have gone down anyway—but I can't help thinking that there must have been another, cleaner way.

Payton Link kept shaking his head. "Still . . ."

"It's me or nothing," I said. "Gunnar's just not available right now." That much, of course, was true.

Finally Payton opened his spotless briefcase, took out eleven stacks of hundred-dollar bills, a hundred and ten thousand dollars total, and dressed them in a neat line across the parade ground of Gunnar's huge desktop.

I counted the bills twice, put them in my purse, then looked up and smiled. "So I guess you'll need some kind of receipt?"

One of the interesting secrets of the insurance business is that when valuable insured properties are stolen—jewels, paintings, antique silver services—they're often ransomed right back to the insurer. No cops involved. Thieves know that the insurance company would rather pay them thirty cents ransom on the dollar than paying the full claim to the rightful owner. It's easier for everybody this way: the claimant gets her priceless heirloom back, the thief gets paid, and most importantly the insurance company gets off easy.

It's not precisely legal. But it's not precisely illegal either. It's what we in the investigations business like to call a "gray area." In investigative work, gray areas are where the money is. As Gunnar is fond of saying, "If it was all clean air and bright lights, the clients would do this shit themselves, wouldn't they?"

In ransom cases insurers aren't always comfortable doing the exchanges—liability problems, don't you know—so they hire an intermediary to do the dirty work. Someone like the legendary Gunnar Brushwood, chairman of Peachtree Investigations. Since Gunnar, as is so often the case, had wandered off to God-only-knew-where without bothering to tell anybody, this particular job had devolved to me.

Payton Link was the head of security for a third rate insurance company called Reliance Insurance that specialized in property insurance for weird and marginal businesses. Art galleries, for instance. Reliance Insurance had insured the Charlie Biddle Gallery, which had been ripped off three days earlier. The thief had nabbed a painting called *Late Afternoon, Pont Aven, Brittany*—probably the ugliest painting ever done by a semi-obscure American impressionist named Childe Hassam—and was now ransoming it back to Reliance.

After a day and a half of negotiations with Darth Vader, we were finally coming to the end of the process. The painting had been insured for three hundred and fifty thousand dollars—though, ugly as it was, I suspected nobody would really pay that much for it. But then, what do I know? I'm not an art connoisseur or a multi-million dollar insurance company or a shrewd and sophisticated gallery owner. I'm just a private investigator.

I pulled my 1974 Cadillac Eldorado into the parking lot of the bedraggled fried chicken restaurant, wrestled my red anti-theft club onto the steering wheel and went inside. With the exception of a mob of industriously buzzing flies, the place was empty and free of activity.

A white guy with an undershot chin stood at the register. He wore a blue polyester shirt and a hair net, and his eyes were full of dim calculation.

"WeckomnaPopeye'smaheppyou," he mumbled.

"Yeah, I left my coat in here this morning. A leather coat. I think it was in the bathroom."

The register guy stroked his cookie-duster mustache. "Your name Sunny Childs?" he said. He looked at me as though he'd been expecting somebody else. A man, maybe.

"Yep," I said.

He looked around furtively, reached under the counter and came out with a 32-ounce plastic cup that said POPEYE'S on it, and slid it across the stained formica.

"That'll be a dollar thirty-seven," he said.

"Yeah, right," I said sarcastically. He just looked back at me blankly and so I gave him the money anyway, made him print out a receipt on the register. I'm a bear for paperwork. In a business like mine, these little expenses can nickel and dime you into the poor house.

I went out to my car, sat down in the front seat and pulled the lid off the drink cup. Inside was a piece of paper with a laser-printed message on it that said, "A cab will arrive in a few minutes. Get in and tell the driver you're feeling short of breath. He'll suggest that he take you to a hospital. If anyone follows you, or if the cab driver sees you use a cellular phone, or if any police show up, the deal is off."

Everything was spelled correctly and all the punctuation was in the right place. A literate thief, what a pleasant novelty.

As I was putting the note back in the plastic cup, a battered yellow cab pulled up next to me. The cab driver, a black guy with the broad cheekbones of a West African, looked at me expectantly.

"Hi, there!" I said, getting out of my Caddy. "I ah, I'm feeling kind of funny. Like, short of breath."

"Look, man," he said as I climbed into the cab, "I don't know what's going on, and I don't want to know." He had a thick accent—Nigeria, Ghana, something like that.

"Just take me wherever you're going," I said.

I was starting to feel pretty nervous as the car slowly pulled out into the road. Up to this point all I'd had to do was talk on the phone. We were finally reaching that spooky point where things started getting unpredictable and dangerous. I had a gun in my purse, of course, a snub-nosed LadySmith revolver. But that wasn't much consolation.

A muscle twitched in my leg and my hands shook slightly.

The cab drove around for a while, barrelling through black neighborhoods on the south side of Atlanta, places I'd never been in my life even though I'd lived in the city since I was a little girl. Call it the ill effects of cultural apartheid, call it whatever you want, but it made me nervous being down in that part of town. Atlanta has a per capita murder rate three times that of New York City—in fact we had the highest rate in the country last year—and sad to say, most of those murders took place in the part of the city we were driving through.

My cell phone rang.

"Uh, what do I do?" I said.

"Sorry?" The cab driver looked at me in the rear view mirror.

"The phone. They said I wasn't supposed to talk on the phone."

The cab driver shrugged. "Didn't say nothing about that to me."

I flipped open the phone.

"Where *are* you, sweetie?" It was my mother, talking to me with the affected English accent she uses when she's had an early afternoon cocktail or three.

I hunched down in the seat in case someone was following, trying to keep an eye on me. "Mom, now's really not an ideal time."

My mother sighed theatrically. Everything she does is theatrical, but her sighs have a particularly winning thespian quality. "This is terribly, terribly important." She sounded a little hurt.

"Look, I'm in the middle of a ransom thing."

"How ripping!" Mom said, laying on the English accent. Obviously she didn't believe me. She assumes that everyone invents their lives the way she's invented hers. "But this is really *crucial*, sweetie. As you know, your brother is up for partnership at Underhill Tabb this year and I know it's aw-fully late notice for you to get something to wear, but there's a function I'd like desperately for you to attend this weekend. Walter's date fell through—"

"Seriously, Mom. I have to go."

She kept talking.

"I'll call later, Mom," I interrupted. Then I flipped the phone shut. It sounds heartless, I know, but with my mother you have to be firm or you get trampled.

The phone rang again immediately. I answered, and Mom launched into her spiel again.

"Bye, Mom. I have to go ransom a painting." As I hung up for the second time, the cab slid to a stop.

"We're here," the cab driver said.

The phone rang again.

"Mom!" I said, still hunched down in the seat. "Now is not the time!"

"What?" a voice on the other end said. An electronically altered basso profundo.

"Oh, sorry," I said. "I thought you were my Mom."

"You, too, huh?" the thief said.

"What is it with women and their mothers?" I said, trying out my pet theory that the thief was a woman, too.

"I don't know," the thief said. It wasn't a response that told me much of anything. Not that I really cared if Darth was a he or she at this point: I just wanted to get the painting, give the thief the money and get the hell out of this sad neighborhood.

"So look," I said. "What if I hadn't answered? That note I got at Popeye's said I wasn't supposed to answer the phone."

There was a pause. "I hadn't thought of that," the thief said.

Ah, I thought. Another criminal mastermind.

"Well, anyway, I'm here," I said, straightening up to look around me.

I didn't like this place at all. We were parked inside a high, rusting chain link fence on a weedy parking lot. The

fence was so overgrown with honeysuckle that you couldn't
see in or out of the property. As far as I could tell there was
only one way in or out—though the parking lot did extend
around the corner of the warehouse. Still it was a good place
for a rip-off trap. I considered telling the cabby to leave. But
I didn't. I couldn't face telling Payton Link that I'd wimped
out at the last minute.

In the distance there was a small rise covered with row
after row of identically drab brick apartments. From where I
stood it reminded me of scale clinging to a rock. George
Washington Carver Homes? Perry Homes? I wasn't sure. As
if this whole business wasn't scary enough already I remembered a newspaper article I'd read recently about violence in
Atlanta housing projects: one of them had twenty-six homi-
cides last year alone. There were entire suburban counties
around Atlanta that had fewer murders than that.

Flanking the lot was an old brick warehouse with the
barely legible ghost of some long-forgotten company's name
painted in fading letters on the side. DANE BROS.
FREIGHT. Or maybe it was TRANE BROS. It was hard to
tell.

"What do I do now?" I said. My voice seemed thin,
frightened, girlish. I hated the sound of it.

"You see that little shed over in the corner?"

I looked around, saw a small metal building on one side
of the lot. It was covered with gang graffiti that looked nearly
as old as the Dane or Trane Brothers sign.

"Okay."

"Get out of the cab and go inside."

"Then what?"

"Wait. There's a walkie-talkie in there. We'll talk next on
that."

The phone went dead.

"You gonna wait for me?" I asked the cab driver.

He smiled, nodded vaguely. I got out of the car and the
Nigerian guy threw it in reverse and peeled out of the lot.

He was obviously about as happy to be in this neighborhood as I was.

"Thanks, bud!" I called sarcastically to the disappearing car. "Appreciate the honesty!"

As soon as he was gone, I felt like some kid whose parents have deserted her at the mall. My heart bounced wildly in my chest. I walked over to the shed, my hand inside my purse, one sweating finger wrapped around the trigger of my Smith. The air was fat with honeysuckle.

The shed had a rusted steel door that opened with a metallic scream and then jammed halfway open. Inside the dark shed was an ancient wooden table with a walkie-talkie on it. I picked up the walkie-talkie—a Motorola, solid and heavy as a brick, with lots of buttons on it indicating it had scrambler circuitry. Presumably so nobody could listen in to our conversation. We had a couple like it at the firm that we used occasionally when we were feeling paranoid during a surveillance operation. I pressed the key and said, "Hello. You there?"

"Hold on," a tight voice said. This time there was no distortion box on it. And it was a man's voice. So much for my theory that the thief was a woman.

"Like for how long?" I said.

The walkie-talkie went click-click, like somebody on the other end had pushed the talk key. But nobody said anything.

I pressed the talk button. "Hello? Hello?"

Still no answer.

Somewhere (over in the projects? it was hard to tell . . .) there was a loud pop. A gunshot. I supposed it was the kind of neighborhood where gunshots went off now and then, and nobody paid it much mind. Still, it was not comforting. Actually, saying that it was "not comforting" is less than completely accurate: it scared the crap out of me.

Another gunshot. This one seemed awfully close. Somewhere I heard a couple of kids laughing. Gangbangers having a little fun with their shiny new pistols? Great. I just hoped they didn't decide to come my way and engage in some friendly target practice.

I was starting to get a very bad feeling about this. It felt more and more like a rip-off. That was the eternal problem with ransoms. If the thief decided to scam you or hold you up for the cash and then fence the painting anyway, there really wasn't that much you could do. That kind of thing just happens sometimes when you wander into gray areas. Price of admission, you might say.

There was nowhere to sit in the shed other than the table—which looked a little rickety anyway. Besides, the place stank of urine. It was mid-May, a beautiful day, warm enough to make the shed uncomfortably hot. I carried the walkie-talkie to the door, leaned against the rusting frame and let the fresh, honeysuckle-laden air play across my face.

I waited.

Waited and waited. After a while the soft wind stopped and I started feeling really warm and sticky. I kept sweating. The more I sweated, the more nervous I got—cheered only by the fact that the gangbangers seemed to have had their fill of gunplay after two shots.

Presently I checked my watch. It seemed like an hour since the cab dropped me off, but it had only been five minutes. The five minutes stretched to ten, the ten to twenty. Then to twenty-one then to twenty-two and twenty-two and a half. I told myself to stop looking at my watch. I looked at my watch.

Finally I put the walkie-talkie to my lips: "Hey, people. Let's get the show on the road."

But there was still no answer.

As it had earlier, a second after I spoke, the walkie-talkie emitted a brief, crackling noise—*click-click*—like someone on the other radio had pressed their talk key. But, again, if they had, they didn't say anything.

I went back in the stinking shed, yanked on the jammed door until it closed with a metallic howl, and then called

Payton Link on my cellular. "I don't know what's going on here," I said, "but something's not right."

"Where are you?"

"I don't even know. Somewhere down in Southwest Atlanta."

"Give it till 14:30 hours. If they don't make the rendezvous, sound a general retreat." Payton Link talked like this all the time and didn't intend it to be funny. I don't think the guy had an ironic bone in his body.

I rang off and went back outside. Again I pressed the button on the side of the walkie-talkie. "Anybody home? Calling all cars. Calling all cars."

A brief pause. Then: *click-click.*

I was starting to feel a heaviness in my arms and legs, a premonition that something really shitty was about to happen. I decided to scrap the waiting-until-fourteen-thirty-hours plan. (I had to add it up—fourteen minus twelve equals two plus thirty is 2:30 P.M.) That was ten minutes away. But a lot of ugliness could go down in ten minutes. Executive decision: it was high time I got out of there. I took the revolver out of my purse and started trotting toward the gate in the chain link fence wondering what all the junior gangbangers in the neighborhood would think about some skinny little white woman blundering through their neighborhood with a drawn weapon.

Before I reached the fence, though, it suddenly occurred to me that the thief couldn't be too far away. Walkie-talkies have a limited range. So maybe the thief was already around here somewhere. But if so, why hadn't they made the exchange? It didn't make sense. But then you never knew in a situation like this. Maybe they were just waiting to make sure I hadn't been followed.

Just so that I could go back to Payton Link with a clear conscience and tell him that I done everything in my power to earn the 250-buck-an-hour quadruple-rate pay I was charging him, I turned around and walked back toward the far side of the lot, over by the brick wall with the Dane or Trane Brothers sign peeling into oblivion. When I got to the end of the wall, I stopped, hesitated. The walkie-talkie crackled again. *Click-click.*

"Hello?" I said. "Hello?"

Nobody answered.

So I walked around the corner of the building and found myself on a long strip of tarmac just wide enough to turn an eighteen-wheeler around in. There were three graffiti-covered loading docks along the side of the warehouse. Parked beside the middle dock was a ten-year-old Japanese car with the trunk open. The engine was still running. I walked up to the trunk and looked inside. There was a flat cardboard box lying on top of the jack. It was just about the right size for the painting I was looking for. But it had been ripped open and there was nothing inside.

Again, my radio crackled. *Click-click.* I jumped, pointed my gun around. But there was no one anywhere near me.

Working my way around the car, I found, at long last, what it was all about. A young woman lay on the ground next to the driver's side door, her head pushed up against the side of the car.

"Hey!" I yelled. "What are you doing down there?"

It was a stupid thing to say. What she was doing was obvious enough: she was dying.

Her eyes were open, staring, and blood ran down the side of her head, down her neck, staining the front of her white cotton T-shirt. In her outstretched hand was a walkie-talkie. I stared at her for a moment, unable to move. After a few seconds her fingers twitched, pressing the talk button on her radio.

Click-click, went my radio. *Click-click.*

CHAPTER 3

WHAT IS WRONG with me?

The short answer, I guess, is that I'm afflicted with a deep emotional obtuseness. I get out of bed and I think about Ron. I brush my teeth and I think about Ron. I spit the water out in the wash bowl and, by God, if I'm not still thinking about Ron. All day he breaks into my thoughts and I get flushed, I get distracted, I get to feeling this . . . well, let's not get bogged down in the details.

I was making a point: let's put aside the fact that I believe it's deeply immoral of me to be involved with a guy who's married and has two wonderfully sweet and beautiful twin girls. Let's also put aside the fact that I know, not just as a matter of dry intellectual fact but as a bone deep emotional truth, that the guy will never leave his wife. Let's put aside the fact that he's not exactly addicted to honesty. The thing that really dogs me is that in my occasional sane moments, I'm not even sure that I like him. Oh, I know, he's polite and respectful and has read all sorts of fashionable books about how men are a bunch of jerks, and so he tries to remedy his behavior accordingly by engaging in fitful bouts of extravagant attentiveness. But that's no substitute for a good heart.

And yet I'm crazy for him. Six months this has been going on. Mad sex at noon; whispered phone calls at midnight;

sudden, desperate rendezvouses; cryptic beeper messages. It's like living inside one of those John LeCarre books where everything's in code and nobody has real feelings. That's why I say that I'm an emotional moron. I don't think this whole thing is about Ron at all; I'm intoxicated with the sneaking around, the excitement, the spy-novel foolishness. If I were a believer in all that 12-step crap, I'd be tempted to say I had a sickness. But I'm not and so I won't. I'll just fess up to being flawed and weak and human. And I'll leave it at that.

What's funny is that for the most part I'm a really responsible and decent person. Loyal to kith and kin, friendly to strangers, generous tipper, I donate money to Public Radio and don't mind friends sleeping on my couch for inordinate stretches of time when they're in dutch with their husbands or landlords. It's just when it comes to men that I'm deeply, profoundly, irretrievably, enduringly, persistently, Faulknerianly dumb.

I'll say this much though: when I finally start moping around in the housewares department at Macy's and start showing interest in wedding china patterns, I generally experience a sudden flash of lucidity which leads me to conclude that it's time to break up with my worthless boyfriend of the moment. It's the china that does it: china leads you to thinking about cooking, cooking to cleaning, cleaning to kids and houses and air-conditioner repairs and chicken barbecues and pressure-washing the deck and that whole domestic thing. And then when I plop the face of my clinically undomesticatable boyfriend *du jour* in the middle of a gee-hon-should-we-pressure-wash-the-deck-this-weekend? scenario, I realize in a flash how ridiculous the whole notion of spending my life with this guy is.

I call this my wedding china moment. High delusion meets brutal common sense in one spine-wrecking flash of insight.

I hadn't had a wedding china moment with Ron. Yet. But I could feel it coming on. Occasionally I would allow a

thought to sneak into my mind before angrily brushing it
away, a thought that it was probably only a matter of weeks
or months before the whole mad affair went down the drain
in the usual depressing pattern. At which point I would once
again swear off men for all eternity, take a vow of chastity,
start wearing shapeless black clothes and practicing karate
with a moderately sick fervor. Then that phase, too, would
pass.

And next time, dammit, I would find him. *Him*—you
know the one I mean: the guy who will unlock my soul and
pour me full of poetry.

Oh, shit, but I wish he'd hurry up.

Meanwhile, there's Ron. And as long as I don't attempt
to think lucidly or commonsensically I can believe that Ron's
the one, the soul-unlocking, poetry-pouring guy who he
couldn't really be in ten lifetimes.

Well.

I mention all of this, not in passing, but to explain why,
before talking to the two detectives down at the Atlanta PD's
homicide unit, I didn't call O. Wayne Dupree, Esquire, my
ludicrously expensive lawyer, but instead beeped Ron at
work. Three times.

When he finally called back (there was some vague excuse
about a pressing meeting with the vice-president of human
resources), I told him about what had happened.

"Whoa," Ron said. "That's horrifying."

"Yeah," I said.

There was a long pause.

"Ahhhh, okay, okay," Ron said, sounding more than a
little distracted. "Is there something you want me to do about
it?"

I thought about it and realized that what I really wanted
was to have him fold me in his arms and tell me lies about
how much he loves me, that I am his all, and that everything
is going to be fine. I also realized that at three-twenty on the
Friday afternoon before Memorial Day weekend, there was

not a prayer in hell that this was going to happen. He probably had big weekend plans cooked up with his family. Steaks on the hibachi, martinis with the wife, frolicking with the kids in the big backyard. Maybe he'd even get a chance to pressure-wash the deck.

So I said, "No. There's nothing. I just wanted to hear your voice."

"Me too," he said.

I thought: Me too, *what*?

"Oh by the way," he said, "while I've got you on the phone, have you given any thought to that thing I was telling you about? With my brother-in-law?"

Ron had been bugging me for a few days to interview his brother-in-law for an investigator job with the firm. I had been putting him off—but the truth was, we didn't need anybody right now. And even if we had, Ron's brother-in-law didn't sound quite like the kind of guy we were looking for. It irked me a little that Ron would bring it up at a time like this.

"Honestly?" I said. "Now's not precisely the perfect moment to get into that."

Then I said goodbye and went in to talk to the cops.

They led me to an interview room and we all sat down. The detective who did most of the talking was a white guy with neat blond hair and a nice double-breasted suit, blue with a white banker's stripe. The second man was black, with heavy features and a bad hair-straightening job that had started to grow out. He wore a cheap, baggy corduroy sport coat, scuffed brown Rockports, a polyester tie with a police-issue tie clip, and chinos that hung down at the seat. As a class, Atlanta police detectives are a pretty dandified bunch; he was hands down the worst-dressed Atlanta cop I'd ever come across. His eyes seemed vague and unfocused, and he had a matchstick perched on his lower lip.

"I know we spoke at the crime scene, but just to refresh your memory, I'm Lieutenant Hagee," the white guy said, smiling a little too broadly, "and this is Major Carl Fontaine." I shook hands with both of them. Hagee's handshake was firm and crisp. Carl Fontaine's was limp, dry, and reticent. He reminded me of the old men who do my mother's yard, eyes averted, all yes'm and no ma'am, showing nothing. Lt. Hagee sat across from me, while Maj. Fontaine sat back in the corner picking his teeth with the matchstick and staring vacantly at the floor. I had a strong suspicion that Fontaine's tired-old-geezer thing was all a big act and that he was actually the brains of the outfit. But it was hard to be sure.

I told the two detectives about everything that had happened to me that afternoon, including the ransom we were planning to pay for the Childe Hassam painting.

Lt. Hagee walked me through the entire ransom process, asking the same questions over and over with a big Officer Friendly smile on his face. First he'd ask the question one way, then he'd kind of change the wording a little and ask it another way and then another way and then another way. Then he'd move on to something else. When he'd pretty much gone over the same ground three or four times without finding out anything new or different, his tone started getting nasty. He implied that I hadn't told him I was carrying a weapon (I had), that I was changing my story (I wasn't), that I was concealing something (I wasn't), and that I knew who the dead girl was (I didn't).

"You're telling me that you don't know Leslie-Anne Gilmartin?" he said finally.

That was the first time they'd let on to me that they knew the girl's identity.

"That was Leslie-Anne *Gilmartin*?" I said.

It was hard to believe. The last time I'd seen Leslie-Anne, she must have been ten or eleven years old, living down the street from my mother and her rich-husband-of-the-moment. I guess I'd been in college at the time.

Leslie-Anne's mother was named Jocelyn Gilmartin. Or

Mrs. Duane Gilmartin, as she preferred to be known—Mr. Duane being the Chief Something-or-other Officer for the Georgia Power Company. She was a friend of my mother's—or at least they fluttered around in the same elevated social circles.

Fontaine looked up from the floor suddenly. "How do you know her, Miss Childs?"

"Our mothers are friends. She used to ride her bike through our flower garden and piss my stepfather off."

Fontaine appraised me for a moment. "When was the last time you saw her?"

I shrugged. "Probably when I was in college sometime. My stepfather died during my senior year, and Mom moved to another neighborhood."

"So you haven't seen her in like a decade."

"At least."

"You mind taking a residue test?" Fontaine said.

Gunshot residue tests are used to see if you've fired a weapon recently. "Not a problem," I said.

"We'll have an evidence tech take care of it. Then you're good to go, Miss Childs."

His partner Hagee looked slightly peeved and said, "Yeah, but—"

Fontaine cut him off. "Nope. She's done."

After that an evidence technician swabbed my hands with some sort of solution that left an acrid smell on my skin.

As I was leaving homicide headquarters, I saw Jocelyn Gilmartin across the room, sitting quietly by herself in the waiting room. To look at her you'd have never known her only daughter had just been shot to death.

I went over and sat down beside her.

"I don't know if you remember me," I said softly. "Sunny Childs. I'm Miranda Wineberg's daughter."

She looked at me blankly for a moment then said, "Sunny Childs! Look at you! My my my!" She was in her late fifties, part of the last generation of rich Southerners to retain the beautiful drawl and manners of the old South. For people like Mrs. Duane Gilmartin, good manners were the *ne plus ultra* of existence: even violent death wasn't allowed to interfere with them. She wore unobtrusive blue wool pants, unobtrusive blue Guccis, and an unobtrusive red cardigan over a silk turtleneck. Her pearls were unobtrusive as were her diamond earrings. The whole ensemble probably cost about as much as a slightly used Toyota. Her gray hair was cut in a barely updated version of the flip she'd probably worn since right after she graduated from Sweet Briar or Vanderbilt or wherever back in 1962.

I smiled and put my hand on hers. "I'm so sorry," I said.

She gripped my hand fiercely, then raised her eyebrows and looked to the side as though if she just didn't look at me, didn't acknowledge my pity, she could somehow make the whole thing un-happen. It didn't work of course, and tears started rolling down her face. She blinked, daubed her eyes with a linen handkerchief. "I'm still in shock I suppose," she said finally.

"Is anyone with you?"

She shook her head slightly. "Duane's in New York. I called him, but he's still *en route*." Pronouncing it the French way.

"Let me stay with you."

"That's lovely of you, but I'm sure you have things to do. You're mother's told me all about you, you know. She's terribly proud."

I took a brief, selfish moment to wonder why Mom never bothered to tell *me* that.

"Really, darling, I'll be just fine," Jocelyn Gilmartin said. "Duane's *en route*. I'll be quite all right." But she didn't loosen the painful grip she had on my hand.

We sat in silence for a while. I stroked her shoulder, and she perched on the edge of her chair, back straight, knees tight together, legs crossed at the ankles—just like they taught her at Miss Whoever's School for Girls all those years ago. Her eyes were bright and wide with expectation, and there was just the hint of a smile on her face. Except for the gray hair and the wrinkles, she could almost have been a young girl waiting on her handsome date for the Dogwood Cotillion.

Some cops trooped through, but they didn't look at us. For them we were just the grieving people—anonymous and unchanging as the furniture.

"I was the one who found her," I said finally. "I don't think she was in any pain."

"They've said terrible things about her," Jocelyn Gilmartin said, looking at the door to the Homicide Unit offices. "They've said she's a . . ." She seemed not to be able to get the word out. ". . . a *criminal*! But I know in my heart that it can't be true."

"The police will sort it out," I said softly.

She looked at me with a curious expression. "Have you *talked* to those people? One of them looks like a high-class Chevrolet salesman and the other is a colored—" She hesitated. "—and the other one picks his teeth in public."

In times like this, it's marginally easier than it might otherwise be to forgive people like Mrs. Duane Gilmartin for being who they are.

"They're good men," I said. "Good cops. They'll sort it out, that's their job."

She shook her head. "No. They'd just love to make out that the daughter of a good family in this town was some sort of criminal. Those kind of people just *glory* in tearing us down."

I nodded vaguely. I couldn't think of any other way to respond. Not one that wouldn't have been pointless or mean-spirited at any rate.

"Oh, what am I saying?" The ugliness went out of her eye. "I just . . . I just want to *blame* somebody! That's wrong of me, isn't it?"

There was a long silence and then she spoke again.

"Leslie-Anne and I haven't seen eye to eye for so long. We hardly speak. If anyone's to blame for *that*, I suppose it's me. I never understand what the younger people want. She was born so late. I was forty, you know, when she was born. Mr. Gilmartin and I were probably far too rigid with her." She stared into the distance.

"Sometimes I turn on the television, Sunny, and I watch the things that are showing and it's so terribly bewildering. Honestly, out of curiosity, I did that one day, just sat there on the couch for hours and hours and hours watching MTV. It was like looking at one of those programs about some cannibal tribe in New Guinea. And then suddenly I was so nauseated I had to run into the powder room! I'm quite serious!" She blinked her wide blue eyes at me. "But Leslie-Anne wasn't bewildered by any of that, the music and the cursing and the drugs and the bosoms hanging out of your shirt and the snotty tone all these young people take today. That's where my daughter lives I think: she lives in a world where these horrible snarling boys with their, oh, their baggy pants and their loud guitars and their outlandish tattoos just seem perfectly normal. And *my* world? My world is as unfamiliar to her as ancient Greece. How did I manage to raise a child like that?"

She shook her head sharply. "It's a terrible world out there, Sunny. Maybe the Catholics have it right. Sometimes I think it would be quite consoling to check into a nunnery and never come out."

Suddenly she let go of my hand, and turned to look at me.

"Sunny, is it really true what your mother says about you—that you're a private investigator? That you work for that famous fellow . . . ah . . . what's his name?

"Gunnar Brushwood," I said. "That's his name."

"Well maybe I'm just a suspicious old fool, but I don't trust those little police creatures. I'd like to retain Mr. Brushwood to look into the matter of my daughter's murder. I want him to find out who did this to my little girl."

I cleared my throat. "I don't know how to say this, Mrs. Gilmartin, but we probably couldn't accept that assignment. We have a conflict of interest."

She waved away the problem with her linen handkerchief. "Oh don't be silly."

"Mrs. Gilmartin, listen to me. Please. I was hired to pay someone so that they'd return a stolen painting. Like a ransom. It was during that ransom exchange that your daughter was killed. As long as I'm involved in trying to get that painting back, I'd really be putting myself in a position where I couldn't look after your interests properly. Why don't you just let the police take care of it for now?"

"Nonsense!" she said sharply. "These things can't be related. Leslie-Anne and I may have had our problems, but I know how I raised her. MTV or no MTV, I did not raise a thief."

"Tell you what," I said. "I have to talk to my client about the painting this afternoon. It still hasn't been recovered. They may want me to continue involvement in the case or they may not. But how about this—I'll look into the matter of Leslie-Anne's death as best I can. But only on an informal basis."

Mrs. Duane Gilmartin smiled brightly. "You see? There's always a way, isn't there? My father used to say that endlessly."

"I'm not promising anything."

"How much do you need?" She reached into her clutch and took out a checkbook with a leather cover that matched her purse. "We can pay anything."

"No, no." I put my hand on her wrist. "For right now money's out of the question. All I'm doing is keeping my eyes open." Then something occurred to me. "Mrs. Gilmartin, how much do you know about Leslie-Anne's friends? Did she have a boyfriend? Are you aware of any acquaintances she had that might have a criminal background?"

Mrs. Gilmartin looked sourly into the distance. "There are still nice, young people in the world, you know. But Leslie-Anne didn't seem to want to know them. She could have pledged any sorority she wanted when she was at UVa, but what did she do? Spent every waking hour with rock musicians and writers and all sorts of other useless no-account people."

"Does she have a boyfriend?"

"Terry. Her boyfriend's name was Terry Yokum." The way she said his name, you'd have thought that in her judgment he ranked about half a step higher than a child pornographer.

"Anyone else you can think of?"

Before she had a chance to answer, a big stolid-looking man in a nice charcoal gray suit came into the lobby of the Homicide Unit. I recognized him as Leslie-Anne's older brother, a guy a couple of years older than me. I couldn't remember his name. He had looked forty when we were in college, and he looked forty now. He'd probably look forty when he turned a hundred. There was nothing childish about him, and nothing entirely mature.

"Charles!" Mrs. Duane Gilmartin said. "Oh thank goodness!"

"Mother. I'm sorry it took so long." He had a dazed look on his face.

They embraced clumsily. Charles was so blinded with grief or shock that I don't think he even noticed me.

"I'll run," I said.

Mrs. Duane Gilmartin grabbed my arm. "You find him," she said. "You tell Mr. Brushwood to find the monster that did this terrible thing to my little girl."

"I can't promise anything."

Her china blue eyes were wide and bright and furious. "Tell Mr. Brushwood!"

"I'll do what I can."

◆　　◆　　◆

I could have kicked myself. I am way, *way* too much of a soft touch. I should have just said absolutely no way, forget it, not possible. I should have fobbed off the names of some good investigators on her and left it at that. Instead, now I'd let myself get talked into a no-win situation—making a wishy-washy commitment that I probably couldn't follow up on while putting myself into what could conceivably develop into a conflict-of-interest situation with Reliance.

On top of which, if I *did* find something out about who killed Leslie-Anne, odds were it would show Mrs. Duane Gilmartin a side of her daughter that she was not particularly interested in uncovering. On the other hand if I didn't find out anything, she'd think I was a just a silly girl playing at private investigator.

Smooth move, Sunny.

CHAPTER 4

SWUNG BACK by the office to call Payton Link. For about the fifth time since I found the dead girl I was only able to reach his voice mail. That seemed a little odd. This should have been the top issue on his agenda today, and I was expecting he'd be waiting on tenterhooks for my call. Not wanting to leave the bad news on a recording, I decided to drive by his office and break it to him in person.

Before I could get myself together to leave the office for the day, my assistant Keesha came in and dropped six or seven pink message slips on my desk. "Girl, this man from the bank kept calling and calling!" she said. "He was trying to reach Gunnar, said it was real important, but I told him maybe he should talk to you."

I looked at my watch. Four o'clock. Where had the day gone? I hadn't even eaten lunch yet.

"I'll call him first thing Tuesday," I said.

"Actually he's out in the lobby right now. Kind of barged in." Keesha put her hands on her hips indignantly. "Getting all *insistent* and everything."

I sighed. "Okay, send him in."

I sat back in my chair and closed my eyes. My mind kept flashing up a picture of that girl lying on the weedy concrete with all the blood coming down her neck in a lacework of red-brown stripes. The thing that nagged at me was that she was still alive when I got there, barely breathing. By the time the paramedics showed up, though, she was gone.

Leslie-Anne Gilmartin had been a strange kid, always in trouble over some trivial thing. I remembered my stepfather, Joe Brenner, yelling at her one time for messing up the yard with her bike. She'd jumped off her bike and squirted him with a hose, then he'd gotten all purple in the face and looked like he was going to have a heart attack. (In fact, two months later he *had* suffered a sudden and fatal one. My mother has many talents, but her singular genius is an uncanny ability to find, and then marry, men who are not only rich and childless but unhealthy. Which was why she was on husband number five right now. My father had been her first—the only healthy one, and the only one whose pockets weren't stuffed with money.)

Those two gunshots I heard, they must have been what had killed Leslie-Anne. I wondered whether it would have saved her life if I'd found her as soon as I heard the gunshots. She must have been signaling me with that clicking noise on the walkie-talkie. Or maybe not. Maybe she'd already been on her way out, the fingers opening and closing in some kind of involuntary spasm.

I opened my eyes, and found myself staring at a young man in a neat blue suit. Very young: in fact he looked about fourteen. Man, I'm getting old.

"Mike Van Slyke!" the young man said enthusiastically. "From NationsBank!" I shook his hand and gestured for him to take a seat. "Actually I was hoping to see Mr. Brushwood."

"Gunnar's in the field right now, Mike," I said. "But I'm pretty familiar with our financial operations. What can I do for you?"

Van Slyke pulled on his earlobe, set his business card delicately on my desk and said, "I, ah, don't know if you knew, but Donald Jefferies—your account manager at the bank? He took early retirement this month. Ah, and I'm taking over for him."

"Congratulations."

"Yes, ah . . ." Van Slyke gave me a wincing smile. He looked very nervous, very fourteen. The knot of his tie was slightly askew and an arc of moist hair stuck up from the back of his head.

"I have a hunch I know why you're here," I said. "I don't know if you've completely familiarized yourself with our operations, so let me fill you in. The firm of Peachtree Investigations employs four full-time investigators, plus me and my assistant and our bookkeeper, plus a few freelancers, and then we have a security guard business which employs another forty or so people. The security guard business runs about a month behind in cash flow. As it happens, the investigations business is kind of a feast-or-famine thing."

"Cyclical," Van Slyke said helpfully.

"Cyclical! Exactly." I gave him what I was guessed was a syrupy and insincere smile. "And right now we're in kind of a slow period. As you probably know, the firm has a quarter million dollar line of credit with NationsBank—and right now frankly we're pretty deep into the credit line." I auditioned my syrupy smile again. "But then . . . that's what credit lines are for, right?"

We both laughed perfunctorily, two jolly business people yucking it up about money. Ho ho, ha ha. Then Van Slyke opened his briefcase and took out a fat manila folder which he opened in his lap. I noticed a dew of sweat on his hairless lip. "That's why, see, ah . . . well, that's kind of why I had to bust in here on such short notice."

I felt a sudden sinking feeling. "There's not a problem with the line of credit is there?"

Van Slyke did his wincing smile, squeegeed some sweat off his lip with the back of his thumb. "Here's the thing. I don't know how much you know about our financial relationship with Mr. Brushwood. . . ."

"A great deal, actually," I said coldly. As it happened, I had negotiated our relationship with the bank myself. Gunnar wouldn't know a line of credit from a hole in his head. Gunnar is the firm's chief selling point and very little else.

"Sure," the young banker said. "Okay. So, then you're familiar with the fact that this is what we call a collateralized line of credit?"

I nodded tolerantly. "I'm familiar with the concept of collateral."

"Okay, so the deal is that we extended the line of credit to the *firm* is based on, ah, collateral supplied by both by the firm and by Mr. Brushwood *personally* . . ." Van Slyke messed around in his manila folder. Some papers spilled out on the floor and the poor kid had to jump out of his chair and scrabble around on the carpet. He got back in the chair, brushed off his knees. "So the collateral on this loan consists of . . ."

"All of our receivables, plus Gunnar's jumbo certificate of deposit."

"The jumbo! That's right!" Van Slyke looked at me as though he were relieved I had mentioned it first. "Mr. Brushwood holds a one hundred thousand dollar certificate of deposit issued by NationsBank of Georgia. As a condition of the loan, the extension of credit under the terms of the, ah, the loan, the documentation here . . ." More scrabbling in the file. Another paper fell on the floor. This time he let it go. "As specified in the loan agreement, ah . . ."

I jumped in. "Gunnar has the hundred thousand dollar jumbo CD. That's your main source of liquid collateral. If Gunnar cashes the jumbo, you guys call the loan and we have to write you a check for the outstanding balance on the line of credit."

Van Slyke blinked in surprise. "That's right."

"Well!" I smiled and looked at my watch. I wanted to get out to Reliance before I-85 turned into a parking lot. "You're clear on that, I'm clear on that, we're all clear on the terms of the loan agreement. If there's anything else I can do, just feel free to drop by, but I've got an important appointment I need to run off to.''

''Wait!'' Van Slyke had a look of terror on his face. ''That's what I'm trying to tell you. Mr. Brushwood cashed the jumbo!''

I leaned forward. ''He *what*?''

''Mr. Brushwood cashed the jumbo CD. So, you know . . . it's out of our hands.''

''What's out of your hands?''

''The loan. We're calling the loan.''

''Calling the loan,'' I said. Because we were running way behind in the investigations division right now, I'd been slow-paying our creditors lately and they were starting to get a little annoyed. If the bank called the loan, that meant we were broke. Today. So not only would the electric company be turning off the lines and the building manager throwing us out of our office and the copier company hauling off the Xerox machine and the coffee company sneaking away with the coffee maker—problems which could be staved off for many, many weeks—but every single employee's paycheck would bounce. And that would happen this very afternoon.

This was a serious problem.

''As of when?'' I said finally.

''As of when, what?''

''As of when are you calling the loan?''

Van Slyke squeegeed his sweaty lip again. He was now looking positively prepubescent. ''As of, ah, right now.''

I stared at him.

''What I mean is, I'll need a certified check for one hundred thousand dollars by close of business today or we call the loan.''

''Which, in practical terms means . . .''

''We freeze your checking account at 5:00 P.M. and file a lien against your receivables first thing Tuesday.''

Translated: *in a little less than an hour, we're going to squash you like a bug.*

Finally I managed to speak. "Mike, it's four-oh-five on the Friday before Memorial Day. How am I supposed to get you a certified check by close of business? Explain that to me."

Van Slyke cleared his throat. "Look, ma'am, I'm a little new at this, so I have to apologize. There was a miscommunication, and I guess I should have gotten hold of you earlier in the week, but . . . maybe if I could speak to Mr. Brushwood . . ."

"Forget Gunnar. It's just you and me, Mike. We've got like fifty-five minutes to solve this problem."

"Yeah, but if Mr. Brushwood is the one who cashed the jumbo, then he's the one with the, ah, with the funds that would be required."

I didn't say anything to Van Slyke, but I did take the moment to dial the number for our bookkeeper and tell her not to give out any more paychecks.

"You, ah . . . you *do* know where Mr. Brushwood is, of course?" Van Slyke said.

I smiled patronizingly. "Of course I do."

See? See how easy it is?

Because the fact was I hadn't seen Gunnar in over a week, and had not the slightest clue where he was. Montana? Tibet? Borneo? The South Bronx? He could have been anywhere. There was nothing especially unusual in this: he had a way of wandering off without telling anybody. My guess is that it makes him feel free and manly and full of testosterone to inconvenience the hell out of me this way. He always shows up again, of course, but it could be a couple days, a couple weeks, a month. There's no knowing, no predicting. All that I can count on is that when he finally does return, he will be certain to corner me somewhere and waste at least half a day regaling me endlessly about the wildebeest that charged him while his gun had jammed, or the sherpa that had nearly

fallen off the mountain and died, or the airplane engine that
had gone out somewhere over the Gobi desert. Or whatever
bullshit macho adventure he's been up to for the past few
weeks.

The stories are always the same: one of his companions
on the safari or the climb or the trek or the expedition was
always a fool or a tyro or (worst of all!) a woman—who
naturally didn't know how to act in life-and-death circumstances; thereby bringing calamity down from the heavens
. . . which, however, was conveniently averted at the penul-
timate moment when the legendary Gunnar Brushwood
stepped in with his legendary swampcraft or marksmanship
or bravery or fortitude or whatever macho virtue was required . . . and—praise be!—all was made right.

But I have to say, Gunnar had never taken off with a
hundred thousand bucks before. That was a new one on me.

"I'm sure this is just a little mix-up," I said airily. "Gunnar has several investment instruments that he dips into occasionally. I'm sure he just put his finger on the wrong one."
Another shameless lie. (Man, do I hate lying! But as we'll
get into later, I seem to be very good at it.) If you knew
Gunnar, the idea of his having investments lying around
would be so ludicrous as to beggar belief. But then Van
Slyke didn't know Gunnar.

"Then you have the funds," the child-banker said, much
relieved.

"Well of *course* we have the funds! I just don't know that
I can put my hands on them in fifty-five minutes."

Van Slyke put his face in his hands. "Oh, God!" he said
finally. "My boss is gonna kill me. Two weeks I've been on
the job, and my boss is gonna tear my head off."

If the kid hadn't come here on a mission to throw me into
personal and professional bankruptcy, I probably would have
felt sorry for him.

"Look," I said. "Call up your boss and tell him that
Sunny Childs, the chief financial officer of Peachtree Inves-

tigations, personally assures you that we'll have the hundred grand by next Friday. Minor mix-up, everything's under control, the legendary Gunnar Brushwood is on the case, yadda yadda yadda. How's that sound?''

Van Slyke looked up, his eyes wide with trusting innocence. ''You think that'll work?''

''Hey, sure.'' I smiled broadly, turned my phone around and pushed it across the desk. ''Dial nine to get out.''

Van Slyke made the call to his boss while I sat there stewing. This was a disaster. What in God's name had that moron Gunnar been thinking? I must have explained how the loan worked at least a dozen times. And he kept saying: 'If it's *my* money, then how come I can't take it out of the bank?' To which I kept responding that if I could answer questions like that, I'd be head of the Federal Reserve and not a lowly private investigator. But I thought it had finally sunk in, that he had finally understood that he absolutely positively couldn't touch the jumbo.

Van Slyke finally got off the phone.

''Good news!'' he said.

''Oh?''

''He's giving you until noon on Tuesday.''

''Noon!? Tuesday!?'' It was Memorial Day weekend. That meant I had about four and a half business hours to come up with a hundred thousand dollars. Or find Gunnar, whichever came first.

The prospects for either were distinctly not good.

''Well, this is terrific, huh?'' Van Slyke jumped up, face shining. ''Great meeting you, Sunny! You mind my calling you Sunny? I'll see myself out.'' Then the child-banker was gone leaving only the sour odor of pubescent fear.

I dialed our bookkeeper. ''Go ahead and give out the rest of the paychecks now,'' I said. ''But tell everybody to cash them today. Straight to the bank, do not pass go, do not collect $200—you hear me? Cash them *now*.''

I grabbed my purse and headed for the door. Time to give

the bad news to Payton Link. I had a hunch that when I finally had about six straight seconds to reflect on my day, I was going to fall apart like a wet paper bag. Maybe I could page Ron at home, get him to slip away from his family on some trumped-up pretext. The thought left a bad taste in my mouth. But not as bad as the thought of being alone tonight.

There wasn't time to think about it though—not yet, not with clients to placate.

CHAPTER 5

I DROVE OUT to Norcross, the Atlanta suburb where Reliance Insurance has its grandly named ''international headquarters.'' Reliance is like a million other businesses in Atlanta: small, entrepreneurial, and about three years away from either bankruptcy or the big time—whichever fate washes over them first. I know people that run companies like this. (Hell, I'm one of them.) They're always swinging between giddy talk about their company car and their huge bonus and the impending initial public offering which will make them rich beyond dreams of avarice, and doleful stories about having to personally fire two thirds of the people in the customer service department because the firm has blundered into an unexpected cash crunch.

Reliance's offices are located in a bland single-story office park of anemic reddish brick that could have been designed by an unimaginative five-year old. They share the sprawling place with a distribution depot for a Japanese camera manufacturer and a bunch of local companies with inscrutable names like MerComm Finance and Electro-Switch Engineering.

As I pulled into the parking lot, I reflected that this place was modern Atlanta's ground zero, the very quintessence of the city. Maybe even of modern America itself. I find life out here in the suburbs both appalling and fascinating.

Though I suppose the only difference between Reliance Insurance and Peachtree Investigations—or, for that matter, between me and Gunnar on the one hand and people like Payton Link on the other—is that Gunnar and I have dumbly refused, so far, to bow to what is so obviously our fate: we haven't abandoned our anachronistic glass and steel tower downtown for the safer, cheaper low-rise blandness of suburbia. I still live in a loft downtown instead of moving into a gated and (need I mention?) all-white community with a bellicose neighborhood association and lots of stay-at-home mothers. Gunnar and I have, in other words, failed to face reality. Suburbs and McDonalds and low-rise office parks— these things are reality. The American city is nothing but a romantic fantasy, as foolish and backward-looking as Mad King Ludwig's castle. If it weren't for the federal government, the city centers of Atlanta and Cleveland and Dallas and Chicago would have been abandoned to the deer and raccoon years ago.

I sat in the lobby for a while and looked at the framed picture over the receptionist's desk. It was a pastel landscape executed in choppy squiggles—a general type which can be found in every one-story office park in Atlanta. The sound of two people shouting at each other was coming from the hallway beside the receptionist. The receptionist and I politely pretended not to notice.

After a while two young women walked out the front door, both of them carrying cardboard boxes full of employee-of-the-month plaques and coffee cups and framed photographs of smiling children. One of the women had a bad run in her stocking and the other's eyeliner had trickled down her face.

"Downsizing?" I said to the receptionist.

She looked up from the copy of *Us Magazine* she was reading. "If that's what you call firing nice, hardworking people and giving them one week's severance, yeah." Then she looked back down at her magazine.

The shouting stopped, and then Payton Link came out with

a stiff look on his face. "Sorry," he said. "It's been a little tense around here lately." He shook my hand and led me back to his office.

"Bad news," I said when I said down.

"Shit!" Payton Link said. I had never heard Payton Link curse before. He was a former Marine MP, a graduate of the Citadel, a deacon in the Baptist Church, one of the stiffest, most correct guys I've ever met in my life, the kind of man who wears fitted shirts which I suspect he changes twice a day so they won't show any wrinkles where they meet the waistband of his pants.

I dumped out the hundred and ten grand on his spotless desk and explained what had gone wrong with the ransoming of the painting. Payton put the money in a safe built into his credenza and then sat with his hands folded across his flat, military-issue stomach.

"I'd like to point my finger at you and tell you that you messed up, but that's not fair," he said finally. He took off his rimless glasses, prodded his eyes with his fingers. "What's it mean, Sunny?"

"Here's what I think happened. Leslie-Anne Gilmartin was the thief we've been talking to on the phone. She had at least one partner, a man. They had a dispute. The partner killed her and took off with the painting."

"You don't think it was kids in the neighborhood? Carjacker types?"

"Highly unlikely. Carjackers would have taken the car, wouldn't they? Keys were in the ignition. Or even supposing they shot her then got scared and ran away, they wouldn't have gone to the trouble of taking the painting out of the trunk of the car."

"Right, but it doesn't make sense that the killer was an accomplice of hers," Payton said. "Let's suppose you're in a gang of art thieves. You're five minutes away from having a hundred and ten thousand dollars in your hands. Why in

the world would you choose that moment to kill your partner?''

"Because you don't want to ransom the painting," I said.

"Shit shit shit!" Payton said. Then he looked up at me as
though startled. "Pardon me, Sunny."

"That's okay," I said. "I've heard the word once or
twice."

"So if the killer doesn't want to ransom the painting, he
must figure he can get more money fencing it somewhere.
Otherwise he would have waited for the ransom, exchanged
the painting for the money, and *then* shot the girl."

"Presumably."

Payton toyed with his glasses, pushing them around on his
desk with his knuckles. "This is bad," he said finally. "We
really can't pay that claim."

"What do you mean?"

Suddenly he looked guarded. "I don't mean we *can't* pay
it," he said. "I just mean we don't *want* to. That would be
a highly undesirable outcome. We need to get that painting
back."

"I don't know what to tell you, Payton."

After a minute Payton got up and said, "I'll be back."

I sat for a while, studied the pastel over his desk. It was
pretty much the same idea as the one over the receptionist's
desk. I was just beginning to really loathe the picture when
Payton came back into the room. He was accompanied by a
middle-aged woman with a soft-serve whirl of bleached
blond hair, a golfer's freckly tan, and a red suit with large
peplums over small, gym-toned hips. I recognized her as
Marion Cheever, the president and founder of Reliance Insurance. I'd never met her, but I'd seen her picture in the
Atlanta Business Chronicle or someplace like that.

We smiled and shook hands. Without asking Payton, she
plunked herself down in his chair and said, "So I hear you
fucked up, Sunny."

Payton looked mortified.

I studied Marion Cheever for a moment, figuring what tack to take with her. If you back down with somebody like Marion Cheever, they bulldoze you. She was one of those women who had come up in business when there were very few women around—and those who were, weren't taken seriously. She had learned to compensate by acting like an asshole. Or maybe it came naturally.

I decided the best strategy was to bulldoze back.

"Bullshit," I said, then I smiled pleasantly and stood up as if to go.

"Wait, wait, wait," Marion Cheever said. Suddenly she was all sweetness and light. "That came out wrong."

I let my smile cool a little, then sat back down.

"Let me be frank with you, honey," Reliance's president said in a confidential we're-just-putting-on-makeup-in-the-girl's-bathroom sort of tone. "We really need that painting back."

"Uh huh," I said.

"Now I realize that y'all generally work on an hourly compensation basis," she said. "But with this murder and everything, I think maybe we're getting into a special situation here."

"Uh-huh," I said.

"What I was wondering is if you might consider flipping back to page one here and trying another approach on this case?"

Which is when a couple of thoughts came to me. Based on what I'd seen and heard in the lobby, Reliance had hit a patch of bad ice. When that happens, the regulators come around and tell them that if they don't get their losses down and their capital up within a few months, some little guy in a cheap blue suit is going to drop by and padlock the front door.

My other thought was that the policy they wrote on this painting didn't get reinsured. Most small insurers sell off their policies to bigger companies, a process that's called reinsurance. Reinsurance is the safe way to play the business, but it's not all that profitable. If you don't reinsure, your risks go up. But so do your profits . . . assuming you don't get stuck with a bunch of fat claims.

For an outfit the size of Reliance—especially if they were in a tough financial position—the three hundred thousand dollar claim for the painting could be the difference between staying in business or getting shut down by the regulators.

All of which was good news for me.

"You're talking about a bounty arrangement," I said.

Marion Cheever grinned. "Well, I'd put it this way. If you can locate the painting—by hook or by crook, so to speak—we'll pay you a nice healthy, ah, finder's fee."

"How much?"

Marion Cheever looked at me beneficently. "How's twenty-five thousand dollars sound?"

"I'll do you a favor," I said. "I'll waive all the fees and expenses you've already accrued in this matter. And I'll get your painting back. And I'll save you ten grand in the process."

"Ten thousand."

"That's right," I said. "You were willing to pay a hundred and ten thousand to the thieves. I'll get it back for you for a hundred grand even."

Marion Cheever raised her eyebrows, lowered her chin, and blinked several times in rapid succession. This was supposed to indicate to me that she thought I was insane. I knew that she didn't really think that, though. If she'd been me, she'd have asked for the full hundred and ten.

I just sat there.

Payton finally broke the silence. "Look, uh, Sunny . . ."

"Shut up, Payton," Marion Cheever said.

"One hundred thousand, payable in the form of a cashier's check on delivery of the painting," I said. Then I stood up and walked out of the room. As soon as I got into the hallway, I broke into a cold sweat. Either I was really smart, or

I had just alienated Gunnar Brushwood's third best customer in the name of a preposterous long shot. I mean how on God's green earth was I supposed to find this painting anyway? Much less over Memorial Day weekend!

Another way of looking at it, of course, was that if I didn't find some way of coming up with a hundred thousand dollars by Tuesday morning, Peachtree Investigations would not have *any* customers.

Payton Link caught up with me at my car. "Marion wants to know if Gunnar is going to work on this."

"Ah," I said.

"Personally. Will Gunnar give this thing his personal attention?"

I looked at him for a minute and thought about personal integrity and honesty and a lot of vague stuff like that. And then I said, "Absolutely."

"Okay. If Gunnar's on top of it, then Marion says okay. A hundred. But we're in kind of a situation here, and we need it by *yesterday*."

Me too sweetheart, I almost said. Instead, I said, "Hey, don't worry. We'll have the painting by Tuesday morning." Then I gave him a quick peck on the cheek.

He blushed scarlet.

CHAPTER 6

FROM THE CAR, I called the office, asked Keesha to connect me with Earl Wickluff, our senior investigator. "Call out the troops," I said to him. "Cancel all vacation plans, everybody's racking up doubletime this weekend."

"Hold the phone, darling!" Earl said in his throaty hill country accent. "I'm going fishing with my boy up at Lake Allatoona this weekend. Besides, it's already five-fifteen!"

"I'm counting on you," I said. "I'll be there to brief everybody in about half an hour."

I hung up the cellular, cranked up the radio, and started singing along with Reba McIntyre at the top of my lungs. It didn't make me feel any better for screwing up all my employees' vacation plans.

I've never understood people who actually *wanted* to "be in management." To me there are few things worse than messing around in other people's lives: having to tell people that their jobs are at stake if they decide to take their son fishing or go up to Mama's for the weekend is no picnic, believe me.

In an attempt to appease everybody, I took my investigators out to Pilgreen's, an old family-run steak place on the south side of town. I had the waiter bring a round of beers, and then I held up a picture of the painting. Sitting to my right was Tawanda Flornoy, a former Atlanta PD vice detective, who had to quit the force when a parole violator she was trying to arrest for pimping his wife drove over her ankle with a stolen Lincoln Town Car. Tawanda is a six-foot-tall black woman, large in every dimension, who wears a prosthetic foot, long fake nails, and a huge wig which is generally red but occasionally changes shades. Aside from being funny and acerbic, she is probably the shrewdest interviewer I've met in my life. Next to her was Earl Wickluff, our so-called senior investigator who was an old campadre of Gunnar's. If it had been my decision, Earl would have long ago gone back to checking parking meters for the Gwinnett County Police—which is what he was doing before Gunnar hired him years and years ago. Sadly, it was the one decision in the firm I was not free to make.

The other two investigators, Leesa Powers and Barry Wine, had only been with us for a couple of years. They were mostly good for driving around taking pictures of wayward husbands or talking to people who'd seen customers of clients of our clients slip on a piece of lettuce in the vegetable aisle at some grocery store. Domestic discord and bruised sacroiliacs—the foundations of our noble profession.

"This picture is called 'Late Afternoon, Pont Aven, Brittany'," I said, showing them a photograph of the painting. "It was painted in 1897 by an American guy named Childe Hassam, and stolen from the Charlie Biddle Gallery on Monday night. We are going to find it this weekend. And when we do, all five of you will get a cash bonus of a thousand bucks." I looked at them soberly. "You will also get to keep your jobs." That sounded way harsh, so I backed up and explained in rough detail what was going on—something to that effect that if we didn't find this painting by Tuesday morning, Peachtree Investigations would turn into a pumpkin.

Then I handed out assignments: "Tawanda, you and I will conduct interviews. Earl, you'll liaise with the Atlanta PD—

and the FBI, if they haven't all gone home for the weekend—to find out all we can about art thefts of this type. Barry, you'll start doing background checks on everybody with any connection to the gallery where the painting was stolen, and Leesa, you'll be the floater.''

"Uh, I really can't," Leesa said. "I've got the kids this weekend."

Leesa was divorced and in a constant tussle with her ex-husband over custody. "This is really important," I said, I explained again in meticulous detail about how the firm was about to collapse.

"Yeah, but I just I can't do it," she said. "Mo and his bimbo just flew off to fucking Cancun and my Mom's back in Florida and I've got that custody hearing coming up and—''

"I know, I know," I said. "But I really need you."

"I can't," she said firmly.

"Everybody else is ruining their weekends," I said.

"These are my *kids!*" She had a glint of desperation in her eyes.

"Well, can you kind of . . . work around them?"

She looked at me with that pained, unbelieving expression that mothers use as a weapon against those of us who've never had children.

"Alright, alright," I said. "You're out. But obviously I can't give you a bonus.''

"Hey," Barry Wine said, "if she doesn't have to do it, I'm not doing it either."

"Me neither," Earl Wickluff said. "I promised the boy. We s'pose to be fishing, Sunny."

"Thanks for setting such a good example as our senior investigator," I said peevishly.

Earl shrugged, slurped noisily on his beer.

I leaned my elbows on the table, closed my eyes and tried to think. What would Gunnar do, Gunnar the legendary master of finesse, Gunnar the legendary people person? Probably he'd split for Timbuktu and leave me to bail his ass out.

"Look," I said finally, "I mean it's just not fair for me to ruin Tawanda's holiday and not everybody else's."

"So what are you saying?" Barry Wine said.

"If you go, you go. It's y'all's choice. But don't expect a job come Tuesday." As soon as I said it, I felt like the most horrible person in the world. But what choice did I have?

Leesa looked like she was going to burst into tears as she folded her green napkin, set it in front of her and got up from the table. Barry Wine watched her, then he smirked slightly. "Fuck it," he said and stood up, too. Only he didn't fold his napkin. He threw it at me.

When I pulled the napkin off my face, they were both gone. "Earl," I said. "You going, too?"

Earl licked his lips. "Hell, my kid's a pain in the nuts anyway." Then he waggled his finger and thumb at the waiter. " 'Nother Michelob over here, podner."

"Well," Tawanda Flornoy said, helping herself to a huge pile of deep fried squash, "I never liked them two much anyway. Always bitching and carrying on about something."

It didn't make me feel the least bit cleaner in my soul.

"Alright, forget about liaising with the cops, Earl," I said. "After we finish eating, you can get onto the computer, start running background checks. Tawanda, you call the homicide people and see if they'll share anything with us. I'm going talk to this gallery guy, Charlie Biddle."

CHAPTER 7

HE GALLERY GUY turned out not to be a guy at all. Charlie Biddle was very much a she.

The Charlie Biddle Gallery was located in the swank Buckhead section of Atlanta on a sidestreet off East Paces Ferry. The lights were burning when I drove up and there were lots of beautifully dressed people inside, most of them drinking out of glass champagne flutes. A security guard with a thick neck stood by the door looking silly in his rented tuxedo.

He let me in grudgingly when I told him I didn't have an invitation. "Don't move from right there," he said, pointing to the spot where my feet were planted. I suppose he was trying to sound kind of threatening, but his voice was surprisingly high and delicate, and I had to stifle a laugh. He locked the door, waded through the crowd and disappeared.

After a minute he came back with a woman. She was willowy, ash blond, dressed in a clingy black Donna Karan (and no underclothing of any sort as best I could tell) that showed off a serious devotion to the gym and a very tasteful boob job. Her face was shaped like an inverted teardrop, and her skin was flawless. If she'd been an inch or three taller, she'd probably have made vast piles of money as a model.

"This is a bit inconvenient," Charlie Biddle said, smiling brightly. "I'm in the middle of a show."

"Sure," I said. Then I explained how the ransom meeting had gone bad that day. "So anyway," I concluded. "I've been retained by the insurer to try and recover the painting."

Charlie Biddle's smile stayed as bright as ever, but her eyes were restlessly scanning the air over my shoulder. "That's all very nice, but now is not good." She had an odd accent, five parts Northeastern old money to one part middle Europe. I wondered if she was connected to the Biddles of Philadelphia, an old money family if there ever was one. I imagined a rich but dour American father, a beautiful mother from a family of fallen European nobility, Swiss boarding schools, that sort of thing. My imagination has probably seen too many bad movies.

I said, "What if I just sort of follow you around and ask you some questions while you work the room? Or whatever it is that you do." Then I threw my brightest smile right back at her.

Her eyes seemed a little clouded, but she said, "Well, I suppose that would be okay. I *do* want that Hassam back. I've got a client who's simply desperate to buy it."

"You know, though, I could get this over quicker if we could sit down in your office for a few minutes."

Charlie looked slightly annoyed. "Ten minutes," she said. Then she crooked her finger at me and I followed the faintly bitter wake of her Chanel No. 5 through the crowd of art buyers and into a doorway in the back of the room.

Charlie's office was small, simply furnished, the walls empty except for two small but elaborately framed paintings of hunting dogs which hung directly above Charlie's head.

"You like dogs?" I said, nodding at the painting.

"Do *I* like dogs?" Charlie looked at me coolly. "What a silly question. My clients are very traditional, very unimaginative people. They like dogs. They like horses. They like ships. They like happy nymphs and happy cherubs and happy peasants. They like pictures they understand." Suddenly she laughed, a happy goat-like bray that you wouldn't have expected out of someone as polished as she was. Then again, I noticed that as soon as the door closed it seemed like a healthy portion of her polish dropped away, as though it was just a role she played for her clients. "I just give them what they want."

I laughed, too.

"So what can I tell you?" she said.

I took out a legal pad, set it on my lap. "First tell me about the painting. Where you got it, how long you had it, that sort of thing."

"Childe Hassam was a pretty famous American painter in his day. Not in the same league as, say, Sargent or Whistler—but he had his good days. He was somewhat neglected during the midcentury, but now that prices on all the French Impressionists have gotten so insane, there's been more interest in the Americans. Hassam is one of the few painters in the Impressionist realm that a more or less normal human being can buy. His best oils go for around a million."

"Normal human beings can buy million-dollar paintings?"

"Well, by normal I mean as opposed to being the sort of person who owns half of Tokyo—which is about what it takes to buy a Van Gogh or a Manet. Anyway the crummier oils and the minor watercolors would go in the mid-six figure range—and *entre nous,* 'Late Afternoon' is probably the ugliest fully finished oil he ever did. The draftsmanship is awful even for Hassam . . . though God knows I'd never tell that to *them . . .*" Here she cocked a thumb at the door. "Anyway, as I'm sure you know, I insured it for three hundred and fifty."

"I see."

"Anyway, I bought the painting from a private dealer in Eastern Europe. As a result of the second world war, frankly the provenance is a little, ah, problematic."

"I'm not sure what you mean."

"Provenance means the history of a painting's ownership. The more you can back up the ownership history, the better for the worth of the painting. You know, bills of sale, catalog listings, connoisseur's marks, that kind of thing. It's part of the authentication process so that you can avoid misattribution, forgeries, so on, so forth."

"Yeah, but what's that got to do with the war?"

"Okay, here's what we know. Evidently Childe Hassam painted it while on a European tour in 1897. It's documented that he stopped at an artist's colony in Pont Aven where he sold several paintings to fellow artists. After that there's no record of who owned the painting until a really bad black-and-white reproduction shows up in a pre-war French auction catalog. Apparently 'Late Afternoon' was sold to a Jewish industrialist named Pierre Stein—this would have been in 1926 or 27—by a small auction house in Paris called J. Montmorency et Fils. The war comes along and unlucky Pierre ends up dead. There are no extant records of what happened to his collection. So the end of the war comes and the painting appears to have vanished. But frankly it's not the caliber of work that anybody four or five decades ago would have been knocking themselves out trying to track down."

"I see."

"Anyway, since the end of the cold war, a lot of stuff that got looted by the Nazis has started surfacing in Eastern Europe. The Old Masters and things like that tended to end up in Moscow. But more minor works? Sometimes they just fell through the cracks, ended up on the wall of some minor party functionary in Bulgaria, or the collection of a provincial art academy in Russia, or God knows where. I mean there's some very interesting stuff floating around . . . if you know where to look." A brief smile touched her lips, then went away.

"And you know where to look?"

Suddenly she was looking at me very closely. "There's a

whole network of people out there—mafia, quasi-mafia, Chechens, starving artists, former dissidents, underemployed jerks that used to be with the Ministry of Culture in Moldova, you name it. And they're all looking for a way to drive a Mercedes and give their fat little wives a fur coat for Christmas. You go over there, you ask around, you flash a little cash . . . you'd be amazed the things that start to surface."

"So the Hassam surfaced."

"Last year in Kiev." She took a key out of her desk, unlocked a filing cabinet and pulled out a brick-red accordion folder from which she took a stack of papers as thick as my thumb. She leafed through them briefly, then handed them to me. They were all typewritten in cyrillic alphabet and had a bureaucratic look to them. Some were yellowed and brittle, some were old-fashioned carbon copies on onionskin paper, and many were covered with official seals and stamps. "The KGB had an art recovery operation after the second world war. They went after art owned by the Nazis, by collaborators and industrialists, by big landowners in Eastern Europe, you name it. There was usually some kind of official transaction or requisition to make it legal—but basically they just stole whatever they wanted. Just like the Nazis had done. Then the stuff got parcelled out all over the Soviet Union. These papers you're looking at document who had this painting and when. Theoretically it kind of got shuffled through a couple of ministries and then buried in a minor museum."

"*Theoretically?*" I said.

Charlie's eyebrows went up just the tiniest fraction of an inch. "Frankly, knowing the people I got this painting from? This documentation could all be bullshit."

It was my turn for the raised eyebrows. "How so?"

"Everything in the East is shady. Everything. Where did things come from? Who owned them? Were they stolen, 'expropriated,' requisitioned, whatever? You don't necessarily want to know. But if you ask these smelly little characters for provenance, they'll say, 'No problem, come back tomorrow.' You come back the next day or the next week or the next month and suddenly they've got a nice big stack of paperwork. Is it live or is it Memorex? I have no idea. Sure looks good though, huh?" She grinned briefly. "And frankly I don't give a damn, as long as whoever buys it from me is happy." She looked at me coolly.

"Wow! And here I thought selling art was a nice clean business for debutantes who didn't like holding down real jobs."

Charlie smirked. "That's what we like the world to believe. The truth's a little more sordid."

"How much did you pay for it?"

"A gentlewoman never tells."

"Seriously, how much?"

Charlie's eyes narrowed a little. There seemed to be very little Swiss boarding school about her now. "I'm being so serious you wouldn't believe it. You can be damn sure it was a lot less than I'm offering it for. Beyond that, I wouldn't tell my priest."

"You got it for dirt, huh?"

Charlie just leaned back in her simple leather chair and looked at me, legs crossed, one ankle swinging languidly. "I'm offering it for four twenty. I insured it for three fifty. I suspect it'll bring something in the high twos. Subject closed."

"Moving right along," I said. "When did you get the picture here?"

"Well, that's kind of complicated. I bought the picture in Kiev last December, had it crated and flown to Atlanta. Went through customs, all the usual bureaucratic hoops, had it here for about a week. Flew it to New York where I had it authenticated and cleaned, and a little minor restoration done. It was in atrocious condition. Then I flew it back down here and reframed it. That would have been back in April. Obviously it sat for a little while while I had it photographed and printed up the catalog. I didn't actually put it on the wall of the gallery until, let's see, I guess it was last Saturday. That was, what, the seventeenth of May.''

"Did you show it to anyone before that?"

She looked at me cagily. "A couple of long-standing clients."

"Could you give me their names?"

"Absolutely not."

"Hey, look," I said. "We've got to follow up with every single person who's had contact with that painting. Framers, restorers, your employees, the carpenter who put the nail in the wall that you hung it from, you name it. Most art thefts are inside jobs."

"No, this wasn't an inside job. The people who stole this were idiots or crackheads or something."

"I'll need the names anyway."

Charlie shook her head. "I can give you the name of the framer, the restorer, my employees. But I'm not going to have you hassling my clients. I mean seriously, you'd be wasting your time anyway. These are rich, reputable people."

"Still."

"Forget it."

I sighed. "All right, tell me about the theft itself."

"As you might expect, we've got pretty elaborate security precautions here. Motion detectors, window and door alarms, those foot treadle things—probably twenty thousand dollars worth of equipment. Plus a security service that checks on the property at frequent intervals. When I left on Monday night, I set the alarm, locked up and left. I think it was around ten-thirty. I went home, went to bed. Around two in the morning the phone wakes me up, it's some detective telling me the place has been broken into. I drive down there like a madwoman, and voilá, no more Childe Hassam."

"Okay, I'll get to that in a minute," I said. "But what about the condition of the place? How did they get in? They set off the alarm I assume?"

"Yeah. These crackhead morons thought they were being clever. They bashed a hole in the wall with a sledge hammer. You should have seen the mess I had to clean up. Probably thought they wouldn't set off the alarm if they didn't go through a door or window. I mean, hello! have you pinheads ever heard of motion detectors?" Charlie Biddle was seething.

"Okay. What else?"

"That's it really. Big hole in the wall. I guess they crawled through. As soon as they go inside of course they set off the motion detectors and the alarm starts blasting. So I guess they just grabbed the Hassam and hit the road."

"And that's the only thing they took?"

Charlie nodded.

"What's the most valuable painting here?"

Charlie squinted, as though thinking. "I guess the Hassam."

"You *guess*? How much more valuable was the Hassam than anything else you've got?"

"I've got a Howard Pyle watercolor, a couple of Remington oil studies."

"How much would those be worth?"

Charlie shifted in her seat. "Seventy-five? A hundred?"

"So the Hassam was far and away the best thing to steal."

"I suppose."

I frowned skeptically. "And you're still thinking crackheads? I hate to say it, but it seems obvious these people knew what they were doing."

"Yeah, but if it was an inside job, surely they'd have figured out a way of walking out with at least two or three more pieces."

I looked at her curiously. "I didn't say it was an inside job. I was just saying it sounds like they knew which painting to take."

"Hmmm," Charlie said. "You've got a point."

I don't know what it was, but it seemed like Charlie was being a little obtuse about this.

I turned to a fresh page in my legal pad and scribbled the following list:

    Restorer
    Close friends of yours
    Framer
    Authenticator
    Photographer for show catalog
    Printer for catalog
    Gallery Employees
    Cleaning Staff
    Gallery Customers
    Security Guards
    Any subcontractors (plumbers, carpenters, gas com-
        pany, etc.) who have been in the gallery in the past
        month
    Others with contact with painting

Then I tore the list off the pad and handed it to her.

"My God," she said, "you're certainly being thorough. Well, how about if I get this to you by Tuesday."

"How about now?"

Charlie looked a little off-put. "Sunny, no offense, but this is my most important show of the year and I really need to get back to my clients."

"I've got a guy sitting at a computer twiddling his thumbs at this very minute, waiting to start running names. We really need to get moving."

Charlie clamped her mouth shut, looked at me angrily.

"Every day that goes by, the trail gets colder," I said. "You want to sell that painting or not?"

Charlie stared at the yellow piece of paper, then picked up a Mont Blanc pen and started scribbling furiously. When she was done, she flung the paper onto the desk. "My Rolodex is right there. Feel free to get the addresses and phone numbers out of it.'' Then she stalked toward the door. She paused with her hand on the knob and looked at me curiously.

''You're working for Reliance, right?''

I nodded.

''What makes them think you can find this painting any better than the cops?''

I shrugged. ''Simple. It's a numbers game. The Atlanta Police Department probably responded to a hundred burglary and robbery calls last night. Sure, most of them are just car thefts, snatch-and-grabs, penny ante stuff. But one or two of those calls probably involved, oh, a fifty-thousand-dollar baseball card collection or a seventeen-carat ruby necklace or a vintage Mercedes. The cops don't even dust for fingerprints unless it's major loss; they just file the paperwork. Even a case like this, every robbery detective is juggling a couple or three cases as big as yours. But me, I've got a team of four people on this, and that's all we're going to do until we find this painting.''

''Really?'' Charlie said. ''You wouldn't think an insurance company would care that much.''

''Usually they don't.''

After I finished digging names and addresses out of the Rolodex, I called Earl Wickluff at the office and read the list to him to run through the computer. ''I want credit bureaus, judgments, D&Bs, anything you can dig up on these people.''

Earl sounded a little groggy, but he read the list back to me without any major errors.

''Have you heard anything from Tawanda?'' I asked.

''Yeah, she called a few minutes ago. Said the cops aren't giving her much.

''I don't suppose you've heard from Gunnar?''

Earl just laughed.

CHAPTER 8

I T WAS ELEVEN o'clock by the time I got back to my loft down on Luckie Street. I'd been working nonstop since seven o'clock that morning but the adrenaline was still racing around in my veins. I checked my messages. Six of them, all from my mother. She was still badgering me about this fancy shindig that was happening on Saturday night. Something about how some of the bigwigs at my brother's law firm were going to be there and he needed to make a good impression since he was up for partnership in a few months. It's axiomatic in my mother's book that no man can make a good impression without a dolled-up woman on his arm.

I fast-forwarded through her messages, hoping each time that the next message would be from Ron. But each time it was just Mom, an escalating assault of chiding and shaming and cajoling—her full repertoire of manipulative techniques. I love my mother, but God she's a pain in the ass sometimes.

After I got through all six messages I stared at the red light for a while and replayed the whole thing, hoping I'd somehow missed the message from Ron.

I hadn't.

I was really, really, really, really not in the mood to be alone. Call me a wimp, but screwing up a dangerous assignment, flirting with bankruptcy, lying to a client, firing a woman for wanting to be home with her children, and watching a beautiful young woman bleed to death—this kind of day takes its toll on you.

I went into the bathroom, washed my face, brushed my teeth, and thought about Ron. I thought about his nice manners and his lovely long eyelashes and the way you could see his ribcage when he lay on the bed with his hands behind his head (as he always did after we made love).

When I was done in the bathroom, I walked into the big open living space of my loft and stood there for a while, trembling. I don't know how long I was there, but it must have been a good while. Finally I rallied and called Ron's pager, punched in the nonexistent phone number that was our secret code for him to call me. Then I lay down on my queen-size bed and stared at the ancient timbering in the ceiling. My blood made a whooshing sound in my ears and I kept waiting for the emotional floodgates to open, but they didn't: I just felt this numb fluttering in my head as though someone had injected the base of my brain with novocaine.

Ron never called back.

After a while I started to drift off. I imagined myself talking to the dead girl, asking her why she'd stolen the painting. In my reverie, she didn't answer, just sat there squeezing the talk button on her radio. *Click-click. Click-click.* She was quite beautiful—you could see that even with the blood on her face. My mother would have had something to say on that score, something wonderfully retro: a pretty girl never has to steal or something like that.

Click-click.

Somewhere along the way, the clicking became a ringing and I realized someone was ringing the bell so they could come up to my apartment. I went over and pressed the button for the door without even using the intercom to ask who it was. The old freight elevator wheezed and clacked and then someone was knocking at my door.

It was Ron, of course.

I stepped aside and let him in. He's forty, a little older

than me, but he looks younger. His hair is black and glossy as a seal's pelt, and he looks out at the world through long lovely eyelashes. He wears a neat mustache with a fleck of gray above the left corner of his mouth, which gives you the impression he's smiling wryly at you even when he isn't. As a rule I'm not wild about mustaches, but his suits his face nicely. He also dresses both meticulously and beautifully—a rare quality in a straight man: chocolate browns, olives, tweeds, muted burgundies.

Ron gave me a deep sucking kiss and handed me some cheap flowers and a bottle of Beaujolais Nouveau. I put the flowers in a jar, let him pour the wine, and then he put his arms around me and kissed me again and it was all fine until he told me he loved me. I guess I didn't believe him, so I'd just as soon he skipped that line.

Still, it was a lot better than being alone.

"You want to talk to me about it?" he said finally.

"Not really," I said, surprising myself. I had figured my long-postponed emotional meltdown would begin as soon as Ron walked in. But nothing happened. I still felt half-drugged.

So instead of talking we groped our way to the bed where we kissed and fondled and knocked over a glass of wine and finally made love. Ron was slow and tender, and it was the nicest thing that had happened to me all day.

After it was over Ron put his hands behind his head, crossed his ankles and snoozed. I stared at the ceiling and started thinking what a shit I was. I'm not usually a gloomy or self-critical person, but I guess it was just that kind of day. After a while I started wondering what kind of bogus excuse Ron made to his wife after I beeped him. I wondered if she believed him. I wondered if he thought about his two beautiful daughters while he was buying the flowers and the seven-dollar bottle of wine at the Winn Dixie store. I wondered why someone would kill a beautiful young girl over an ugly old painting.

Finally Ron got up and put his clothes on again, and we talked a little. I didn't tell him about Leslie-Anne Gilmartin getting shot, I just told him about the smaller bumps in the road—including the two people I had to fire.

"Hey," he said enthusiastically. "You need a couple of new hands, how about talking to Sean?"

I mentioned before that Ron had been trying to convince me to hire his brother-in-law, Sean. I wasn't quite sure how to take it: Ron always said that Sean was a good guy—but then he'd go on to tell about what a screw-up the kid was. Not in so many words, but enough to give me that impression. Sean had dropped out of Georgia Tech, spent a couple years as a cop in this dinky little town in north Georgia where he left under some sort of cloud that Ron had never completely explained. After that he'd been a security guard and some other stuff like that, just kind of knocking around, never holding onto a job for very long.

I couldn't figure out why Ron thought he ought to be able to fob off his useless relative on *me*.

"Hm," I said. "I don't know. We're in kind of a down period right now, and I've got a couple of freelancers who've done good work for me in the past—"

"Yeah, but you could use an extra couple of hands on this painting thing couldn't you?"

"Sure but—"

"Then why not try him out on a freelance basis? If Sean goofs up, no harm done. But if he does a good job, then you can decide whether you've got a place for him."

He had a point. I shrugged. "Okay. Why not? Send him by around noon tomorrow."

Ron kissed me on the lips. "Thanks, babe! Ellen's been bugging me to help him out for months. She's going to be ecstatic."

Ellen, being his wife. Call me ungenerous, but she's not a person whose ecstasy I'm supremely interested in fueling.

Ron didn't seem to notice the lack of enthusiasm in my face. But boy was *he* suddenly full of great good cheer.

I followed him to the door where he kissed me and, for the second time that night, told me he loved me. He'd said it before a few times, but it wasn't until that night that I realized how much it rubbed me the wrong way. I mean, it may or may not have been true—these things are so mysterious, aren't they?—but it *seemed* like a lie to me. And as I've said, I hate a lie, passionately.

After he was gone, sleep was out of the question. I listened to Patsy Kline sing "I Fall To Pieces." She may have, but I didn't. Finally I gave up and called my little brother Walter at home. When the answering machine kicked in I hung up and called his office. Surprisingly, he answered. I looked at the clock: 1:15 A.M.

"Damn!" I said. "Midnight oil, huh?"

"Hey!" he said. "Big sister!" His voice was bright with adrenaline. I guess practicing law at 1:15 in the morning will do that to you.

I grabbed two frozen bean burritos out of the freezer, put on a shoulder holster with my LadySmith in it, and hiked through the spooky, deserted canyons of downtown Atlanta to the tall spire where my long-suffering brother spends the vast majority of his life. He was waiting in the lobby, talking to the security guard.

We took the elevator up to the 49th floor without speaking, then I followed him back to his office. Some sort of legal document flickered on his computer screen.

"So what's going on?" Walter said. "Kind of late for you, isn't it?"

Which is when—finally—my thumb came out of the dam and everything started busting loose. Walter held me for a long time while I cried and cried, stroking my hair and murmuring things to me. When I find a man with a heart as good as Walter's I will drag him to Las Vegas the next day and marry him. Screw the white dress, the silverware, the engagement ring: there is no substitute for decency and loyalty in a man. Why is it so hard to come by?

And maybe that was part of what I was crying about, too.

After I was done sobbing I felt somewhat restored, so I told Walter about the girl and the painting. "It's just not right," I said finally. "Who would do a thing like that?"

Then I made some brave noises about how I wasn't just going to get the painting back, I was going to find out who killed that poor girl. Even if she was a thief, I said, nobody deserved what had happened to her.

To his credit, Walter never once looked over my shoulder at the computer screen, never once indicated that he was worried about whatever grand litigation emergency was keeping him here at one-thirty on the first morning of Memorial Day Weekend. He just nodded and held my hand and said all the right things. I would wish every woman in the world a brother like him.

When I'd finally run out of steam, Walter said, "So I guess you heard about this thing tomorrow? This party?"

Here was where Walter and I differed. Where I made a point—maybe too much of a point—of keeping my mother out of my life, Walter let her completely rule his. Walter was one of the brightest, sweetest kids I've ever known. He was also a wickedly talented musician. But Mom had long ago convinced him that only a nitwit would try to make a living whanging on a guitar and singing in bars every night. She browbeat him into grade-grubbing his way through Dartmouth, and then after graduation when he threatened to move to Nashville and flirted briefly with the singer-songwriter life, she pulled out the big guns (guilt, tears, begging, Right Reason, and whatever else she could lay her hands on) until finally he had caved and applied to law school.

He had told me back then that he would never actually *practice*, oh no no no, God forbid! It was just a safety strategy to keep himself occupied and solvent until he finally got his musical career rolling. Well, here he was nine years later, working on some awful brief in hopes of becoming the umpteenth partner at Underhill, Tabb, LaFollette, Gold & Pearcy, not quite the largest but certainly the most prestigious and most white shoe firm in Atlanta. It made me depressed and angry every time I thought about it. So I just didn't think about it much. Only on days like today.

"Yeah, Walter," I said. "Mom told me about the party. I didn't listen too carefully, though."

"Well, it's a fundraiser. Good cause and all that. AIDS or something. Mom put the whole thing together and she's made sure that half the partners in my firm are there. The whole thing's shameless, I know, but she's really just trying to help."

"Help what?"

"Help me make partner."

Silly me. Now I understood. I sighed somewhat obnoxiously.

"Partners have to bring in clients," Walter said. "Mom just wants me to put on a good front. Nothing too serious."

"Oh God," I said.

Walter got a hangdog look on his face. "So . . . uh . . . what do you think?"

"About what?"

"The party. You think you can come?"

"So Mom will get off your back."

Walter shrugged.

"Don't you know any girls?"

"Yeah, but they're mostly like art freak types, rock and roll hangers-on, that kind of thing. Mom hates everybody I date, you know that."

"I'm really going to be busy this weekend," I said. "It's terrible timing."

"An hour and a half?" he said. "You eat, you shake

hands with my boss and his boss and you giggle at their jokes and then you split.''

"That's my forte, you know—girlish chatter, all the feminine virtues.''

"Please? Pretty please with sugar on top?''

I couldn't help cracking a smile. "Okay, okay.''

He poked me under the arm. "I think you could lose the shoulder holster, though,'' he said. "It ruins the line of nice a sequined dress.''

After a while I went into the kitchen at the end of the hallway and nuked the two bean frozen burritos and took two Cokes out of the freezer.

Walter and I ate the horrible burritos, and then he put a Sheryl Crow CD on his boom box. When "Every Day Is A Winding Road'' came on he cranked it up really loud and we went out into the hallway and danced, grinning like apes.

"Every day is a winding road!'' we yelled joyously along with Sheryl. "Every day I get a little bit closer to feeling fine!''

And for a minute it was like we were ten years old again, before the world had been damaged.

CHAPTER 9

THE NEXT MORNING I woke up on the couch in Walter's office. I jogged home, dumped about a gallon of Visine in my eyes, took a shower and headed back over to the office.

Tawanda Flornoy was waiting for me. "Somebody named Marion Cheever called from Reliance Insurance asking for a heads-up from Gunnar. What's that all about? I thought Gunnar was out of town."

"Oh dear," I said.

"She really seemed hot to talk to him."

"Oh dear," I said again.

I called Marion Cheever, updated her on the piddling amount of progress we'd made. She was insistent about talking to Gunnar.

"I think he's out at Krispy Kreme getting a bag of doughnuts right now," I said. "You might check your e-mail, though."

"Just tell him to call," she said.

After I got off the phone, I logged onto Gunnar's e-mail account and sent a note to Marion. I signed it, 'Affectionately, Gunnar Brushwood.' Then I put, 'P.S. I have messengered a bounty agreement to your office re: amount to be received by this firm upon your receipt of the stolen painting. Don't forget, payment is to be by cashier's check.' "

As far as I know, Gunnar has never used his e-mail account in his life. I set the thing up in hopes he might use it to keep in better touch with our clients. Dream on, Sunny! The result, of course, was that I now masquerade as Gunnar on the Internet. It seems to make our clients happy, getting all these expansive notes from Gunnar, so I guess there must be some virtue in the ruse.

Anyway, I figured it might hold Marion Cheever off for a while.

Tawanda Flornoy came into my cubicle and heaved herself into a chair with a rich sigh. She was holding a stack of computer printouts, the ones Earl Wickluff had run last night on the people Charlie Biddle had listed as having come in contact with the painting. "I took the liberty of glancing through these before you got here," she said.

"Anything interesting?"

"Oh yes," she said, smiling broadly. Today she was wearing a black wig, the one that looked like Gladys Knight, circa 1965. She had a different wig for each day of the week.

"Who do you like?"

Without looking at any of the papers she said, "Our friend Charlie's right hand man is guy named Roland C. Porter III. I don't know what a salesman at an art gallery makes, but I'm guessing it's not enough to sustain a consumer debt load of forty-six thousand five hundred and eleven dollars spread across nine different credit cards. Seems like a brand new Mercedes 420E would be a little rich for his blood, too."

"Interesting."

"Better yet, this ambitious young man has four judgments outstanding against him, including three for bad checks, one for nonpayment of rent."

"Excellent. Who else?"

"This person she lists as a house painter? They had a personal bankruptcy a few years back, a pretty good pile of bills. But nothing that really sticks out."

"What's his name?"

"It's a her. Jillian Silver."

"Anything else?"

"The authenticator. Fellow by the name of Milton George. His financial picture is also pretty interesting. Had a lot of debt up until about three months ago. Plus two judgments. Caesar's Palace and Circus Circus—both in Las Vegas, Nevada."

"A gambling problem."

"Well, he got worse problems than that now."

"Like what?"

"He comes up deceased."

"I guess that takes him out of the running," I said.

"But here's my favorite piece of evidence." She held up a piece of paper. From where I was sitting, it looked blank.

"What's that? I can't see."

"This is everything the computer knows about Ms. Charlie Biddle, gallery owner extraordinaire."

I squinted at the page. Nothing. "You think Earl just messed up the search parameters?"

"Nope. He ran the Dun & Bradstreet on the gallery. She's got a lot of bills, no doubt about that, but nothing running behind. Her personal credit bureau, though, that's the strange one. He tried about ten different ways and she appears not to exist. I took the liberty of retracing his steps."

"And?"

"Nada."

"Damn. That's strange."

"Isn't it, though."

"Might be interesting to see if we could get the cops to take a look at that list. Do an alias search on Charlie Biddle, then get them to run all the names through the crime computer. You got any sway with that guy in Homicide, Carl Fontaine?"

"I was working on that old fox yesterday, didn't get too far." She ran her fingernails through her wig. Today they were painted yellow with red polkadots. "I could give it another shot now that they have the crime scene processed. Way I'd play it, we're both working the same side of the street; we want the painting, they want whoever killed the girl. I'll go with how we got a team of professionals working twenty-four hours a day on this thing, we scratch their back, they scratch ours. You know the routine I'm talking about."

"Will he go for it?"

She clamped her eyebrows down, mock serious. "You talking to Tawanda Flornoy!"

"Go to it," I said. "Oh, here's another name." I wrote TERRY YOKUM on a sticky note and gummed it onto the stack of computer paper. "That's her boyfriend. I don't have a Social or an address on him, but you can run it down on the computer. Meantime, I think I'll see if I can track down this guy Roland Porter that works at the gallery."

The Charlie Biddle Gallery, as I'd expected, was closed. I walked around the alley on the side, found a patch of unpainted brick where the thieves had smashed their hole in the wall. I wondered how long it would take to do something like that.

As I was staring at it, a silver Mercedes pulled up and a gorgeous blond boy got out and stood watching me with his hands on his hips. He had the look of a Roland C. Porter III: six hundred dollars worth of casual Italian clothes, razor-cut hair that was a bit too fashionable for my taste, broad shoulders, nice pectorals, and the kind of bronze skin that you only get from a tanning booth. If he wasn't gay, then he was sure sending out the wrong signals.

"Yes?" he said sharply. "Is there something I can help you with."

"Sunny Childs," I said, flashing my PI's license. For some reason I get a childish pleasure in doing that. "I'm an investigator with the insurance company."

"Yes?" Same snippy, demanding inflection.

"Obviously we're trying to get back the Childe Hassam. Charlie suggested I talk to you."

"I doubt that," he said.

"That we're trying to get back the painting? Or that Charlie suggested I talk to you?"

He ignored me, walked over to a large steel door in the back of the gallery, unlocked two deadbolts and walked inside. I followed him, watched as he punched in a code on the security panel by the door and turned on the lights. We were in a cramped storeroom with racks of paintings against one wall and a stack of cardboard boxes on the other. The floor was concrete.

"So how many people besides you and Charlie have the code to the door?" I said cheerfully.

He continued to ignore me so I followed him through the next door and out into the gallery.

"I'm just trying to find out a little about the security precautions and that sort of thing," I said.

There was a counter at the back of the room with several expensive-looking leather chairs behind it. He sprawled in one of them, then looked up at me as though wondering why I was still there.

I dropped my cheerful expression, leaned my arms against the counter, and stared blankly down at him for a minute. "Roland, I don't know if you heard, but a young girl was murdered yesterday when I tried to ransom that Hassam. That means this is not just about a stolen painting. It's about murder. So let me fill you in on something. If you keep acting like an officious little jerk, here's what's most likely going to happen next: a couple of cops will come in here, and they will make you get in a squad car and they will transport you to an ugly little building downtown that says Atlanta PD Homicide Unit next to the door and they will put you in a room and give you two cans of Coke Classic and then they will sit around shooting the shit for several hours while you're wondering what the hell they are doing and then at the exact moment you realize that you really really really need to take a whiz, they will come in and say to you, 'Roland, you owe your creditors over forty-three thousand dol-

lars and you have four judgments outstanding against you
and you're a worthless little faggot check kiter, so how about
telling us why you ripped off the painting and killed that
beautiful sweet little girl.' ''

Roland C. Porter III blinked. I seemed to have gotten his
attention.

"That's not me talking, okay? I'm just telling you how
cops operate, how they think. You understand me, Roland?"

He looked frightened now—but he didn't say anything.

"The reason I mention this, Roland, is that I'm not an
idiot. I don't think like a cop. Obviously you didn't steal that
painting. Maybe you've got a weakness for credit cards, but
anybody with half a brain can see you're not the type to get
involved in something illegal. So the more you can help me
right now, the more I can do to help steer the police toward
whoever really stole the painting."

"How do you know all that?" he said in a shaky voice.
"I mean about the credit cards. And my . . . ah, that problem
I had with the checks."

"It's what I do for a living. Now did you steal that painting?"

"Of course not!"

I tried to sound motherly—something I'm not particularly
good at. "Then help me out. Please. I don't want to have to
jerk you around. I hate getting put in a position where the
next time I'm chatting with Lieutenant Hagee or Major Fontaine down at the homicide office I end up having to agree
with them when they tell me what a squirrelly suspicious
little creep Roland C. Porter III is."

Roland Porter was just a kid, twenty-four or -five. And I
could see he was nervous. "What do you want to know?"

"Just to get the question out of the way, where were you
the night the Hassam was stolen."

"The gallery's closed on Mondays so my, uh, roommate
and I went up to the mountains." He scowled at me. "You

want to check it out? The Dogwood House—it's a B&B up near Asheville, North Carolina.''

"Fair enough," I said. "So tell me about security at the gallery. Does anybody else know the code for the alarm system?''

He shook his head. "No. Just me and Charlie."

"Not the mailman, not the carpenters, not the bookkeeper?''

"I *am* the bookkeeper."

"The maid."

Roland looked at the floor. "There's not much to clean here. So as far as that goes, I'm the maid, too."

"You sound like a pretty irreplaceable employee. How long have you worked for Charlie?''

"About two years."

"She a good employer?''

He pouted for a moment. "She's all right. She's got a little bit of a diva thing going on, but I don't mind that.''

"What about the gallery? How long has she had it?''

"I think she started it about ten years ago."

"Tell me about the gallery generally—what kinds of work you represent, who your customers are, that kind of thing.''

"For the most part there are two kinds of galleries. It's not a real firm distinction, but on the whole you've got contemporary galleries that represent modern artists, and more traditional galleries that tend to represent stuff that's more in the figurative realm. We're the latter type.''

"So you sell . . .''

"Third-tier impressionists. Maybe some Brandywine school. When we're lucky maybe an occasional Old Master drawing or a teeny little Turner watercolor. And of course lots of whippets and stallions and frigates scudding across the watery main. Most of our clients are rich but not . . .''

"Not too sophisticated."

"Frankly, yes. Most of them wouldn't know John Singer Sargent from Jackson Pollack. They just want something to put up in their horrible two-million-dollar house that won't clash with the furniture. You know, a ship that looks like a ship, a dog that looks like a dog.''

"I see. And where do you get the paintings?"

"Charlie does all the acquisitions. A fair amount of our work is sold on consignment. We've probably got a dozen local clients who buy and sell art as a hobby—old Bryn Mawr graduates, that sort of person. They don't like modern art, but they're reasonably sophisticated. Some of these paintings in here have sort of made the rounds.'' He pointed at a small watercolor on the other side of the room. ''That horrible little sketch over there is a Turner. They all buy it because it's a Turner and then they hang it on the wall for a while and finally they realize how wretched it is, so it comes back here and we sell it to somebody else.

"The rest of the collection Charlie has picked up hither and yon. Dealers, auctions like Christie's or Sotheby's, once in a blue moon even from other galleries.''

"What about Eastern Europe?"

Roland looked surprised. "How'd you know about that? She's made several acquisitions from the Ukraine and Russia in the past couple of years. I guess the deals are good if you're in the right place at the right time. But there's a lot of red tape—customs and whatnot.''

"Who does the paperwork?"

"On this end? Me, mostly. That's not Charlie's forte.''

"What is?"

"Selling.'' The boy smiled slyly. "Selling and selling and selling.''

"Does she have good taste?"

"Taste!'' Roland looked vaguely offended. "Taste really isn't an issue in a place like this. A horse by Stubbs is worth more than a horse by Ward. It's that simple. Who cares that it's the worst horse Stubbs ever painted. You just have to have a nose for what the average surgeon's wife will want to hang over their endtables.''

"Surgeon's *wives*? That sounds a little retro."

"The world hasn't changed as much as we'd like to think," he said archly. "Most surgeons in this town are still men. And Southern men—*straight* Southern men—are afraid of art. Okay, sure, the occasional ship of the line, full sail, guns blazing. Or maybe Bobby Jones swinging a three wood on the ninth green. But the average Southern man figures people will think he's a swishy little queer if he looks at a painting." He laughed. "And they're probably right. So they let their wives run the aesthetic aspects of their lives. *Plus ça change . . .* "

"Have you had any unusual or suspicious customers recently? People who didn't seem like they were really who they claimed they were? People who asked about security precautions?"

Roland shook his head. "I wish I could think of somebody like that, but I can't. We mostly deal on an appointment basis, referrals, that sort of thing. There's not a lot of walk-in business for fifty-thousand-dollar oil paintings."

"Then why have the gallery at all? Why not just sell out of your house?"

"Makes you look more solid this way, more prosperous. In New York there are gobs of dealers operating out of apartments on the upper west side. The typical Atlanta art patron finds that slightly suspect, you know—as though you might be ready to rip them off and then head for Brazil. Southerners are reassured by brick and mortar."

"What about tradesmen? Any of them hanging around at odd times of day or taking an unusual interest in a painting?"

"You know, funny you mention that. There was this girl, a painter . . ."

"Like a house painter or a *painter* painter?"

"House painter. Charlie had the walls painted before this show she just put together. And this painter kept kind of wandering off. I thought maybe she was going out behind the building to smoke dope or something, but then I found her back in the back staring at one of the paintings.''

"The Hassam?"

"No. The Hassam wasn't here then. It was locked up somewhere.''

"This painter. Was her name . . ." I checked my notes. "Was it Jillian Silver?"

"How do you know all this stuff?"

"I talked to Charlie."

"Oh. Well, anyway, yeah, I think that was her. Kind of slobby looking.''

"What did she say when you found her in there?"

"Nothing. I just told her to get back to work.''

I asked a few more questions, but none of them led anywhere. As I left I thought of something else. I put my little notebook in my purse and got ready to go.

"You, ah, you'll tell those homicide people, won't you?" he said. "That I'm being cooperative?"

"Sure." I smiled and headed for the door. As he let me out I said, "Oh, yeah. One other thing. What's Charlie's real name?''

His face was blank. "Huh?" he said.

CHAPTER 10

I HAD MADE a vague promise to Leslie-Anne Gilmartin's mother, and while of course it was *well-intentioned* bullshit, it was still bullshit: I didn't have any real expectations of finding her killer. Or of even especially trying, for that matter. In fact I had made a point of *not* thinking about Leslie-Anne Gilmartin at all. Not just because I felt sick to my stomach whenever I remembered the look of her blood, the twitch of her hand, her dying smell, but because the thought of her annoyed me. It was a lot easier to focus on finding the painting. A nice, clean Gunnar-like hunting expedition: going out to track down something with a simple and clear— but not too intimate—relationship to my life.

Self-centered? Hell, yes. But if you've ever seen anybody murdered, or thought in practical terms about committing yourself to finding out who killed a human being, you'll know that it's a complicated, scary thing. It weighs heavy, believe me. And I was all for dodging that burden.

Which brings me to the envelope.

When I got back to the office, somebody had left a large manila envelope by the door, the kind that's lined with plastic bubble wrap. It had my name written on it in green magic marker, so I tore it open. Inside was a high school yearbook, a video tape, and some photographs. I looked at the pictures first.

There's something cloying and obnoxious about being shown photographs of someone who's just died—particularly posed professional shots. And even more particularly if she's a pretty girl. Maybe it's because that's the first thing we always see on tabloid TV when some poor young woman gets strangled or shot. She is immediately reduced to some kind of icon. We see her vacant, smiling face and we close our eyes and we are left with nothing but the thumping accents of bad Victorian poetry: Suffering Womanhood! Virginity Tarnishéd! Youth Destroyéd! At which point some young woman is forever stripped of everything about her that was unique and beautiful and strange, everything that was human.

What I'm saying is that even though I knew who the girl was and even though I'd seen her die, I was prepared to be angry when I looked at her pictures. I presumed those pictures would show some sanitized, smarmy, bogus version of this child that would be at odds with her real character, with the bad judgment or avarice or anger or self-hatred or whatever it was that had put Leslie-Anne Gilmartin in that place on that day, where she had hoped to run off with a hundred thousand dollars that she hadn't earned.

But it didn't happen that way.

The first photo I looked at was Leslie-Anne's school picture from first or second grade. She had a missing front tooth and her hair was a mess and she looked at the camera with her teeth bared in what appeared to be more challenge than smile. It looked like it had been a fight to get her to sit long enough to take the picture. This was unsanitized Leslie-Anne Gilmartin, the real deal, the same kid I remembered tromping furiously through my stepfather's flower bed.

I looked at a couple more of the small photographs, then I flipped through the yearbook, several pages of which had been paper-clipped where there were photographs of her. What was remarkable about her was that she *never once* seemed to give the lens what it asked from her, never surrendered to the bland self-extinguishing sameness which is the one quality that yearbook photographers (and all too many mothers) want from every child. Instead there was always defiance in her eyes—defiance and a certain sad vulnerability, as though the central fact of her life was that she would be judged again and again and again, and always she would coming up lacking. Always her hair would be wrong, her collar askew, her eyes glaring off in the wrong direction.

Her story was boringly familiar: a smothering mother, a father who wasn't around much—and when he was, didn't do much but criticize. It was the story of half the girls I'd gone to high school with. With a few significant variations, it could have been my story, too. Most of my classmates finally just gave in, fixed their blush, took the shine off their nose, smiled for the camera, and married well. For whatever it was worth, Leslie-Anne never gave in.

I didn't bother looking at the video tape. Home movies, birthday parties, proms, beauty pageants—whatever was in there, it didn't really matter. I'd seen enough.

Enough to feel a funny sort of kinship with this child. I guess I'd expected to find a smug and spoiled little rich girl. What I found instead was a kid whose whole life was probably a struggle to free herself from smugness, a struggle to find something meaningful outside the staid, self-satisfied, well-trampled ground that was the life her parents wanted to give her.

Maybe I'm just being self-absorbed, but it seems worth explaining why this struck such a chord in me. My mom was born on the poor side of Atlanta, went to the University of Georgia where she got pregnant by—and promptly married—a young ROTC student named John Childs. My father served in the army for almost a decade and was killed in Vietnam two days before my ninth birthday. At that point Mom moved us back to Atlanta where we lived in a deteriorating neighborhood on my father's death benefits until Mom finally cashed in her chips—a pretty face, a quick mind, a certain manipulative desperation—and bagged the first of her four rich husbands.

For the first ten or twelve years of my life, we lived in circumstances that were anywhere from spartan to flat-out poor. Then suddenly Mom hit the jackpot. The rest of my growing up took place in the ''good'' parts of Atlanta, the ''good'' schools with the ''good'' people. But all those good people always smelled something on me, a whiff of something that gave me away, that told them I wasn't comfortable in their world.

What I'm getting at is that those pictures suddenly made me feel something for that dead girl that I never expected to feel. I could see it in her eyes, that same feeling I've always had: that I am an alien everywhere. Here, but never quite *of* here.

Call it a melodramatic reaction, but suddenly I wanted to catch the son of a bitch that killed her.

I put the pictures of sad little Leslie-Anne back in the envelope and stuck it in the bottom drawer of my desk. I haven't checked lately, but I believe it's still there. Not as Reminder, not as Cautionary Tale. They're there as Leslie-Anne Gilmartin. They're there because every one of us counts, every one of us has a story. Even the screw-ups, the weaklings, the liars, the thieves, even the smothering mothers, the angry daughters, the weak and decent sons.

I checked my voicemail to see if Tawanda had gotten anything from the people in homicide, but apparently she hadn't. A few minutes later Earl Wickluff finally straggled in.

''Well, here I am, Sunny,'' he said peevishly. ''What you need me to do?''

I gave him a run-down of my conversation with Roland Porter and then told him to check on Roland's alibi at the Dogwood House in Asheville, then to track down Leslie-Anne Gilmartin's boyfriend.

''His name's Yokum,'' I said. ''Like the country singer,

but spelled differently. His first name's Terry." I had to spell it for him twice.

"Got an address?"

"Try the phone book."

"Thank you for that red hot tip, boss," Earl said.

After he went away I picked up the phone and dialed Mom. "Hi, it's me."

"Thank God!" she said. "Walter tells me you're coming tonight."

"I have agreed in principle to make a showing," I said. "A showing amounts to precisely one and one half hours and not one second more."

"Why do you have to be like this? You'll meet so many nice people tonight. People who could do you a world of good."

"In what respect?" I said.

"That's not funny," she said. "Now look, we don't have much time."

"For what?"

Mom let a moment of what was presumably supposed to be appalled silence hang in the air. "Your *dress*, sweetie! We've got to get you a *dress*."

"What do you mean 'we'?"

You see how our game works? She says things, and then I pretend like I don't understand what she means, and then she acts insulted. We've been doing this since roughly the moment I learned to speak.

More appalled silence. "Well, you've *got* to have a dress! I'll be busy with the arrangements for most of the afternoon, but I could slip out for a couple of hours starting at—"

"I have a dress," I said.

"Don't be ridiculous. You need something new. We'll meet at Phipps."

"I have a nice little black thing that I bought a couple years ago. It'll do fine."

Mom chuckled indulgently. "*Fine* will not do, sweetie. Tonight nothing but smashing will suffice. We'll get you a

Miracle Bra, too. It's high time you showed a little cleavage.''

"Mother," I said. When I start calling her Mother instead of Mom, I know I'm reaching my limits. "I don't need a push-up bra. It's ridiculous. I am a virtually boobless woman."

"Which is precisely why you need a Miracle Bra. You'd be amazed at the difference they make."

"Let me tell you my problem with those things," I said. "You come to a party and you meet some cute guy and he stares at these fake hooters all night, and then you go home with him and you take off you boob assistance apparatus and the guy looks at your flat little chest and rightly gets peeved because you just sold him a bill of goods. You might as well make an honest pitch from the get-go and take the consequences."

Mom sighed loudly. "Which just illustrates your whole problem. You're such a lovely girl. If you would just quit jumping in the sack on the first date, you could hold on to a decent man. Why should they buy the cow if they're getting the milk for free?"

"Jesus!" I said. "Mother! Is that the way you think of yourself? A goddamn cow?"

"You are altogether too literal, sweetie," Mom said cheerfully. "Anyway, the point is, I need to have you sparkling tonight. I'm thinking maybe gold lamé . . ."

By this point I was speaking through clenched teeth. "I *have* a dress, Mother. It is black and pretty and it does not have any holes in it, so it will work *fine*. Moreover I will *never* wear gold lamé, not in a million *billion* years. Furthermore I do *not* require the services of a push-up bra. And finally I have *extremely* important work to do and very little time to do it. Therefore I do *not* have time to be *traipsing* around in some froofy-ass—"

"Two thirty, sweetie!"

Mom hung up on me.

"AAaaggghrrhhrhhhcchh!" I said. Or something like that. I tried to call her back, but of course she conveniently didn't answer.

A few minutes later I took the elevator down to the parking garage, got in the car, and drove over to see my old friend Honey Chanteuse.

Well, maybe "friend" is not precisely the word. Honey is one of the most vastly entertaining, profane, original, and generally useful people I know. It is a testimony to the intensely weird way that her mind works that she seems to really like me. But more on that later . . .

As soon as I knocked on Honey's door, I realized that ten o'clock was probably far too early on a Saturday morning to be talking to her. But I didn't have much time: after all, I had to meet Mom in four and a half hours so she could buy me a push-up bra and a gold lamé dress.

Honey lives at the top of one of these high-rise apartments in midtown. Her place is huge. My guess is that the rent runs an easy four or five grand a month; I have no idea where she gets the money. She damn sure doesn't have a job, though.

I took the elevator up, rang the doorbell twice. Some shuffling and thumping and cursing noises filtered into the hallway and finally the door opened a crack. Honey shrieked when she saw me. "Well, God *damn*, there she is!" She threw open the door. "Come on in, stranger!"

Honey goes about six feet, with dyed blond hair that was in a certain amount of disarray at this point due to the earliness of the hour. She is probably forty-five or fifty and very beautiful in an aging redneckish linebackerish whorish sort of way. Despite her name and her size, she is not a drag queen.

She lit a cigarette and made herself a bloody mary that was about two fingers of bloody and three fingers of mary, then we caught up on things for a while. Eventually she said, "Well, baby, I know you didn't wake my fat ass up to shoot the shit."

I looked around her apartment, which was beautifully decorated. I suspect she paid someone else to do it: there would have been a lot more mirrors and gilt curlicues if she'd been completely in charge. My guess was that it was really somebody else's apartment and she was just staying there for the duration. But then with Honey Chanteuse, you never knew. She was just one surprise after another.

I pointed at a small drawing on the wall, a dove painted in blue ink. "That one," I said. "Is it real?"

"It's an original Picasso," she said. "Isn't it awful? He used to draw shit like that and pay his bar tabs with them. It's devoid of any originality or feeling, isn't it?" She made a rich phlegmy noise which was her rendition of laughter. "Still, it's worth an assload of money so I keep it on the wall anyway."

"Ah," I said. That was the thing about Honey. She could reduce everything to its essential quality . . . which, from her perspective came down to one thing. Money.

"Where'd you pick it up?" I said.

"Provenance," Honey said, smiling. "The word is provenance. You gonna ask me about art, you got to talk the right lingo."

"Okay, tell me about its provenance."

Honey raised one eyebrow coyly. "Baby, you don't want to know."

"You're telling me it's stolen?"

Honey arranged her nightgown delicately across her large and still very perky bosoms, fluttered her eyelashes a little. "I'm shocked—shocked!—that you would think such a thing." She took a drag on her cigarette. "Why the sudden interest in my art treasures?"

"Well, as it happens, I'm trying to find out about art theft. Now I'm sure you have no personal knowledge of such matters . . .'' I smirked. ''. . . but maybe you've read up on the subject.''

Honey pressed her fingertips to her chest, widened her eyes. ''Moi?''

We all have our shameful secrets. And mine is philosophy. After I graduated from college, I worked for a year on Wall Street, a truly horrible experience, which led me to the equally horrible idea that I would enjoy life a lot more in graduate school. What to study? Philosophy, I decided. I'd dated one of my philosophy professors when I was a soph-omore (don't ask!), which had led me to major in the subject. So after a year of spending forty-six hours a day staring at spreadsheets for Salomon Brothers, philosophy seemed like a wonderful retreat into sanity.

Of course I had about as much business being a philoso-pher as I did being an investment banker—to wit, none. So after a year of grad school at Johns Hopkins I dropped out, came back to Atlanta with my tail between my legs and lived with my mother. It was by far the longest three months of my life. Worse than Salomon Brothers, worse than Kant, worse than anything. During that time Mom set me up with at least twenty stupendously boring men (where do you even *find* six dentists?), bought me somewhere in the neighbor-hood of ten thousand dollars' worth of clothes, counseled me on how to wear my hair, how to improve my posture, how to take better care of my nails, how to get a job, and—most of all—how to find, tease, please, flatter, and retain a man.

For all my little annoyances with Gunnar Brushwood, I will be eternally grateful to him: he was the man who saved me from that living hell. After sending me to at least a dozen interviews with her friends and flunkies and stooges (interior decorators, real estate brokers, owners of exclusive china shops and boutiques, and various other approved jobs for young women of a certain class, don't you know—a class of which I never considered myself part, by the way) for which I showed up hostile, sullen, and unprepared, Mom finally broke down and sent me to Gunnar. I am still unclear on how she knew Gunnar, but she did know him from somewhere. Maybe he owed Mom something, or maybe he just wanted to get inside my pants, but for whatever reason he hired me.

It was the turning point of my life. In those days, Gunnar actually showed up for work with relative frequency, and he taught me a hell of a lot. At the time most of his business consisted of bounty-hunting jobs that he did for bail bondsmen, but he also did some investigative work. Unlike Gunnar I was not much of a bounty hunter—the average scofflaw felon is not all that afraid of me, even when I'm pointing a gun at him—but I *was* a natural at investigation.

One of my first assignments involved going undercover at a liquor distributor which had a hundred-thousand-dollar-a-year pilferage problem. I worked in the warehouse, letting slip occasionally to other employees that I had served a few years at the Metro State women's prison down on Constitution Avenue for receiving stolen property. The idea was that I was going to ingratiate myself with whoever the scumbags were that were stealing all that liquor, and then I would tip off the cops.

Now I have to mention here that the main requirement in any undercover assignment is that one be a resourceful bullshitter. Which I found, to my surprise, I was. I made up stories about prison. I made up stories about a former husband who used to beat me with a belt. I made up stories about my insane twin sister who had spent the past five years in a loony bin obsessively making multi-colored confetti with a hole puncher. One story after another. And what was the harm? It was all good fun. Besides, I was there to bust the bad guys.

Something you'll hear undercover cops talk about is "drawing lines." What they mean is that when you take on a false identity, you have to have a strong sense about when to quit. You have to go home and turn off the false identity; you have to make decisions about who you lie to and who you don't; you have to think about your family and the things that are important to you. If you don't, you get carried away.

Well, I hadn't learned about drawing lines. I *lived* my new persona—started dressing like a redneck slut chick, talking like a redneck slut chick, listening to heavy metal, driving a Camaro T-top, the whole bit. Not just when I was at the liquor warehouse. I mean, all the time. In retrospect I suspect I was on the verge of coming unhinged.

Fortunately the undercover assignment started costing the liquor guy about as much as the pilferage, so he canceled the job, and we never caught the people who were stealing all the liquor.

Before it was over, though, I met Honey—who, at the time, was married to the guy that owned the liquor distributorship. For some reason she took a shine to me, and one night we went out to this bar where she got me very drunk. I guess her husband hadn't told her that I was working undercover, because when I told her some ridiculous story about how I'd helped this woman hire this guy to kill her wife-beating scumbag of a husband, Honey believed me. Honey kept pumping me and pumping me about this story, and I got drunker and drunker and just kept embroidering the story.

At five minutes till one, the bartender yelled last call and Honey Chanteuse took my hand and said: "Baby, you think you could get hold of that guy again?"

"Huh?" I said.

"You know. The guy. I think I want to get rid of my husband."

Suddenly I wasn't feeling quite so drunk.

Anyway, the upshot of it was that I got the cops involved and they had me wear a wire, and with my help they sent Honey for a several-year stay down to Metro State for conspiring to kill her husband.

That's why I say Honey is a pretty odd fish: most folks don't keep a warm place in their heart for people who send them to jail for extended periods of time. But Honey isn't most folks. After she got out of the pen she came by my office one time and told me she didn't hold a grudge, that she'd been hitting the booze a little hard at that time and had kind of lost perspective. I've never asked her, but I suspect she was the one who was stealing all that liquor, too.

For a while I kept waiting for the other shoe to drop. Honey is the sort of person who uses other people, and so I kept waiting to find out what she was using me for. Finally I think I figured it out. Just as she is my pipeline to the world of thieves and prostitutes and drug dealers, I'm her pipeline to a world of where people tell the truth most of the time and play by the rules and respect the laws and at least make a pretense of treating each other decently.

Anyway, Honey has turned into my best source. She knows a lot of dirtbags in Atlanta, and when I need to get information about that world, she's the first person I turn to.

I explained to Honey about the case I was working on, and about Leslie-Ann's murder. I concluded by saying that it now appeared the thief didn't want to ransom the painting. So I was looking for an overview of the art theft business in hopes of figuring out the most fruitful avenue to pursue in the case.

"When you consider any sort of theft business," Honey said, "there's one thing you always have to ask: where's it going?"

"I'm not sure I follow you."

"Let's say I steal ten TVs. Obviously I don't steal them so I can watch them. I want to turn them into money."

"Okay."

"So I have to find a buyer, right?" Honey stood, grunted softly, and went in the kitchen to freshen up her drink. When she came back, her bloody mary was such a pale, translucent pink that you could hardly tell there was tomato juice in it at all. She sat down on her chaise lounge and took a healthy sip off the top of her drink. "In other words, you've got two ways to go. You can try to find the person who stole the painting, or you can try to find the person who *buys* the painting."

"I hadn't thought of that."

"I have to tell you, baby, that stolen pictures are really not my area of expertise. So I'll tell you everything I know. And it won't take long. The first thing that's working for you is that the art world is not that big. More or less at the top you've got the two big auction houses—Sotheby's and Christie's—and then a handful of smaller ones. They're all pretty legit. They've been around for literally hundreds of years and they are definitely not interested in being in the fencing business."

"Parallel to that you've got a handful of really big, really reputable galleries. From what I understand, they're a bunch of sleazy bastards. But they're more into screwing their artists and their customers than into selling stolen merchandise. For a big reputable gallery, there's no percentage in selling stolen goods. The downside is way too high."

"Next you've got smaller New York galleries, regional galleries, smaller auction houses. These guys are probably a little less careful about the stuff they buy or represent, whether it's got good provenance or not. But still, these are people with a fixed address and a lot to lose. If it's obvious something's stolen, they won't go slapping it up on the wall. Bottom line, nobody that's big enough to represent a piece worth several hundred grand is going to be dumb enough to try moving a stolen piece by a prominent artist.

"So what you're left with are private dealers. These are people who operate out of their houses. They buy here, they sell there, they're on the phone all the time, on planes all the time. They don't advertise, they don't pay rent. If they feel like it, they can do business out of a suitcase, out of the trunk of a car. Tricky people to find.''

"How many people like that are there in the world? I mean, ones that could handle a half-million-dollar sale.''

"Hold on, hold on. I'm not finished. Okay, now most private dealers are just like anybody else. They have no interest in going to jail. So your average private dealer, hell, he's not interested in moving stolen shit.''

Honey lit another cigarette, waved the match in the air. "So here's what I'm getting at. For a painting like this, the buyer's mostly likely gonna be in this tiny little group of dealers who are big enough to have the contacts to sell a half-million-dollar painting, but who are also are shady enough to take the risk. That's who you want to talk to.''

"Great.''

"Yeah, but here's the problem. There's not some directory of people like that. If you don't know who they are, you'll never find them.''

"Damn.''

Honey looked out her window. "Too bad you don't know anybody who's got some contacts in that world,'' she said airily.

I didn't say anything. Honey had her own way of doing things and there was no point putting a hitch in her rhythm.

"Yeah, baby, if you knew somebody like that, if there just happened to be somebody in that little subset of scumbag art dealers who lived in Atlanta, well hell, *that* might give you a leg up, huh?''

Again, I just sat there in my chair and waited.

"If you had a friend who knew somebody like that and your friend could maybe give you an entree, warm them up a little, I bet that could work out to being very valuable to your investigation, what do you think, Sunny?''

"I think you might well be right.''

Honey sucked an ice cube out of her bloody mary, crunched it loudly between her teeth.

"So," I said finally. "How much do you want for making this introduction? Would ten percent of my bounty be about right?"

Honey shook her head. "You think I would do something like that for *money*?" she said.

"I know you would."

"I guess you don't know me too good, huh?"

Once again she surprised me.

She winked in my direction, then picked up the receiver and dialed, waited, then punched in some more numbers and hung up. The phone rang about thirty seconds later.

"Sugar!" she said into the receiver. "My God, how are you?" Then she buttered up the person on the other end of the line for a while. When she'd finally gotten through with the flattery phase of the conversation, she said, "Well, look I have this friend, I must have mentioned her, Tawny Cheeks. She dates that guy Jay Lowensteen from New Orleans? Sure. Well, here's the thing. She's recently become very interested in art. She took this night class at Tulane, Art Appreciation, and now she's just crazy about the stuff. And so she might be interested in . . . right, right. Well, old Jay has pisspots of money and he's just letting her write checks. Uh-huh. Uh-huh. So what's my end if I send her over? No, no, sugar, speak English so I can understand you. I don't . . . nope, nope, I'm just having a hard time understanding that number you're using. Try another one. Okay, okay. That's a better one. See how easy it is?" There was a long pause. "Right. Her name's T-A-W-N-Y. Cheeks. As in . . . right. She'll call you, baby."

Honey hung up the phone.

"*Tawny Cheeks?*" I said.

Honey laughed. "It's just a name."

"So who is this guy?"

"His name's Winston Percival," Honey said. "He sells big paintings, jewelry, sculpture, antiquities. Serious stuff.

And some of it is stolen. The good news is, he lives two blocks from your Mama.''

"A local boy."

"That's right. I figure unless your thief is tapped into the international scene, Winston's your only game in town."

"That's great," I said, "but I'm still a little puzzled here. If this deal goes the way I need it to, we're going to have to bust this guy Winston Percival. Obviously there's not going to be any money involved, so he can't give you a cut."

"Of course not," she said. "Winston screwed me once. Bigtime. So now I'm screwing him back. If he can get you that painting, I want him busted. I want that little douchebag playing drop the soap down at Reidsville."

"I just hope you don't feel that way about me," I said.

"You're different," she said, waving her cigarette regally at me. "You're my hero."

And I think she half-way meant it. But like I say: with Honey you really never know.

CHAPTER 11

IT WAS AN interesting lead, but I decided to save Winston Percival until later. First I thought I'd keep working the people who had contact with Leslie-Ann Gilmartin and with the gallery.

I dropped back by the office, found a thin blond man sitting in the lobby reading a copy of *American Investigator*. When he saw me he stood up quickly, wiped his palm on his pants and stuck out his hand.

"Sean McNeely," he said. His hand was moist but his grip was firm. "Ron Widner said you might be willing to talk with me about a job?"

Ron's brother-in-law. I'd completely forgotten.

"Oh, sure, sure!" I said. "Come on back to my office."

I checked my messages—there was nothing that couldn't wait until Tuesday—then turned to appraise Sean McNeely. He was a tall gangling man, blond almost to the point of a towheadedness, with a face that was more pretty than handsome. He wore a blue jacket that sagged slightly at the elbows, a white shirt that was a little frayed at the collar, a red tie, and olive drab Dockers that any idiot would know should have been ironed before going to a job interview. Sean, however, had not ironed them.

We made small talk, mostly about Ron. I maintained the

fiction that Ron was just a client of mine and that I didn't know him all that well.

Sean gave me his résumé, which ran two pages. I was a little surprised at his age. Ron had given me the impression he was in his mid-twenties. In fact, however, Sean was 32. And he'd held an awful lot of jobs for a 32-year-old guy. He'd also helpfully included the fact that he was a National Merit Scholarship Semi-finalist in High School and the winner of the Jasper High School Good Citizenship Award, which I thought was reaching back a little far for a 32-year-old guy. Then again, he didn't seem to have accomplished much since.

He'd spent two years at Tech where he claimed to have been a Criminal Justice major. After that he'd gone back to his home town of Jasper and served in the police force for three years. Then there were some security guard jobs around Atlanta, three months as a deputy for the Fulton County Sheriff. Then it was lots of stuff like meatpacker, shipping clerk, computer programmer, security guard, movie projectionist, and so on.

Now I have to say a little something here about screw-ups. It's my belief that any human being who hasn't been at least a moderate screw-up somewhere in their lives has probably got some deep psychological problem. In fact I'm a hesitant about trusting anyone who didn't flounder some in their early twenties. But fifteen years is a long time to be a screw-up: it starts to indicate a basic tendency in your character.

"So tell me about yourself," I said.

"I've always been interested in law enforcement and, ah, you know, stuff like that. You can see from my résumé, that's been my focus."

I couldn't precisely, so I just said, "Sure."

"Yeah, I was with the PD up in Jasper for three years, then I served in Fulton County for a while. Plus, when I had the opportunity, you know, there's been the security business. Kind of a fill-in type of job." He smiled weakly. I got the impression he'd given this same spiel to a lot of people and that it had started to wear very thin about five or six years ago.

"Why'd you leave Jasper?" I said.

He made a face. "Oh. Jasper. Gosh. Bottom line? I got squirmy up there. It's a little country town, and I guess I just wanted to move to Atlanta."

"So if I called the chief up there and asked him why you left that's the story he'd give?"

Sean turned a deep red and he avoided my eye. "Look, I was twenty-one years old. There was some question about certain reports and stuff. I was pulling a lot of double shifts and quite honestly they caught me sleeping a couple times when I had filed a report saying, you know, that I was downtown twisting doorknobs to make sure nobody was breaking into the VFW post and stuff like that. It was a long time ago. We could have worked it out, but I just used it as an excuse to move to Atlanta."

"And the Fulton County Sheriff's job?" Fulton County was the county in which Atlanta was located. By police standards, the Fulton County sheriff's department was the lightest of lightweight jobs: they were mostly in the business of ferrying prisoners to jail and providing security in the courthouse. "What happened there, Sean?"

Sean sighed, shook his head. "I honestly don't know. It was one of those deals where you're hired on a probationary basis. I didn't get along too great with the supervisor, but I didn't think anything was wrong. But then they just . . . the end of my probationary period comes up and they go, 'See ya.' You can check, there's nothing in my personnel file. But after that I've had a hard time getting law enforcement jobs. They look at my record and they think there must be something wrong with me." He looked me in the eye. "That's why this job would mean a lot to me. I'll be honest, you look at my résumé and you say, whoa, this guy must be useless. Skipping from job to job and everything? But I've just been looking for a chance. I hope you'll give me a chance because I promise I'll repay you with dedication and, uh . . . uh . . ."

"Hard work?"

"Hard work. Right." He shook his head eagerly.

The big L. Primo loser. You could see it a mile away, practically tattooed across his forehead. But I had a hunch Ron would get annoyed at me if I just blew Sean off completely. I figured I could tell Ron that I gave him a shot and that he just wasn't what we were looking for in a permanent employee.

"Here's what I can do," I said. "I need an investigator today. Just for a short-term project. It pays ten bucks an hour. Just a temporary thing. Right now I've got no permanent positions available. But if you do a good job and we're looking to pick up some more permanent staff, you'll be on the A-list so to speak. Can you start today and work through the weekend?"

"Really? I got the job?"

"Like I said. It's just a three-or four-day gig."

"Wow! Private investigator!" Sean smiled happily.

"I take it that's a yes?"

Sean jumped up and shook my hand again. His palm was moist and warm as bread dough.

"Go get some lunch," I said. "I'll get you started doing computer research this afternoon."

I went into the break room where I found Tawanda eating lunch with her husband Gerald. Actually they weren't eating per se. They had Subway sandwiches and barbecue potato chips and cloth napkins neatly laid out on paper plates at the table and they were both praying. Gerald, a tiny and intensely shy man with very light brown skin, is a lay minister in a storefront church somewhere in Southwest Atlanta, and he makes a big thing about praying before he eats. I watched them for a while. They were on their knees, heads bowed, holding hands, and the prayer went on for quite some time. Gerald is probably the most devoted husband I've ever known. I wondered briefly if I'd ever meet a man who loved me like that.

They stood up and I tried to pretend like I hadn't been staring at them.

"Gerald brought you a sandwich," Tawanda said.

"Turkey," he said. His voice was surprisingly large and rich for such a tiny man. "I hope you don't mind turkey."

"Turkey's fine." I kept standing there looking at them.

"What?" Tawanda said.

"What's the secret?" I said.

"Of what?"

"Being in love the way you two are."

"There is no secret," Gerald said. "That's the secret."

Then he started eating his sandwich, dabbing at his mouth after each bite with a deft, economical, and precise motion.

I opened the refrigerator and pulled out the sandwich he'd bought me, then laid a five-dollar bill next to Gerald's elbow. He didn't touch the money or even glance at it. I unwrapped my sandwich.

"So what did you learn from the police?" I asked Tawanda.

"As you might expect, they were not excessively happy to hear we was poking around in their investigation," Tawanda said. "I was forced to rely on my feminine wiles."

Gerald grunted but didn't look up from his sandwich. I remember one time Gunnar saying that the closer Gerald got to Tawanda, the smaller he looked, until finally he diminished into complete invisibility.

"I'm guessing they didn't turn down that list of names you gave them."

"Matter fact, they did not." Tawanda and I laughed, then she pushed a small pile of computer printouts across the desk. They were the results of NCIC searches run by the Atlanta police on the names we'd given them.

"When are you going to give me permission to clone your wife?" I said to Gerald.

Gerald smiled very briefly, showing off one gold incisor.

Tawanda said, "They did an alias search on this Charlie Biddle woman. Guess what her real name is? Comes up Ludmilla Rutskoi. DOB, twelve two fifty-eight, Kiev, Ukraine. She got a bunch of aliases."

"Why would she have aliases?" I said.

"Look at the next page."

I flipped over to the next piece of paper and found her crime computer records. She had a shoplifting conviction back in the late seventies, no big deal. Then the good stuff: 1983, convicted of receiving stolen property in Cook County, Illinois. Paroled. In 1985 they threw the book at her: theft by taking, theft by receiving, theft by deception, fraud—this time in Fulton County, Georgia. She got a three-year sentence in 1985, for which she spent a little over a year inside. Nothing since.

"Man," I said, "I'd sure like to look at the case files on those convictions."

"Too bad Superior Court Records is closed today," Tawanda said. Then she ran her hands down the front of her shirt. "On the other hand . . . I know this poor girl over there, got two young children, no husband. Tragic situation. She's always in need of something for the kids."

"Uh-huh."

"You know how that is. Occasionally you willing to add a little something to the scholarship fund, maybe somebody find time to break away from their weekend holiday activities, do a little work off the clock."

"You're saying you bribed her to sneak in and pull records for you?"

Tawanda's eyes widened. "That type of thing sounds highly illegal to me! But while I'm thinking about money, you need to voucher me a hundred dollars for . . . how does miscellaneous expenses sound?''

"How miscellaneous?" I said.

She handed me some xeroxes. "That's the police report on her '85 conviction. I couldn't follow the whole thing exactly because the detective who wrote these reports seems to have been functionally illiterate. But the gist of it, she and this guy she was working with were selling hot paintings. There's no trial transcript, but based on the supplementaries in there, I'd say her co-conspirator rolled on her and she pled out."

"Well, well, well," I said. "So old Charlie is not exactly Little Miss Squeaky Clean."

"Another thing. You'll notice when we did the alias search another last name came up for her. I figured maybe it was a married name, so I had this girl see if divorce papers came up for her."

"And?"

"Underneath. Turns out she was married to the guy that rolled over on her, sent her to jail."

"Obviously the soul of marital devotion, this guy."

I hunted through the stack of papers until I found the divorce decree. I read the caption: Ludmilla Rutskoi Percival vs. Winston C. Percival.

"I'll be damn," I said. "Sorry, Gerald."

I stood and picked up the phone that hung on the wall near the counter. First I called my home number, forwarded it to the office, then I beeped the number that Honey Chanteuse had given me for Winston Percival and punched in my home number. It was a distant possibility, but this guy Winston Percival might run a check on the number I left for him and I didn't want it leading back to Peachtree Investigations. He called back immediately.

I tried to put myself in the frame of mind of a woman with big hair, a red Camaro Z-28, and a brand new boob job. "Hey!" I said. "This is Tawny Cheeks? My friend

Honey Chanteuse tole me I should call you? Yeah-huh, I have recently took this course, you know? In Art History? At the Tulane University extension program back in New Orleeeeens? And my boyfriend, Jay Lowensteen—you know Jay don't you?—he tole me I should just go out and buy something nice for myself. For our six-month anniversary of being in love! Isn't that the sweetest thing? You think you could he'p me out on that?''

Winston Percival thought maybe he could fit me in. I made a date with him for four-thirty at his place. Honey was right: he was in Buckhead not more than two blocks from the huge pile in which my mother and Husband Number Five lived.

"You so *bad*," Tawanda said. "You *awful!*"

"Said the pot to the kettle." I took out my checkbook and wrote her a personal check for a hundred dollars to take care of her bribe to the Superior Court records clerk. "I want an expense voucher on this by Tuesday afternoon."

"I wouldn't dream of forgetting." She finished up her sandwich and then said, "So what next boss?"

"Roland Porter mentioned that there was a young woman, a house painter, who appeared to be scoping out their inventory. It's a long shot, but why don't you track her down and chat with her."

"Name?"

"Jillian Silver. Here's her phone number." I took out my notes, handed them to Tawanda. "See if she's got an alibi."

"I'll get right on it."

I got up to leave. Then I thought of something. "Say, Tawanda," I said, "did a messenger ever show up with the bounty agreement from Reliance?"

"Not unless they just stuck it under the door." I picked up the rest of my sandwich and walked out to the reception area. Nothing there under the door. As I was going back to the break room I decided to check Gunnar's e-mail and see if Marion Cheever had sent "Gunnar" a note back from the one I sent this morning. She had. It said, Thank you for the note, Gunnar. I'd very much like to speak with you about the missing painting. Also about the bounty agreement.

A bounty agreement was pretty much a form agreement. You typed Peachtree Investigations in the blank space at the top, then you filled in the next blank with the words "Painting—Late Afternoon by Childe Hassam" and then you put "$100,000.00" in the next blank. And then you signed it and messengered the thing over our to office. So what was this woman's problem?

I swallowed a mouthful of processed turkey and dialed Marion Cheever's direct line at Reliance.

"Hi, Marion," I said in my most chipper voice, "Gunnar wanted me to give you a buzz. He got your e-mail and said you had a question about the bounty agreement."

"Where is he?" Marion said.

"Good question," I said. "Could be interviewing the dead girl's boyfriend. Could be talking to Charlie Biddle. He's on one of those patented Gunnar Brushwood rampages right now. No sleep till he's got his big capable hands on the painting, that kind of thing." I chuckled in what I hoped would be an infectious manner. Marion Cheever did not catch the infection, however.

There was a moment of silence.

"Why do I have the feeling I'm getting the runaround?" she said.

"Huh?"

"Don't play stupid, Sunny. This is very simple. I asked for Gunnar to return my call, and I keep not hearing from him."

"Sure, sure," I said. "Gunnar likes field work, and tends to leave the administrative and client contact to me."

"Are you saying Gunnar Brushwood is not the president of Peachtree Investigations? That he's not the man in charge?"

"Well no. But—"

"Fine. Then let me put it to you this way. Either Gunnar

calls me, or I don't send over that bounty agreement.''

"Message received," I said.

When I was done I tried to figure a way out of this. In desperation, I called Gunnar's pager number and left a priority message—but he'd already ignored it all week, so it seemed kind of pointless.

As I expected Gunnar didn't call back. I suppose I could have just called Marion back and said Gunnar had to leave town or something and either I was in charge or the deal was off. But I didn't. Instead I had an idea. A silly idea, sure, but . . .

Tawanda was in the break room washing her hands—a laborious and delicate process with her long fingernails—when I walked in. "You ever seen these electronic voice distortion boxes that you put over a telephone," I said. "The kind that makes your voice lower."

"Sure. Probably get you one at Radio Shack. Or that Spy Store place out at Cumberland Mall." She started drying her hands, finger by finger. "Hey, if you need one now, try Earl Wickluff's office. He always checks out all the electronic surveillance equipment and 'forgets' to gives it back. Maybe he's got something like that."

And sure enough he did. In the bottom drawer of his desk—underneath a Motorola walkie-talkie very similar to the one I'd used at the failed ransom the day before, a chin mike, a Nikon camera with a 400-mm lens, a handset phone like the ones telephone linemen use, and two copies of *Hustler*—I found a small black box with a little speaker on one side that said "Sound Bender" on the front.

I wrote HAPPY READING! with a little smiley face on a sticky note and put it over Miss May's face, then picked up the sound bender, took it back to my office and hooked it up to the phone. I dialed the break room. There was a little setting on it that let you adjust the pitch up or down. I set it so my voice would be an octave lower, then dialed Tawanda's extension.

"Guess who this is?" I said when she answered.

"Girl, you really need to lay off them steroids," Tawanda said. "You fixing to turn into something scary."

I laughed.

"By the way, this Jillian Silver, the house painter that Roland Porter found staring at all the paintings? We can cross her off the list. I just got off the phone with her old roommate. She left Atlanta two months ago, moved to Israel and joined a kibbutz."

"Thanks."

I hung up, took a few deep breaths and then dialed Marion Cheever's direct line. When she answered I put a big smile on my face—just like they tell you to do when you sell time shares or penny stocks over the phone—and shouted into the phone like Gunnar does. "Marion by God, Cheever! How the hell are you? I'm sorry as a lame mule about not getting back to you, there's something wrong with this goddamn sumbitching piece-a-shit phone. The reason that—" Then I hit the off button, waited about five seconds and redialed.

"See what I mean, Marion? Sumbitch keeps cutting out on me! And when I do get through, it does some crazy-ass thing to my voice, makes me sound like Darth Goddamn Vader!"

"That's all right," Marion said, "but—"

"You and me need to get together and lift a jar!" I shouted. "You hunt quail, darlin'? Or duck? Gonna have to get you down to my hunting shack near Brunswick come quail season, do a little shootin'! I got a thousand acres of shitass swamp and a couple nice Eye-talian fouling pieces cut down for a lady's physique. What you say to that? Bring down the husband, bring down the kids!"

"That's very kind but—"

"Terrific! Out*standing*! Call my seckatary and set it up! Oh and send that bounty form over to my office, pronto, would you? I'm a bear for paperwork! Oop, looks like the subject I'm surveilling is on the move. I got run, darlin', before this slimy little piece of shit starts—''

I broke the phone connection in mid-sentence. Maybe that would work, maybe it wouldn't. All in all I thought I did a pretty creditable imitation of Gunnar. Glib, profane, obnoxious, loud—yet big-hearted and generous at the same time.

I looked up and saw Tawanda's husband Gerald peering at me with a mildly censorious look on his face. I smiled feebly. He nodded once, turned, walked away.

CHAPTER 12

Ron's brother-in-law Sean McNeely came back from
lunch and I got him started doing Nexis searches for stories about art theft. He had some computer experience, so
I was sure he wouldn't have any problem with this kind of
work.

Then I paged Earl Wickluff to see what he'd turned up.
He called back a couple of minutes later and said that Roland
Porter's alibi checked out: the owner of the Dogwood Inn
said Porter and his boyfriend had been sitting in the parlor
until at least 11:00 P.M. on Monday night. Since Asheville
was a good three hours from Atlanta, there was no way he
could have gotten back in time to have broken into the gallery.

Earl was still having no luck chasing down Leslie-Anne
Gilmartin's boyfriend, however.

"I don't know what the deal is with this Yokum guy,"
Earl said. "He moved out of his apartment about three
months ago and forwarded his mail to Leslie-Anne's place."

"So he's been staying with her?"

"Nah. Apparently he sleeps over sometimes, mostly on
weekends. Other than that, he comes by every now and then
to see Leslie-Anne and to pick up his mail."

"Does he have a phone?"

"He's got a pager and a cell phone. But nothing to tie him to a particular address."

"Keep digging," I said.

"I always get my man, boss," Earl said unctuously.

I almost said, *Since when?* but figured that was not recommended in the employee motivation handbook.

As soon as I got done with Earl, the phone rang. It was Ron. It occurred to me that I hadn't thought of Ron all day. I wasn't sure what that augured.

We talked for a little while. I gave him an update on the case, and then he started asking a lot of questions. Which surprised me. I've started noticing that Ron gets pretty distracted in the middle of any conversation that doesn't revolve around himself. I figured maybe he'd been reading some book—*How To Keep Your Mistress Happy* maybe?—and had just come to the chapter on feigning interest in their lives.

When I hung up I realized it was really getting close to the point where I needed to ditch the guy. I could do better, I was sure of it. So, okay, yes I'd done a lot worse before. But still . . .

I looked at my watch. Two-fifteen. Jesus, why had I agreed to go to the mall with Mom? Stupid, stupid, stupid.

Mom was in full shopping regalia. She had a fresh and fairly authentic-looking dye job; there was not a gray root in sight beneath her rust-colored hair—which, incidentally, was cut in the style popularized by a 22-year-old actress on some sitcom that I've never watched. Her make-up, though not precisely garish, was a little too heavy for my taste. And her casual little silk frock probably ran in the thousand-buck range. Mom is sixty-one years old, but her breasts are buoyant, her legs are beautiful and the skin on her face is taut as a thirty-year-old's. I'll give her this: she gets good value for her money when it comes to personal trainers, spas, emollients, lotions, and—especially—plastic surgeons.

"It's okay, sweetie!" she said brightly. "I was late, too. I barely had to wait ten minutes for you."

"I was *extremely* busy," I said irritably. I could already feel the heaviness descending on me. I told myself to be nice. Shopping was fun, right? The great American pastime. Sit back, relax, and enjoy.

Mom immediately launched into a dissertation on the Miracle Bra as we headed off at breakneck speed through the mall. Mom walks faster than anybody I know. Except when she's with a man, at which point she becomes like a Japanese geisha, a dutiful two steps behind. I guess that's so she can steer them wherever she wants them to go.

Normally I would have put my foot down on the bra issue, but since I anticipated the big struggle coming over the dress, I thought maybe it would be best to get the lingerie issue resolved as quickly and painlessly as possible. We were passing Victoria's Secret anyway so I said, "Here why don't we grab a bra first and then worry about the dress."

Mom smiled and showed off her fabulous dental work. "Sweetie, you *know* we can't buy the lingerie until you've got the dress."

"We'll get something in black and something in ivory," I said. "That ought to cover all our bases."

Mom's shook her head mournfully. I suppose she was wondering how her own flesh and blood had turned out to be so excruciatingly fashion-challenged. "Don't be ridiculous," she said.

But when I turned left into the store, she followed.

"So what's this shindig you're throwing tonight?" I said when she caught up to me.

"Pediatric AIDS," Mom said. "Wonderful cause. Five hundred a plate. I've paid yours of course, so don't worry about that. I went to the hospital last week and saw some of these kids. It breaks your heart." A brief wave of sadness passed over her face. Then it was gone. Mom is convinced that sadness causes wrinkles. Hell, she's probably right. "It's

the perfect charity for me really. A little too outré for people
like Betsy Wheat or the Goizuetas. But, *sick children*, you
know—who can turn you down when it comes to sick children?''

''Mm,'' I said.

Then we investigated the lingerie options of the store in
great detail and finally I let her talk me into buying some
push-up bras. She insisted that—since we didn't have the
dress yet—I had to buy one bra with straps, one plunge-back,
and one strapless. In all colors. *All* colors. Black, white,
ivory, red, green, and blue. She even tried to sell me on
matching thongs. ''You have such a terrific little can,'' she
said. ''You really shouldn't let a panty line get in the way
of showing it off.''

I gritted my teeth, relented on the stack of push-up bras
just to make her happy, but dug in my heels on the thong.
Matching briefs, okay. Push-up bra, sure, why not. (Hell, I
wasn't planning to wear a bra tonight anyway.) But no thong.
I am thirty-four years old and I have *some* sense of propor-
tion.

We put three hundred and forty-seven dollars on Husband
Number Five's platinum Amex card and left without inci-
dent.

See? I thought. This isn't so bad.

Then we went to a boutique called Holton Harwell. Since
I don't routinely shop at places where a dress costs more
than seventy-five dollars, I'd never noticed the place before.
The attendants in the shop recognized Mom—she was obviously a regular there—and immediately went into full
fawning mode. While Mom did her regal thing, pointing at
various dresses and making commandments about one thing
and another, I tried to act invisible by feigning interest in a
couple of silk blouses. They were pretty nice—bone white
silk with small mother-of-pearl buttons. One had sleeves and
the other didn't. I checked the price tag on the sleeveless job.
Seventeen hundred bucks. When I looked at the other one, I

almost burst out laughing. Twenty-four hundred. That came
out to three hundred and fifty dollars a sleeve.

Before I knew it Mom had sicced the two attendants on
me, and then they were fawning and fluttering their eyes and
going *oh gosshhhh that must be so exciiiiiting being a private
investigator*, and *oh, gosh, what I wouldn't giiiiive to be a
perfect size two like you* and suddenly I was feeling extremely claustrophobic. Before I could move, though, Mom
was pointing and commanding and the fawning attendants
were holding up dresses in front of me. Red sequins, green
sequins, blue sequins, spaghetti straps, plunging backs,
plunging necks, giant crinoline bows at the butt or the bosom
. . . and lamé, lamé, lamé.

I could feel my heart beating, and my palms were starting
to sweat. I don't know what it was about the experience, but
every time Mom puts me through something like this, it really makes me nervous. I imagine most women in America
would give their eye teeth to have a wacky mother with a
bottomless ocean of credit and a yen to dress her daughter
in ridiculously expensive clothes. Call me a traitor to my
gender, but it gives me the creeps. Maybe it's because I know
where her money comes from.

"What do you have in black?" I said finally. "I'm thinking simple. You know. Simple, black, maybe some little
straps and a neckline to about here." I poked myself in the
middle of my bony chest.

The two attendants looked at me then looked at Mom then
looked at me. They both had large eyes and hair that had
been nudged blondward through chemical means. I seemed
to be breaking some kind of unwritten rule.

"I suppose we might have *something* . . ." one of them
said dubiously.

"Don't be silly," Mom said. "It's not that kind of affair."

They brought out an off-the-shoulder number, black silk,
with one of these big swooping crinoline things around the
chest. Most women wear them with push-up bras. Gunnar

once pointed at a woman who was wearing one and said, "That gal looks like a bowl full of tits, don't she?" And he was right.

I asked for another dress. The next one was a sleeveless fitted mini with fat black and white horizontal stripes and a small oval porthole cut out in the chest so that the dress's high neckline wouldn't deprive you of the opportunity to chum the procreational waters with some tasteful cleavage. It actually looked great on me. I am one of the few women in the universe who can wear fat horizontal stripes without looking like I should be milked at sunrise. That's one of the few benefits of being built like a prepubescent boy with a nutritional disorder.

"I'll take it," I said.

Mom started to protest that it was too dull, too plain, that it didn't sparkle. At which point I made the mistake of asking the attendant—as though this information might help firm up my decision—how much the dress cost.

I should have known, of course, after seeing the price on those blouses—but the number she whispered to me was so vast, so embarrassingly, criminally huge that I can't summon the courage to quote it here. My eyes must have bugged out or something, because there was a moment of silence, and one of the attendants made a little downward twitch at the corner of her mouth, like: Oops, there goes my outlandish commission.

"Mother . . ." I said. I could feel my jaw muscles clench up and my face harden into an ugly mask. I could feel my shoulders seize and my neck stiffen. Then I turned and walked as fast as I could out into the parking garage. Mom was several steps behind me the whole way—which tells you how fast I was moving.

When we had gotten out of earshot of the mall, we had a little blow-up. I called her a thug and suggested that if she gave all the money she was getting ready to spend on my dress to the pediatric AIDS people, we would probably see a cure by summer and so on. She countered by going the guilt-trip route: I didn't care about Walter and his prospects at the firm, I didn't care about making my mother happy, I didn't care about all the little children with their terrible disease, all I cared about was myself. Ta-da, ta-dee, ta-da, ta-da, ta-dee.

Over the years it's all become as ritualized as Kabuki: the more I yelled, the softer she spoke. The more I waved my hands, the more her posture suffered and her voice trembled. When the tears finally came and her make-up ran all over her forty-thousand-dollar face, I finally surrendered.

And, as always, there were kisses and hugs and apologies. My mother fixed her lips and her eyes and her cheeks and threw on a little powder, and I blew my nose and took out some eyeliner and put a firm new stroke of black under each eye.

Then we went back and I had the terrified attendants bring out a silver lamé thing with a very modest front and a scoop in the back that plunged at least to my sacroiliac. I have to admit, maybe we could have fed all of Burundi for a month with the price of that dress, but by God I did look smashing!

I stood there staring at my reflection in the mirror and thought, well hell, there are times when it ain't so bad to be a perfect size two with a sinfully rich mother.

On the way out I put my arm around Mom and told her I loved her. It's something I don't say as much as I should, and Mom had to blot at her eyes again with a Kleenex. I had an odd, wistful feeling that I can't describe except to say that I really wished my mother and I didn't have to go through all this Kabuki horseshit just so we could show some affection to each other.

But the likelihood of things ever changing is pretty slim, I guess. For good and ill, we are who we are.

CHAPTER 13

I WAS A few minutes late arriving at Winston Percival's house. He lived in a faux Mediterranean that was smallish for the neighborhood—which is to say it wouldn't have sold for more than six or seven hundred grand.

The reason I was late was that I had barely had time to stop in at the outlet mall on Buford Highway and buy an official slut uniform—leather mini, clingy sweater, six-inch heels, a couple pieces of garish costume jewelry. Then I quickly teased my hair up a lofty four inches above my scalp, copped a great quantity of make-up from Mom, and borrowed her car (I thought a Jaguar convertible would be a more appropriate car for Tawny Cheeks to arrive in than my far-too-retro '74 Eldorado). Oh, yeah. And I changed into my brand new black satin Miracle Bra from Victoria's Secret. My scrawny little 32-A chest didn't really seem appropriate for somebody named Tawny Cheeks. And I have to tell you, that Miracle Bra was quite an engineering achievement. Suddenly I was damn well *stacked*.

Winston Percival was a tall aristocratic-looking guy of about fifty with a lean handsome face, and a somewhat dissipated look to the eyes. His suit was tweed with lots of odd little pockets in the double-vented coat. I guessed it was handmade in Savile Row.

He led me into his house and offered me a drink. I asked

for a Pink Lady, and then when he didn't know how to make that or a Fuzzy Navel or a Sloe Gin Fizz, I said, "That's okay, hon! Jack Black straight up would be good."

That one he knew. I looked around the room while he poured the bourbon. The antiques were beautiful and eclectic, and lots of paintings crammed the walls in a Victorian clutter. Most of them were muddy still lifes or meticulously rendered landscapes of the sort I vaguely associated with early-19th-century England. I had taken Art History in college, but it was a hell of a long time ago.

"So . . ." His English drawl was so deeply Etonian, I assumed it had to be a put-on. "Jay Lowensteen. How is the old boy?"

"He's *fabulous*!" I gushed. "Just spoiling me to death."

Then I tittered and gave him a flirty look. The way I was sitting gave him a nice view up the very short leather skirt I was wearing. As I may have mentioned, my legs are my one real physical asset and I admit to a certain vanity in that department. I also swayed my back slightly so as to put my miraculous new bustline to best advantage. I was annoyed to notice that his eyes spent a lot more time on my fake boobs than my real legs.

"What's Jay up to then?"

I had neglected to ask Honey who Jay Lowensteen was and so for a moment I felt a vague sense of panic. "You know Jay! Always got something going." I smiled apologetically. "He don't tell me much about business, though."

Winston Percival appraised me. I got the feeling he was trying to figure out if I was for real or not. "Quite so," he said finally. "Quite so."

"Well, shoot!" I said. "Let's talk about art, huh?"

"Marvelous idea." He smiled in a way that was supposed to convey to me that while he was my social and intellectual superior, it wasn't the sort of thing that mattered to him in any profound way. I assumed this was a useful expression for an art dealer. I had noticed, in fact, that Winston Percival had a limited repertoire of facial expressions, all of them no doubt carefully practiced in a mirror. He had an I'm-terribly-fascinated face, and an I'm-thinking-deeply face, and the one I just mentioned. They were fine as far as they went—but when his face relaxed, it took on a sort of rat-like quality. But he didn't let that one out of the cage much. Mostly he stuck with terribly fascinated.

"So what were you thinking of, my dear? Do you have a period or a style that's especially turned your head?"

"Well, I tell you something," I said. "I like a pitcher that looks like something. All them cubisms and everything? With both eyeballs on one side of the head? That stuff ain't me."

"You're a fan of the classics, the old masters."

"Yeah, well, you know I looked into this a little—the prices and everthang?—and I don't think Jay's exactly got in mind paying twenty bazillion dollars for some dang Rembrandt, you know what I'm saying?"

Winston Percival chuckled and crinkled his eyes. Terribly fascinated. Terribly, terribly fascinated. "Would that we all could have a Rembrandt, hm?"

"Right. That's what I'm saying. So you know, I tell you something I sure do love, you know, like Moe-nay? And Man-nay? All them lilies and everything?"

"Ah. Well. Again you are aware that—"

"Oh *shit* yeah! I couldn't get near one of them Moe-nays with a stick, not for the prices them things are bringing. So what I was thinking was maybe like an American Impressionist? Or maybe one of them Brandywine school people."

"Ah, yes. That's terribly clever of you, if I may say so. I think that some of the American Impressionists, especially the women, are simply getting ready to explode in value. As a matter of fact I've got a terrific Jane Peterson you might be interested in looking at."

"That right?" I tried to sound interested. I had never heard of Jane Peterson. "Let's take a gander."

Winston Percival picked up a tiny bell and rang it delicately—an inspired move, I thought—and immediately a small but muscular Asian guy wearing jeans and a black turtleneck with short sleeves came in and set up an easel on the other side of the room, then draped a black velvet cloth over it.

"Gary, if you'd get the Peterson for me?" Winston said to him when he had finished setting up the easel. The Asian guy left without a word.

"I don't know how familiar you are with Peterson, but . . ." and then he launched into the painter's biography. I nodded and blinked a lot. After a while Gary came back in and set up a painting in an elaborate gilt frame on the easel, fussing with it a little to get it perfectly level and centered. It was one of these Arab street scene pictures that were popular back in the late nineteenth century, with lots of sunlight and bright white turbans. While the rest of the room was fairly dim, the easel was under a puddle of unobtrusive but very bright light, making the painting stand out dramatically.

"That's *terrific*, Gary, really," Winston said impatiently. Gary quit fussing and stepped to the side. Winston blathered on for a while about the painting.

Finally I interrupted him. "Uh . . . like how much you asking for this, Winnie?"

Winston cleared his throat delicately. "What *were* we thinking of on this one, Gary?" Winston said.

"Eighteen, I believe, Winston." Gary had a fake English accent, too.

"Ah, yes, eighteen."

I nodded, then wrinkled my nose, leaned forward and patted him on the knee. "Jay told me I wasn't supposed to tell you this . . . You promise you won't tell him?"

Winston smiled confidentially. "You've nothing to worry about on my account, my dear."

"I think Jay'd be willing to go into a good bit higher price range. You know, if I find something really really cool."

Winston looked terribly fascinated and then he looked like a rat and then he looked terribly fascinated again. "How much higher, em, is a 'good bit'?"

"Well. Like have you got anything in the, like, couple hundred thousand range? See I was thinking maybe more like . . . oh . . . Childe Hassam or somebody like that."

"Were you now?" Suddenly Winston was wearing the rat face again.

I shrugged "I mean, Jane Peterson, hey she's okay, but that guy Childe Hassam . . . I mean, he really kicks ass, you know. All those . . . those *colors* and everything?"

"Childe Hassam." Winston ran his hand down the side of his face. "Hassams are rather dear these days."

"Well, you know, see the thing is, Honey was kind of saying that like from time to time you get—you know . . ." I winked at him.

Winston said, "I'm not sure I *do* know."

"Like, special deals."

Winston glanced at his assistant. "Gary could you run upstairs for a moment. There's a Howard Pyle up there . . ."

Gary left.

"I'm not necessarily looking for a Howard Pyle," I said. "I'm more looking for a special deal."

"I'm still not quite sure what you mean."

"Like, this provenance thing," I said. "You know, like if a painting's from a particular place and you know who owns it and where it's been and all that jazz?"

"Yes . . ."

"And like if maybe I was the type of collector who was just looking for something that was pretty. See what I mean? And since I just wanted it to keep, right?—not worrying about selling it?—then maybe I wouldn't care about all that provenance stuff. See? So like if there was a painting that you had that didn't have all that provenance and the papers behind it and everything, maybe there'd be a special deal on it."

Terribly, terribly, terribly fascinating. Winston's aristocratic chin lifted a fraction of an inch. "Ah! So then you're a *long-term* collector."

"That's it exactly!" I smiled brightly. "I'm a long-term collector. And Jay just wants to make me happy."

Winston's eyes took a long, searching tour of my Miracle Bra. "I can understand why, my dear."

"So let me be kinda plain here. I understand you might could get me a certain Childe Hassam. And you might could get me a special deal."

Gary came in with a new painting. "Put it back, Gary," Winston said. "We don't need the Pyle."

"That's why I'm here, see?" I said. "Cause of your reputation."

"My reputation."

"In this neck of the woods, you're the special deal man."

Winston got up and walked around. He had a look of consternation on his face. "Am I talking to you, or am I talking to Jay?"

I quit smiling, lowered my eyelids slightly.

"You're talking to both of us, hon," I said. Then I tossed back my Jack Black, doing my best to look a lot smarter and tougher and more serious than I'd looked earlier, while still maintaining a certain redneck bimbo aura. I don't know if you've ever tried this, but it's a tricky line to walk.

Winston started looking nervous. "I think if I'm talking to Jay, I need to talk to Jay."

My heart started beating faster.

"Gary! Gary! Get the phone."

Gary hustled in with a cordless phone.

I had to head this off at the pass. "The phone?" I shrieked. "Are you out of your goddamn mind, talking on a *phone*? You ever heard of wire taps, Winston? You ever heard of the fucking FBI?"

Winston set the phone down. "Yes, yes, you're quite right. Quite right." He tapped nervously on his front tooth with one of his buffed and manicured fingernails.

"Jesus H. Christ, Winston, what is this? Goddamn amateur night!"

"I'm sorry, I'm sorry."

"We understand what we're talking about don't we, Winston? Childe Hassam. 'Late Afternoon, Brittany,' whatever the hell it's called."

"Yes, but—"

"So can you get it?" I said. "Or not?"

Winston sat down in a chair, put his hand over his mouth. He was thinking now, but it was the rat thinking, not the English gentlemen art dealer.

"What?" I said impatiently. "Talk to me."

Winston spread his hands helplessly. "Look, I—I just don't know. I'd like to help Jay on this but it's just . . ."

"You don't know who has the painting? Or you promised it to somebody else?"

Winston sighed. "Look look look . . . Let me . . . I can make some calls, all right. I'm sure I could chase it down for you. Okay? I don't, it's not . . . I don't have what you're looking for on hand, okay? But I'm sure we can, em, work something out, my dear."

Suddenly it struck me why he acting so funny. The guy didn't have the slightest idea who had the painting or how to get his hands on it.

I decided to press a little bit. "My understanding, this chick Charlie and her boy over there, they paid some girlie-girl to rip off the painting. The girl tried to fuck Charlie over and ransom it back to the insurance company. Only it didn't work out the way she planned and now Charlie's got the painting. That's just what I heard."

Suddenly Winston's eyes narrowed. "If you know that for a fact, then why did Jay send you to me? Why not go straight to Charlie?"

I didn't have an answer for that one. I had the sudden, awful feeling that I should have kept my big mouth shut.

"Uh . . ." I said.

Winston's eyes flicked upward from my face, as though someone was standing behind my chair. Then he nodded. That was when I realized that somebody *was* standing there. I tried to stand up, but I was about a second too late. The Asian guy, Gary, grabbed my shoulders and wrestled me back into the chair. He was a strong guy, and I'm a very small woman and there was not a damn thing I could do to get away from him.

Winston reached into the drawer of an antique secretaire behind him and came out with a long black tube. For a second I had the awful feeling it was a cattle prod, but then I realized it was a metal detector.

"Jay is gonna kill you," I yelled. Then I tried to bite Gary's hand. It was no use.

Winston ran the metal detector up my legs and across my chest. At which point the wand let out an electronic bleat. Winston ripped open my blouse. Then he and Gary stared at the midpoint between the tumescent cups of my Miracle Bra. It wasn't the inauthenticity of my breast size that interested them, however: it was the small black microphone held to my chest with a piece of duct tape.

"Fuck!" Gary said. "She's a cop!" Suddenly his accent sounded very California.

Winston ran his hand through his hair, shook his head. "I should've fucking known. That fucking Honey Chanteuse, man, I knew there was something goofy when she called me this morning." His English accent had evaporated, too. "She hates my ass."

"So what do we do?" Gary said.

"Get this cop bitch out of here before the damn SWAT team busts our doors in."

As Gary wrestled me out of the chair and propelled me toward the front of the house, Winston yelled, "Hold on!"

Gary stopped, turned me around so I was facing Winston. He pointed his finger at me and yelled, "Let me tell you something, cop lady. If it was like you say, that Charlie stole that Hassam from herself so she could get the insurance money, you know who the first person she would have called to get rid of that painting would have been?"

I shook my head timidly.

"Me! She'd have called *me*! But she didn't. So you don't have shit on me and you don't have shit on her. And if I see your skinny cop face around here again, I'm filing for police harassment."

Next thing I knew I was face down in the mulch under some azalea bushes just to the side of Winston Percival's front door.

I stood up, wiped the mud and pine bark mulch off my legs. "Well," I said loudly, in a moderately successful attempt to stave off the shakes, "that could definitely have gone worse."

CHAPTER 14

WHEN I GOT back to the office Sean McNeely hadn't found anything of much use on Nexis, and Earl still hadn't located Leslie-Anne Gilmartin's boyfriend. I told Earl to keep at it and then got Sean started pulling cases off of Lexis. I told him to try finding stuff on all the names on Charlie Biddle's list, plus anything in the past five years that he could find on art theft in Georgia.

Then I typed up a brief interim report on what we'd discovered so far: Charlie Biddle had the means and motive and a background that made her seem suspicious, but my experience with Winston Percival more or less shot down the Charlie Biddle theory. Besides, if this was an insurance scam, Charlie would obviously have ransomed the picture back to Reliance and left it at that. Right now Leslie-Anne's boyfriend still seemed like the most fruitful avenue to pursue. When I was done with the report, I forged Gunnar's signature at the bottom and stuck it in an envelope along with a signed copy of the bounty agreement which Marion Cheever had finally sent over, and called for a messenger.

As usual I was running late. I drove like a maniac across town, slipped into the silver lamé dress, and then gunned it back down to the Buckhead Ritz-Carlton where Mom's AIDS benefit was being held.

Mom grabbed me, told me in a low hiss how embarrassed she was that I had not been there to walk in the door with Walter, and then turned on the high-watt smile while she introduced me to Walter's boss and Walter's boss's boss. They were both smooth men with nice Southern accents and good manners, highly intelligent, well dressed, and bland as tapioca pudding.

Walter looked more or less sick to his stomach. The senior partner in the firm had a wife who was very much in my mother's mold—if a bit more subdued—while Walter's boss's wife was a quiet woman with a round face and round arms. I had absolutely nothing to say to any of them.

I knew what my role was, though, and I dutifully played it: I sent Walter off to caddy some drinks for his bosses, then I flirted with each of the partners for precisely thirty seconds apiece (senior partner first, junior partner second), then I engaged the wives in a discussion of what a sad thing it was for children to have AIDS. It was agonizingly dull. Walter came back with the drinks. I noticed he reserved the double scotch for himself.

Mom angled by, flirted with the senior partner then the junior partner, then talked to the wives about what a sad thing it was for children to have AIDS. She spiced this up with a moving anecdote, and then cocktail hour was over and we all sat down. I looked at my watch surreptitiously. Sixty-nine more minutes and I could split in good conscience.

During dinner Mom spoke and a doctor with thick glasses and a tremor spoke and a wan little boy got up and read a short speech that made my eyes well up.

"You okay?" Walter said.

"I'm fine," I whispered. "Are *you* okay?"

He smiled thinly and took a long pull on his scotch. I looked around the room. The mayor was there. Ted and Jane were there. Also the chairman of Coca-Cola, the president of Georgia-Pacific, Martin Luther King III and his mother, half the bullpen of the Atlanta Braves, the usual assortment of surgeons and lawyers, and a wide assortment of heirs and heiresses who felt no compunction to hold down jobs.

And then Mom congratulated everyone for being the wise and generous and humane people they were. At which point she introduced Walter as the chairman of the event—a move so brazen, so bold, so shocking and brilliant I could barely believe it. She talked about what a wonderful and clever guy he was ("even if he is my son!" titter titter), and most importantly how hard he'd worked to bring together all his dear friends for this important affair.

While she was going on and on about him, I looked over at Walter. His face was white with anger. I could see she hadn't told him that she would do this. If she had, he would never have consented to be there: it was obvious he had no more organized this event than he'd won an Olympic gold in the shot put.

"A few words, Walter?" Mom said.

Walter sat there for a long time, staring at her.

I was proud of my brother. Finally he stood up and he walked to the podium and he made a few gracious comments about the goodness of the cause, then said, "I wish I could take credit for this event, but I can't. It has taken place solely because my mother Miranda Wineberg believed in it and made it happen. Frankly I had nothing whatsoever to do with its success." Then he smiled and he sat back down at our table.

The senior partner stood up and shook his hand enthusiastically, clasping his elbow with his other hand. Walter's boss followed suit, clapping him on the back once or twice for good measure. I imagine the old fox of a senior partner knew the score, that this was all a put-up job by my mother the social climber. But I could see a funny look in the eye of Walter's boss—envy I think it was, but it might even have been fear. He must have thought Walter was just being modest and cagey up there, giving away the credit in a thin attempt to disguise his drive, his precocious organizational skills, and the broad net of his social connections.

And when I saw that look in the junior partner's eye, I knew that Mom's ploy had worked, that tomorrow they might as well print up the next batch of Underhill, Tabb, LaFollette, Gold & Pearcy stationery with Walter's name in the partner's column. For Mom this was an absolute coup, a triumph, a Napoleonic master-stroke.

And for Walter?

After my brother sat down, I watched his face. He looked like someone had just put a rope around his neck, like a man with not much time left to live. I took his hand and squeezed it, but he just sat there and stared at the congealed remains of his food. If I could have strangled my mother then and there, I'd probably have done it.

The minute my mother sat down, I folded my napkin and set it next to the pear confit with walnuts and whipped lingonberry cream on top, told the senior partner and the junior partner and their wives what a marvelous time I'd had, but that I had a terribly pressing engagement, and headed for the door as fast I could get my silver shoes to move.

On the way out a man stood up and grinned at me, blocking my way. I was so blind with anger that it took me a moment to recognize him.

Ron.

I stopped dead in my tracks. "Sunny Childs!" he said brightly.

I couldn't move.

Ron turned to his left, put his hand on the shoulder of a beautiful blond who looked an awful lot like Sean McNeely. "Sweetheart," he said to her. "I want you to meet somebody." Ron's wife turned to look at me. I had this queasy feeling like I was trapped in some awful nightmare. "This is Sunny Childs, the friend of mine I was telling you about who hired Sean today. Sunny, this is my wife Ellen Widner."

"Oh my God!" Ellen said. "The private investigator!"

I did some sort of rictus thing with my face, found myself shaking her hand.

"Sit down," Ellen said. "You just have to sit down. Ron was telling me all about this ransom thing yesterday. I saw on the news about the girl being shot. My God, it must have been terrible!"

I finally managed to speak. "I really have to go," I said.

"Oh, sit, sit!" she said. "I have to hear everything." Ron was still blocking my path.

Maybe if I hadn't been so stunned about Mom's little power play, I would have had the good sense to find an excuse. But I didn't. I just sat down and told her the whole story. Ron was leaning over my left shoulder, listening carefully.

"Any suspects yet in the murder?" he asked.

"We're looking at Leslie-Anne's boyfriend. Hopefully either we or the police will find him soon."

"What about this guy Porter that works at the gallery?"

"I'm not going to write him off as having some involvement. But he didn't do the theft itself. He's got a firm alibi."

"This is so exciting!" Ellen said.

I looked at my watch. "Well it was great meeting you," I said, "but I really do need to run."

"We'll have to have lunch or something," Ellen said. "I've just got to hear how this all works out."

"Give me a call," I said.

"Oh, and thanks for throwing my brother a line."

"Well, it's just a temporary thing. We'll have to see if there's a fit or not."

"Let me see you out," Ron said.

"No, please."

But there was no way I could protest too strenuously without it looking strange, so he took me by the elbow and walked me to the door. I gave my ticket to the carhop, and then turned to Ron, "What possessed you?" I said.

Ron shoved his hands down in his pockets, stared across

Peachtree at the mall on the other side of the road. "I couldn't help it," he said in low whisper. "I was watching you through the whole dinner. Do you realize how hot you look in that dress?"

"Go inside to your wife, Ron."

"You don't have a bra on, do you?"

"Ron. Don't."

He stood there a while longer. I could tell he was going to touch me if the carhop didn't get back soon.

The carhop arrived with my old Eldorado, jumped out, opened the door for me. "*Very* cool ride," the carhop said.

"Thanks." I gave him five bucks and jumped in.

Ron closed my door, then leaned his arms against the car. "Keep me and Ellen posted about this painting thing," he said in a loud voice.

"Sure," I said. Then I laid down some rubber.

The only good thing I could say about the whole experience was that Mom was so intent on pimping Walter to his dull bosses that she didn't notice I'd failed to wear my Miracle Bra.

CHAPTER  15

WHEN I GOT back to the office Earl Wickluff was sitting in the break room playing solitaire.

"Did you ever find Terry Yokum?" I said.

"Sure did," he said, not looking up from his cards.

"And?"

The way Earl was sitting I could only see him in profile. He turned his face toward me. His left eye was swollen shut. By tomorrow he'd have a nice black eye. "He demonstrated a distinct disinclination to talk."

"Ouch," I said.

"Yeah, well you better believe *I* got a couple good licks in on his punk ass."

"Exactly what happened?"

"I finally found him. The reason I never located him, turns out he's been living in this artist studio over on Ottley Drive. He doesn't have a phone or get his mail there. Anyways, I take this freight elevator up to his loft and here's this little son of a bitch painting a picture of a nekkid girl. I say to him, 'Son, would you like to talk to me about Leslie-Anne Gilmartin?' He just looks at me with this empty look on his face. Can't tell if he's sad or mad or glad, you know what I'm saying?"

"I guess."

"So at that point I take out my PI's license and I tell him

my name and I say, 'Alls we're interested in is getting that painting back. We don't care about pressing charges for stealing, we don't care whether you killed that girl.' Still doesn't say a word. Puts his paintbrush down, tells this girl, his model, to put her clothes back on. Naturally I turn to look at this gal—cause I got to admit it's not every day I see that type of thing. I mean this gal's got a rack on her like—''

"Just get on with the story," I said testily.

"Yeah, well, I'm looking at this gal and our buddy Yokum seizes the moment to take a poke at me. Tried to get me right in the old family jewels. I must have seen something out of the corner of my eye, though, because I moved back a step and he didn't get a good lick in. So I pop him with an uppercut and then he—'' What followed was a meticulously rendered blow-by-blow of the fight. I could see why Gunnar liked Earl: they shared the same enthusiasm for all the primitive male pursuits. Guys beating the crap out of each other, for instance.

"Okay, okay, so what was the upshot of all this?"

"Well, I put a good foot in his ribs. I guarantee you he'll feel that every damn time he draws a breath for the next month.''

"No, I mean did you get any information out of him?"

Earl looked at me like I was four years old. "Shoot no! After I rap him a couple of times, he goes booking into the elevator.''

"Did it occur to you that getting in a rumble with this kid was maybe not the world's best interview strategy?''

"What—I'm s'pose to just sit there and let this punk thump the living dook out of me?''

"Maybe you could have calmed him down a little, gotten something out of him.''

"You women," he said, shaking his head in bewilderment. "Y'all are so naive. A man who don't defend himself in a situation like that, hell, he ain't even a man.''

"Better to be a professional who comes back with the information than a big macho man who comes back with nothing but bunged-up knuckles."

"If you was a man," he said, "you wouldn't even *think* of making a silly statement like that." Then he stared at his cards, looking for his next play.

"Jack on the queen," I said.

"I be dog. Don't know why I missed that one."

Apparently Sean McNeely had gone out for dinner, but he came back a few minutes later. "Oh, hi!" he said when he saw me in my office. "I got some stuff on the computer for you."

He hustled off for a minute, then came back with a stack of paper from the laser printer. I searched through the pages. He'd come up with lots of art theft and art fraud cases, but none that seemed immediately relevant. He'd also tracked down the verdict in Charlie's case—which we already knew about—as well as a couple of cases involving Winston Percival. Percival, not surprisingly, turned out to be a long-standing alias. The guy's real name was Joe Lee Nichols, Jr., and he had a couple of receiving convictions for back in the early '70s. But it didn't really add anything to what we already knew about the guy.

Nothing came up, though, for the person I was most interested in: Terry Yokum.

I did a little thinking out loud. "I wonder if the police have run this Yokum guy through the NCIC?"

"Would they tell you if they had?"

"I don't know," I said. "We managed to get some information out of them this morning, but I suspect our welcome will start wearing pretty thin pretty fast."

Sean shuffled his feet and looked like he wanted to say something.

"What?"

"Well, you know, due to my law enforcement back-

ground? Plus computer experience and so on? I kind of figured out a way.''

''A way to what?''

Sean looked around as though eavesdroppers might be
lurking in the corners of my office. ''Hack into crime computers.''

''You can hack into the NCIC?''

''NCIC. Georgia Crime Computer. Atlanta PD central
computer. ID Net. DMV. I can get into a bunch of stuff.''

I took a moment to reappraise Sean McNeely. These were
sources of information that were of huge value to investigators, but we were prohibited from using them. What happens, as a result, is that we end up having to use our contacts
in law enforcement every time we need this kind of information. And sometimes our contacts don't feel like giving it
to us. It's not a very good system.

So some investigators hire people like McNeely who've
figured out ways to hack into the computers. The downside,
of course, is that if you get caught inside one of these computers, you get in big, big trouble. Unfortunately the NCIC,
which is the most useful database of all, is a federal system.
Get caught there, they send the FBI after you.

''Hm,'' I said.

''Look, I've never been caught, if that's what you're worried about. This isn't real high-tech stuff, I just have friends
here and there that slipped me their passwords and stuff.''

It still made me a little nervous.

''Okay,'' I said finally. ''Can you connect to Fulton
County?''

Sean nodded.

Fulton County was the jurisdiction Atlanta was located in.
Their computer system only had records on local crimes, and
it only went back a few years. But it was the lowest-risk
computer to break into. ''Try that first.''

Sean went back to the computer he'd been using in what
used to be Barry Wine's office. I watched over his shoulder

as he logged onto the Fulton County computer. The process didn't seem to be very complicated.

"See," he said. "All you need to know is a couple of passwords and you can get in with a standard terminal communications program."

He went through several menus in the Superior Court Clerk's system until he came to one that said: CRIMINAL RECORDS. I got the feeling he'd done this a few times before.

"Typical government operation," he said in a derisive tone. "Idiotic. It's all set up based on the docket, so you have to do a separate search for each year."

He typed in YOKUM, then did a search for the current year. Two entries came up. Neither one was Terry.

"Nice thing about this, though—unlike NCIC—is you get charges that were dropped, pending charges, arrests, all kinds of stuff that never ended up leading to a conviction."

"Try last year," I said.

He ran another search, which also came up dry.

His third search got a hit, though. Terry Yokum had been charged with DAA. "What's DAA?" I said.

"Driving Away an Auto. It's like a misdemeanor version of auto theft. It's basically so they can give car thieves something to plea down to when the evidence is weak."

"Well, it's something."

He ran one more search and we turned up gold: when Terry Yokum was 19 years old, he had been charged with theft. The charges had been dropped. Then about two months later there'd been two charges lodged against him: aggravated assault and carrying a concealed handgun without a permit. That, too, had been dropped.

"Aggravated assault," I said. "That could mean a lot of things."

Sean tapped the screen with his finger. "Agg Assault, that's a kind of broad charge. In Georgia there's no such charge as attempted murder, so you can get charged with agg assault for whacking a guy in the butt with a two-by-four, or for shooting him six times in the head. My guess, with the concealed weapon thing in there, he shot somebody.''

"Wonder why they dropped it.''

Sean shrugged.

I picked up the phone and dialed an old friend of mine who used to be with the Fulton County DA's office. It was kind of a long shot. "Renee,'' I said. "Hi there, it's Sunny.''

"Sunny, gosh, haven't heard from you in, what, six months?''

It was my fault. I got wrapped up in Ron six months ago and since then I've been bad about calling my friends. "I know,'' I said. "I'm a terrible friend.''

There was an awkward pause.

"So, actually, I'm working a case here and something came up.''

"Oh,'' Renee said.

"Does the name Terry Yokum mean anything to you?''

"Isn't he a country singer?''

"That's Dwight.''

"Right, right.''

"I'm trying to recover a painting. I don't know if you've read about the case. This girl Leslie-Anne Gilmartin got shot and—''

"Oh, yes! I saw something about that.''

"We think this guy Terry Yokum was an accomplice and that he might be involved. I just wanted to get some background. He was charged with agg assault three or four years ago. I don't know if the case came through you or not, but I figured it was worth a stab.''

"Wait a minute, wait a minute. Rich kid, right?''

"I'm not too sure.''

"Yeah, I remember now. Good family, went to Westminster School, all that. He was some kind of artist, wasn't he?''

"I don't know much about him.'' I don't know why I didn't put it together when Earl said he'd found the guy at an art studio. I felt a surge of energy: suddenly I was sure that I was on the right track.

"Well, I didn't handle that case. I think that was Jerry Burkhardt. He was prosecuting cases in front of Judge Crooks back then. Jerry got a real hard-on for that guy, got really pissed when the case fell apart. Why don't you call him?" She gave me a number. Like Renee, this guy Burkhardt had gone into private practice.

I called Burkhardt, who sounded annoyed at being called on a Saturday night. At least he did until I mentioned Terry Yokum's name.

"Terry Yokum! That little weasel. Man, I still get mad when I think about that creep."

"So you remember the case?"

"Oh, yeah. You know Mark Yokum, the litigator over at Bettson, Lumm & Fourchay?"

I didn't.

"Well, that's his dad. Big anti-trust guy, rolling in dough. Anyway this kid Terry is a typical spoiled jerk, one of these kids that's always in trouble, but inevitably manages to slime his way out? Anyway, here's the case. Terry's dating this girl. He's nineteen, she's a minor, like sixteen or seventeen. She shows up in the ER at Piedmont late one night with a GSW in her head. Just grazed her, but of course she's bleeding all over, scared the piss out of her, but she won't talk to the cops. Finally this female detective, Clarisse, damn, Clarisse something-or-other, I hate forgetting all these names, but she comes over there and gets the girl to talk. Turns out she and Terry had a fight over something and Terry pulls a three fifty-seven on her, points it at her head, pulls the trigger.

"Frankly we don't think he meant to kill her. He just wanted to give her a little scare. So the cops roust him. He runs out the back door with the gun. Trying to hide it, I guess. They take him down, charge him with no permit, fleeing, resisting, agg assault, you know, the whole bit.

"So everything's moving along and we're heading for trial. Then suddenly this girl shows up and says she won't testify. Well we've got no bullet, no witnesses, no nothing. Fleeing, resisting, no permit, that's all bullshit, so we *nole pros* those charges and drop the agg assault. The scumbag skates."

I thought about it. "Any idea why she decided not to testify?"

"Who knows? Maybe she fell back in love with him, maybe he threatened her. She was not from the same kind of background as him, though, you know. Extremely bright kid, but from a dirt-poor family. My little fantasy about the thing was that Terry's old man gave her folks a refrigerator or something and told them to get the girl to back off."

"Thanks," I said. "This is a big help."

"So what's your interest in this guy, Sunny?"

"You read about that girl Leslie-Anne Gilmartin that got killed yesterday?"

"The art theft thing."

"Yeah. We're trying to recover the painting. He's our number one suspect right now."

"I hope you get that little douchebag."

"Me too." I circled Terry Yokum's name on the legal pad next to the computer. "I don't suppose you remember what their dispute was about?"

Burkhardt laughed harshly. "Matter fact, I do. He finishes up some piece of artwork, then asks the girl what she thinks of it. She says it's 'derivative.' So he shoots her in the head."

"What kind of art work?"

"Painting. The guy's a painter.

"Hah!" I said.

"What?"

After I hung up I smiled at Sean McNeely. "Great work, Sean. I believe we can log off now. This has got to be our guy."

Sean was beaming.

"So what do we do now?"

"Well, I'll give the police a call. If we've found all of this out, they probably have, too. I just want to make sure that when they arrest this guy, they make finding the painting a high priority."

"How can I help?"

"You could probably head on home. You've done a good day's work."

Sean looked a little disappointed. "Will you be needing me tomorrow?"

"Hm. Truthfully, I'm guessing this will go into the hands of the police now. But I can't be sure. Do you mind coming in? I mean I might end up just sending you home again."

"Hey, no problem."

I sent Earl and Tawanda home, too, messed around with some paperwork and finally told myself to stop being so anal, that it was time for the day to be over with. I tend to have a hard time tearing myself away from the office. I'm told this is a common affliction among people who have no life. Just as I was about to go, I decided to check my e-mail. Half an hour later I logged off. It was closing in on ten o'clock. "Get a *life*!" I said loudly to the empty room.

Of course it then occurred to me that I hadn't checked *Gunnar's* e-mail. So I logged onto his box. There were two messages. One was from Marion Cheever thanking Gunnar for the interim report. The sender name for the second message read: [X2111@FORZZRD.NZ].

I clicked on it and opened the message. There was a bunch of more or less inscrutable header information that led back to a server in New Zealand. I'd never heard Gunnar mention knowing anybody in New Zealand. But that didn't mean anything. He knew a lot of people.

The message read:

>GUNNAR,
>SORRY THINGS GOT FOULED UP THE OTHER
  DAY,
>BUT IT WASN'T MY FAULT.
>IF YOU WANT THE PAINTING, YOU CAN
  HAVE IT.
>AS AN INDUCEMENT TO KEEP YOU FROM
  DOING ANYTHING
>STUPID (LIKE CALLING THE COPS) I'M LOW-
  ERING
>THE PRICE TO $50,000. CASH ONLY.
>I WILL CALL AT 8:00 PM TOMORROW AND
  TELL YOU WHAT
>TO DO.
>THIS IS A ONE-TIME ONLY DEAL.
>I KNOW WHAT YOU LOOK LIKE, SO DON'T
  TRY SENDING
>SOME COP.

I looked over the header information again. I'm not a computer expert so it's no surprise that I couldn't make anything of it. I had a good bet who sent it, though: Terry Yokum.

I hesitated for a minute. What the hell was I going to do? First there was the issue of the $50,000. The bounty agreement made it clear that anything I paid came out of my bounty. Which meant that I would come up $50,000 short on Tuesday.

I dialed up my bank on the computer, logged in, checked the balance on my savings account. There was $7,488. I poked around in my drawer until I found a statement from my mutual fund company. It said I had $36,547. That could have gone up or down a little, but it still left me about six grand short. Six grand was no sweat: I could borrow that much from Walter.

But that was only the first problem. The second problem was that if, as I suspected, the sender of this e-mail was Terry

Yokum, and if, as I also suspected, he had killed Leslie-Anne Gilmartin, then I really needed to get the cops involved.

Oh, yeah. And there was the minor problem that this guy wanted to deal with Gunnar personally. I got on the phone and futilely paged Gunnar. Once again, no one called back.

If I called the cops and they made the bust and got the painting, I was in tall clover. That way I'd get the full one hundred grand. Of course, if they screwed up the bust, or if Yokum got spooked or if he got busted before he had the painting and then clammed up . . . then I'd never see the painting by Tuesday. Probably not by doomsday.

I was still trying to figure out what to do when the phone rang. "Hello?" a woman with a patrician Southern accent said. "Is this Sunny?"

My heart sank. It was Jocelyn Gilmartin. "Hi, Mrs. Gilmartin," I said. "How are you holding up?"

"We're forging on," she said. "I'm sorry I missed the benefit this evening. We were just too cut up to make it."

"You didn't miss anything."

There was a long pause. "So, I was wondering. Has Mr. Brushwood made any progress in finding the killer?"

"Uh. Well, I guess you could say, yeah, there's been some progress."

"I know it's awfully late, but I've been sitting here fretting and fretting and fretting, and finally I just had to call. Do you suppose I could speak to him?"

"To Gunnar?"

"Yes."

"Well, he's . . . he's not around right now. Frankly, uh, he's probably in bed by now. He's one of those early-to-bed, early-to-rise types."

"I see."

"I can't tell you everything, but we've identified a strong suspect."

There was a brief pause. "It's that boy, isn't it? Terry. I never liked that boy."

I hesitated and then finally said, "I'd rather not jump to conclusions. I think we'll know more tomorrow."

"You'll call me then?"

"Sure."

"So I guess you've involved the police?"

"One of my agents spoke to them extensively this morning. As a matter of fact, I was just getting ready to call them again."

We spoke a little longer, then I put the phone down. Talking to her I realized that I couldn't worry about the money. If Terry Yokum had killed that girl, he had to pay. I had to call the police.

As I was reaching for the phone, it rang again. I picked it up and before I even spoke I felt a chill run down my neck. I don't know what it was, but there was a hollow, creepy electronic hum on the line, like falling water heard through a drainage tunnel.

"Peachtree Investigations," I said.

"I want to talk to Gunnar." It was that Darth Vader voice again.

"He's not here. But he got your message. The problem is—"

"Eight o'clock. I'm only dealing with Gunnar," the voice said. "No cops, no flunkies. If I don't see a big white mustache, there's no deal."

"Listen! Gunnar's not—"

The line went dead.

I hung up the phone, cursed, took a deep breath, and called the homicide unit. Carl Fontaine wasn't there, so I left a message, told the detective who had answered that I had some extremely urgent information about the Gilmartin case. Three minutes later he called back.

"It's Sunny Childs," I said. "We need to talk."

CHAPTER 16

THE NEXT MORNING I was sitting around the table in the break room of Peachtree Investigations with six Atlanta Police detectives, waiting for the phone to ring. One of the detectives, a big weather-beaten guy named Sgt. Cyrus Nix, had been given a white wig and a fake white mustache. He wore a bush jacket, lace-up boots, and an Aussie hat. If you knew the real Gunnar, he wasn't that close, but if all you knew was the legendary Gunnar that you'd seen on TV, he'd pass.

So we had to hope that our thief had never actually met Gunnar.

We hadn't slept at all that night. After I briefed them late the previous evening and then waked up Payton Link so he could get the ransom money for us back out of the safe at Reliance, the police had tried to cut me out of the operation to catch the thief. But then I convinced them that they needed me in case he called and asked this guy Nix something that Nix didn't know. As long as they had me hanging around next to Nix, I could feed him any information the guy might test him with to make sure he was really Gunnar.

The call came at 8:15. Nix nodded to me and I put on a pair of headphones to monitor the call.

"You're late," Nix said into the phone.

Darth Vader said, "Go to the Dunwoody MARTA station.

In section A, row 3 of the north parking lot you'll find a white Mustang, license number WLD 901. Reach up under the front left tire and you'll find a secure walkie-talkie. Pick it up. I'll give you instructions on what to do next.''

Before Nix could speak the line clicked off.

"He's gonna drag you all over town to make sure you aren't being tailed,'' Maj. Carl Fontaine said.

The burly sergeant shrugged.

Fifteen minutes later I was sitting in a car out at the edge of the Dunwoody MARTA station. Nix had been rigged with a body mike and a tiny earpiece so small that you couldn't see it unless you were standing right next to him. The wire from the earpiece looped behind Nix's ear, under the wig, and down the back of his shirt. I, too, was given a tiny earpiece with a microphone in my sleeve. I felt like I'd just joined the Secret Service.

Because Nix's radio had a limited range, I had to be fairly close in case I needed to feed information to him. Two other police detectives were on the platform already, one dressed as a businessman, the other—a female detective—dressed in casual clothes. I was wearing a silly-looking curly black wig in case the thief recognized me from the other day.

Maj. Carl Fontaine sat next to me. A black female detective sat in the back. I started to get out of the car. Across the lot I could see the faux Gunnar stoop down to reach under a car.

Fontaine reached over and grabbed my arm. "Hold up a sec. Get back in.''

I got back in the car. "What?'' I said.

Nix stood back up and talked into the radio he'd picked up from the Mustang. In my earpiece I heard him say, "Okay, I've got the walkie-talkie. What do you want me to do?''

Carl reached over the seat back, looked at the detective in the back of the car. "Lucille, you got some make-up on you?''

"What?" she said.

"Make-up. I need some foundation, pancake, whatever you call it."

The detective named Lucille squinted at him. "It ain't gonna make you any better looking, Major," she said.

"It's for her," Fontaine said, pointing at me.

"Uh, Major . . . I don't know if you noticed, but she's white."

"Hurry! Give it to her."

The female detective scrabbled in her purse, came out with a compact of dark foundation.

"Put it on! Put it on!" I felt ridiculous as I started smearing the make-up across my face. The color, according to the label on the compact, was *light ebony*. "Hurry! Hurry! Hands too."

"Might I ask—"

"Lipstick, too."

The female detective handed me some lipstick in a deep red-brown. I turned the rear-view mirror around, put on the lipstick, pursed my lips. "Great," I said. "Al Jolson lives. What's the idea here?"

"See what he's doing? He's gonna take y'all into a black area," he said. "If he sends Nix down to Lakewood or someplace on the south side and a bunch of white folks come jumping off the train with him, he'll spot them for cops in about half a second. Even if you're not a cop at all. I mean white ladies *do not* get off the subway down there, see what I'm saying?"

I looked up and saw a train pulling into the station. "Damn it!" I said.

"Go!" Fontaine poked me not so gently in the ribs.

I could see I wouldn't make the train, but I jumped out and sprinted for it anyway.

The train pulled in as I reached the other side of the parking lot. I didn't have a token and there was a MARTA policeman standing right next to the gate. I pulled out my money, fed it into the machine. In my earpiece I could hear the squawk of Nix's walkie-talkie picked up through his microphone: a voice said, "Get on the train, Gunnar."

The token machine didn't like my dollar bill, so I had to run it through twice. I charged breathlessly up the stairs, cursing to myself. Just as I reached the top of the stairs I heard Nix's radio crackle. He was so close to the stairs that I heard it directly, not through the earpiece, as Darth Vader said, "Now get back off the train, Gunnar."

Nix jumped off the train. At the far end of the platform the black detective in the suit managed to get back out, too. The female detective had not gotten on at all. She had been leaning casually against a post pretending to read a paper. I guessed it was her plan to hop on at the last second. The doors closed as I ran toward the train. I figured if anyone was watching, I might as well keep up the pretense. As the train pulled out of the station, I hammed it up, acting like I was annoyed about missing it. I slapped the door of the moving train with the palm of my hand, and someone inside gave me an ugly look.

It turned out to be a lucky break: Nix's radio crackled. "Nice try, asshole," Darth Vader said. "If the chick reading the newspaper and the black guy in the suit get on the next train, we've got no deal. Tell them to lie down on the platform and don't get up."

So he was watching. He had been smart to make them get on at Dunwoody—the terminus at the north end of the North-South Line. Since it was the end of the line obviously everybody was waiting for the southbound train; anybody who hung around on the platform while the train pulled out was most likely shadowing "Gunnar." His only mistake was that he assumed I was not with Gunnar since I was so late coming up the stairs.

I drifted down the platform, sat with my face in my hands so that my features would be hard to make out. It would be obvious to anybody closer than twenty or thirty feet that I wasn't black. Nix went over to the two detectives, told them to lie down.

Through my earpiece I heard the thief's electronically altered voice. "Okay, Gunnar, I know you're wearing a wire so you can talk to the cops and tell them where you're going. Get rid of it."

The only good news was that he still thought Nix was Gunnar.

Nix looked around helplessly, then he lifted the walkie-talkie to his mouth and said, "I'm not wired. I swear."

"Okay, fuck it," the thief said.

Nix pressed the talk button. "Wait, wait!" Then he reached into his pants, pulled out the transmitter, set it gently on the concrete.

"The earpiece, too."

Nix took off the earpiece, set it next to the transmitter. After that I heard the radio crackle, but since I had no radio contact now and Nix was at least fifty feet down the platform from me, I couldn't make out what was being said. But then I saw Nix walk over to a bench, reach underneath and pull out a plastic shopping bag that said The Gap on the side. Nix opened his briefcase, looked around to see if anybody was watching, then dumped the money into the plastic bag. I assumed this was another precaution by the thief: he probably figured there might be a homing device in the briefcase Nix carried.

Which, in fact, there was.

After that Nix walked down to the end of the platform, stepped behind a big concrete pole for a moment. For a couple of minutes I couldn't see him. When he stepped out again, he was wearing a blue jumpsuit and a pair of work boots. He must have stripped off all his clothes right there behind the pillar. You had to give the thief credit: he was being thorough in making sure that Nix didn't have a homing device or a backup wire on him.

It struck me suddenly that this meant I was now Nix's

lifeline to the other cops. Nix had no weapon, no wire, no badge—nothing but fifty thousand dollars cash in a blue plastic bag. I watched him surreptitiously as he walked disconsolately back down the platform.

I heard Fontaine growl in my ear: "What the hell's going on, Sunny?"

I covered my mouth with my hand, spoke softly into the microphone in my sleeve, explaining the situation.

"Well, stick with him!"

I followed Nix onto the next train. This time there was no get-on, get-off trick. There were plenty of seats as the doors closed and the train took off, but I stood anyway. I figured this way I could leap off at the last second if I had to. My heart was beating fast and my palms were wet.

The train stopped at Chamblee and nothing happened. I saw two more detectives get on. That made me feel a little better. I didn't like having the burden of supporting Nix fall completely on my shoulders. One of the detectives got onto my car. He was a white guy, obviously a weightlifter, with a brush cut and a tight blue shirt. He might as well have worn a sign that said COP in big neon letters. We studiously avoided looking at each other.

At the Lindberg MARTA station Nix got off the train. I didn't move, just maintained my position by the door waiting to make a last-second dive if I had to. I saw the other detective, a black guy, get off the train a car or two down from me.

At the last second, Nix hopped back on the train. The black detective tried to get back on, but Nix held the door open, pointed at the detective and shook his head. Obviously he was blown, too. So we were back down to me and one detective. And I knew from our planning session that morning that there were no more. Fontaine, Lucille, and Hagee were all held in reserve to make the bust. Assuming we ever got to that point.

It occurred to me to wonder how the thief had kept us in

his sights all morning. I decided he must have had watchers at every station.

We rode through a few more stations uneventfully. At the Five Points station, Nix got out again. I waited, pretending to fuss with my bag, then as the door started to close and it was obvious Nix wasn't getting back on, I trudged out, head down—trying to look like someone who was coming home tired after pulling a long night shift. Nix threaded his way up and around through the big station, then headed down to the East-West Line platform. I tried to hang back in case he got instructions to double back . . . but he never did.

On a hunch I decided not to go down to the platform immediately. Instead I walked into the library cubicle above the tracks and looked through their fiction section. The Fulton County Library has a glass-walled cubicle where you can check out books in the subway. As it happens, it's centrally located in the station and has a good view of the tracks. I could see Nix at one end of the platform, the muscular white detective at the other end. The muscular guy took one of these pocket-sized New Testaments out of his pants, knotted up his forehead, and ran his finger slowly down the page.

The eastbound train started sliding into the station. I walked out of the library cupola and got onto the escalator. Nix got on the train, but the white guy stayed put. As the doors began to close, Nix jumped off again. I have to give the musclebuilder credit: he never even looked up from his bible.

The next eastbound train arrived five minutes later. We all got on and this time there was no Chinese fire drill.

After a couple of stops, the train emerged from underground and began running on elevated tracks. I stared out the window, watching the bleak landscape roll by. Once a thriving industrial area, South-East Atlanta was now a depressing jungle of crumbling warehouses and scrap yards and tiny frame houses with bars over every window.

At the King Memorial stop Nix got out and started walking down the platform. I followed him out and trudged along with my head down, doing my worn-out night shift worker routine. Carl Fontaine had been exactly right. Nix, the muscular detective, and I were the only white people on the platform.

After he'd taken about ten steps, Nix turned around and crooked his finger at the muscular guy. As I walked slowly by them I overheard Nix say: "You're blown, Jansen. He wants you to get on the next train and head out to the end of the line."

"Daggum it!" Jansen said.

I kept on walking, trying to figure out how the thief was spotting everybody. Surely he didn't have enough manpower to spy on all these different stations. Which is when it struck me: security cameras! Every MARTA station had security cameras. And those cameras were centrally monitored. Either the thief had hacked into the computer system or he had one of the MARTA security people on his payroll.

That was why nobody had spotted me. Despite the obviousness of my make-up, I had been walking around with my head down the whole time. Which meant that no one watching a security camera could have seen what I looked like.

Sometimes you just get lucky.

At the bottom of the stairs I paused and looked around as though I was waiting for a ride. Nix walked by me quickly, carrying the Gap bag tightly in his hand. It wasn't as bad an area as the one where Leslie-Anne had been shot—but still it wasn't the kind of place where an unarmed white guy with fifty grand in cash would feel excessively comfortable.

I turned my face so as to be as hard to see as possible. My make-up seemed so transparently fraudulent I was kind of amazed I hadn't been spotted yet. It was certainly obvious enough from the funny looks I got from the few other Sunday morning passengers that I was not passing for black to anybody who got very close to me.

"What's happening?" It was Fontaine in my ear.

"I'm at the King Memorial MARTA station. Jansen's blown. Everybody's blown but me. Nix is heading down . . . damn, I don't know what street this is."

"Well, follow him! When you see a street sign, let me know."

Nix turned right and headed briskly up the street paralleling the railroad tracks. I let him go about a block, then started shambling after him shaking my head as though annoyed that my ride hadn't showed up. I'd gotten about half a block when I was suddenly seized by fear. Up until this point I had felt a pleasant nervousness, like this was a lark. But now the neighborhood, the situation, the weight of everything that rode on my not screwing up . . . it was starting to wear on me.

Once again, I realized how smart the thief had been. This was mainly a business district—and not a very busy one at that. On a Sunday morning it was roughly as populous as the moon. Anybody driving by in a white Ford sedan might as well do it with siren on and lights flashing.

The only good news was that the thief was obviously pretty desperate to make a deal: if he hadn't been he would have bailed when he spotted the first detective on the subway platform up in Dunwoody. He had given himself lots of opportunities to weed out people shadowing him. And now he was in an area where any police presence would be spectacularly obvious. I suspected that we were reaching the point where if a police cruiser drove by, the thief would crawl off to wherever he was going and that would be the last we'd hear from him.

Needless to say, the painting would disappear and Peachtree Investigations would crash and burn come noon Tuesday.

Nix was moving faster than I was, but I figured if I got any closer I'd be so conspicuous as to lose any chance of successfully shadowing him. At the next intersection, he turned right and headed into a tunnel that went underneath the MARTA tracks.

I kept far enough back that he had come out the other side before I entered the tunnel. It was dark, old, and narrow— one lane in each direction with a row of concrete pillars running down the center. Plenty of places from which muggers and crackheads and homeless paranoiacs could spring out and do awful things to me.

"I'm going into a tunnel," I said.

Fontaine said something back, but I couldn't make it out. The tiny transmitter apparently had a weak signal: the transmission broke up as soon as I was inside the tunnel. I felt very alone as my footsteps echoed against the concrete. There were aging gang tags all over the walls, stalactites of lime hanging from mortar seams in the ancient concrete, smears of dirt and smoke on the walls.

My heart was pounding. "Can you hear me?" I said. "Can you hear me?"

Nothing. Only an empty hiss from the radio.

Then suddenly I was out into the sunshine again: this side of the MARTA tracks appeared to be more residential. A jumble of smoke-stained brick apartments huddled on one side of the road, while the other was lined with tiny, poorly kept houses. A pit bull on a chain crashed into the other side of a fence next to me, snarling and slobbering, its pink eyes full of a calm hatred. That sped me up a little, and my heart jumped again.

A family drove by on my left in a rotted Chevy, everyone in their Sunday best. I felt absurd, like a walking insult in my black-face make-up. A little girl smiled at me out the back window, her hair sticking out from her head in pointy black braids.

At the far end of the road Nix turned left. He was still pulling away from me so I picked up my speed a little once he had rounded the corner. A smell of collard greens wafted through the air. By the time I got to the turn, Nix had disappeared.

I stood on the corner for a moment.

"I lost him," I said into my sleeve.

"We got to be close," Fontaine said in my ear.

"Yeah, but that doesn't mean squat if I can't see him."

"Stay cool," Fontaine said. "Time to think like our subject here. Okay? Imagine you're the thief. Imagine you're using this neighborhood—its features, its terrain, its buildings. You want a place where you can be concealed, but where you won't get trapped, where you're mobile but safe, where you can make the switch without being conspicuous, where you can command the terrain but not be spotted. Look around. Where would you go?"

I looked around. Dreary little houses, old rusted cars, a small rise with a tree on it, a gulch with a couple of train tracks cutting through a bunch of jungly-looking foliage, a row of flatbed train cars with piggyback trailers chained on top of them.

"I don't know," I said. Suddenly the sleepless night seemed to be catching up with me. "I don't know."

"Safety, visibility. Something unusual maybe."

Which is when I saw it: down and over a block or two stood a tall round tower rising up over a dilapidated warehouse. It must have been a hundred and fifty feet high, with a row of small rectangular windows circling it about two thirds of the way up from the ground.

"Wait!" I said. "I think I got something."

"Get close then. See if you can spot any activity. If you do, just watch from a distance. Do not, I repeat, do *not* get involved. You're our eyes, okay?"

"No problem," I said.

I started walking down the street in the direction that Nix had been walking. But then I decided that was a bad idea. I should take a parallel street so if I got spotted I wouldn't seem to be following Nix's route.

I turned around, walked up past a small clapboard Church of God in Christ. I could hear the choir inside. They were singing and clapping, the heavy beat of drums and guitars and an organ pulsed beneath their voices, loud as a nightclub. It was a good sound, and it picked up my spirits a little.

I continued up the street, peered around the corner of a street that cut through on a diagonal. Two blocks away I saw a flash of tan jacket—Nix!—but then he disappeared behind a chain link fence. I worked my way carefully down the street and Nix came into view again. He was about a block away talking into the radio.

I ducked into the front yard of a scaling clapboard house and peeked over the railing of its sway-backed porch.

The big round tower stood in the middle of a triangular property surrounded by a rusting chain link fence which was topped with razor wire. Nix stood in front of a double gate with a sign on it saying POSTED NO TRESPASSING. Inside the fence was a stack of very old warped boards, a lot of trash, a small building that looked like a two-car garage. The garage-like structure was painted a faded pink. Looming over it all was the huge round tower. I couldn't figure out what the tower was. It was too wide to be a chimney. Then I noticed a pile of old bricks in front of it and decided that maybe it had once been a brick kiln.

Now that I was a little closer, I could see that it was made of either concrete or brick with some kind of stucco on the outside, the tall sides of the tower bowing in slightly. An exposed steel ladder led to the very top, and a row of small windows circled the tower about two thirds of the way up.

I didn't notice the old woman until she spoke.

"What the *hell* you doing, girl?" I looked up, saw an ancient woman in a bright green housecoat and fuzzy slippers staring angrily down at me. When I hesitated, the old woman took a large shiny revolver out of her housecoat and pointed it at me. I felt a sudden need to empty my bladder.

"Uh. Police business," I said as sternly as possible. "Please get back inside your house."

"You ain't no po-lice." She squinted at me. "What you got on your face?"

"Back inside. Now!"

She looked at me acidly. "Shit," she said. "Stepping all up on people property, I file a gotdamn *harassment* on your skinny white ass." But then she went back inside. Twice in two days I'd heard that from people who thought I was a cop. Real cops sure must get tired of that line.

When I looked back at Nix, he was unfastening a chain from around the gate, slipping inside the fence. I still didn't see the thief.

Once he was inside the fence Nix looked around then put the walkie-talkie to his ear, listened for a moment, nodded, then walked over to a small cardboard box. He lifted the box, then threw it aside.

"Okay," I said into my microphone. "Nix is inside a fence area next to this big round tower at the corner of Decatur and Milledge streets. Still haven't seen anyone."

"What's Nix doing?"

"He just picked up a box. Wait, I see, the box was covering something up. Hard to see from here. Oh, I get it. There's a video camera underneath. Nix is taking the money out of the bag and riffling through each one of the bundles in front of the camera. I guess our guy is monitoring it remotely somewhere."

"Damn." Maj. Fontaine's voice in my ear. "This boy does not miss a trick."

"Nix is talking into the walkie-talkie again. Now he's walking over to the tower. There's a ladder that goes up the outside of the tower. He just stuffed the bag in his pants."

"Seen our boy yet?"

"Nope."

"You think he's in the tower?"

"Doesn't make sense," I said. "If you're him, the tower

gives you a nice view and everything. But he's planned pretty carefully. Everything he's done so far has had a fail-safe. Right? So if you're him, what are you most worried about?''

"Getting busted after the exchange."

"Right. So the last place you want to be is in a tower."

"But how's he going to make the exchange if he's not in the tower?''

I watched Nix climbing slowly up the outside of the tower. He looked pretty nervous, hugging the wall as he moved. I didn't blame him. It gave me the willies just watching him. What if it was a trap? The thief could just wait until Nix got half-way up, step out from inside the pink garage or something, shoot him, grab the money when Nix hit the ground.

I took my pistol out of my purse.

That was when it hit me.

"Wait, wait, wait!" I said. "The painting is on the roof of the tower. Nix goes up, sees the painting, verifies it. Then the thief drives by in a truck, stops under the tower and Nix drops the money down. The thief grabs the money and scoots.''

"Hey," Fontaine said. "That might work." A pause. "But looking at it from his view, what's to keep Gunnar from yelling to everybody in the neighborhood once he sees the painting and then sitting up there until a patrol car shows up and chases the thief away?''

For a moment I didn't have a response. Nix was about halfway up now. He looked down, paused for a while, finally started moving again. He was moving very slowly now, like every rung was an effort of will. My eyes landed on the video camera. "Hold on. Look at all this high-tech stuff. The video camera, the secure walkie-talkie. I'm guessing he was also watching us somehow through the MARTA security cameras. What if he's got the painting booby trapped somehow? I bet the thief tells Nix that if he doesn't drop the cash, he'll set off some sort of flash bomb that'll burn up the painting.''

"That could be it," Fontaine said.

After that I waited in silence, watching Nix make his painful way to the top of the tower. When he got to the top of the tower, he disappeared from view. For a minute or two nothing happened. Then I saw him silhouetted against the sky, talking on the radio. After a minute a blue Ford pickup swung slowly around the corner. The driver was a white man. I ducked down behind the porch.

"I was right!" I said into my microphone. "A blue Ford truck."

"Get the tag number if you can."

I listened to the engine muttering as the truck drove very slowly by, straightened up when it had passed.

"F-F-C-two-eight-seven," I said.

But then the truck surprised me by not stopping beneath the tower.

"Hm. False alarm," I said.

"Maybe he's just checking things out."

The truck turned left at the corner down beside a white warehouse, heading him back in the general direction he'd come.

A minute or two went by. Fontaine was right: a couple of minutes later the blue truck showed up again.

"Here he is," I whispered.

The blue truck drove slowly down the street. He was now directly beneath the tower.

I put the mike to my lips. "He's pulling up . . . he's stopping right below the tower."

Nothing happened for a moment, then I saw Nix silhouetted at the top of the tower, talking on the walkie-talkie. Then—just as I'd predicted—Nix dropped the Gap bag off the edge. The bag floated down, tumbled gently in the wind, landed five or ten yards from the truck. The guy in the truck hopped out, ran over to the bag. I was surprised to see that he was no more than four feet tall.

"The guy's a midget!" I said.

"What?"

"The guy. He's a midget."

"So I guess you never heard a physical description of Terry Yokum, huh?"

"What do you mean?"

"Terry Yokum. White male, brown hair, brown eyes, no distinguishing marks. Four foot one inches small."

"I *knew* it!" I said. "I knew it had to be him."

"Look, Sunny!" Carl suddenly sounded impatient. "Has he got the money?"

"Oh!" I said. "Yeah. He's got the money!"

At which point Yokum had just jumped in the truck with the Gap bag in his left hand. The engine roared, and then the truck took off down the street, tires smoking.

I didn't hear anything for about five seconds. Then suddenly it was like the whole neighborhood was surrounded by sirens. They were all kind of distant, but there were an awful lot of them.

At that point I guess my first priority should have been the painting, but I figured it wasn't going anywhere. For the moment this was about catching a man. So I can't say that I gave it any thought: I just saw Yokum's truck tearing around the corner and I ran for the other corner of the triangle of roads surrounding the big tower. In some primitive part of my brain maybe I had a notion of catching up with a hopped-up V-8-driven truck, I don't know—but whatever the reason, I ran.

My guess was that he'd cut through the tunnel under the MARTA tracks so that's the direction I headed. I didn't have a prayer of making it, but off I went anyway. As I rounded the corner I saw that I had predicted correctly: the blue truck was charging toward the tunnel. There were still no police in sight, but the sirens were getting closer. At the far end of the tunnel another car appeared, blocking the exit. For a fraction of a second I assumed it was a policeman. Then I saw a flash of green paint.

"He's heading into the tunnel!" I shouted into my sleeve.

The big blue truck swung into the tunnel with an echoing squeal. A torrent of gray tire smoke obscured my vision. As the smoke cleared, the blue truck's brake lights winked on. I kept charging down the hill toward the tunnel, my breath burning in my chest, but some dumb part of my brain kept hoping that maybe the green car would block Yokum off, give me time to catch up with him.

The tunnel was so dark and long that even as I got closer, I couldn't really make out what was happening at the other end. I saw movement, but that was all, movement that didn't register as making any sense to me. But I didn't have time to do anything. I kept running, gasping for breath.

Then the brake lights disappeared and the far end of the tunnel winked open like an empty white eye. The green car and the truck were gone.

"Son of a bitch!" I yelled, and I slapped myself on the leg. Which hurt a lot because somewhere along the way my LadySmith had gotten into my hand.

Then there were flashing lights all around me, squad cars screaming by, two of them heading into the tunnel, another couple or three heading toward the tower.

Suddenly I had a bad feeling. All that motion at the end of the tunnel: it had been doors opening, people jumping out of the cars. Yokum had switched with the driver of the green car! The cops were probably all still tearing after the truck while Yokum drove calmly off in the green car with his bag full of money. And if the cops didn't get him with the money, there'd be no case against him. No case for the painting, no case for the murder, no nothing.

"The green car!" I screamed into my sleeve. "He switched cars, Fontaine! Can you hear me?"

"What green car?" the voice in my ear said.

"I don't know. There was a green car in the tunnel!"

A cop pulled up next to me, "Hey!" he said. Then he

said something else but I didn't hear it. I just ripped open his front door and jumped in.

"Go!" I screamed.

"You can't get in here with that!" The cop pointed at my gun. He was a sour-looking white guy with big arms and an expanding waist line.

I replied by reaching over with my left foot and stomping on the gas. "Hey! Whoa! Lady!"

The car fishtailed and then the cop got control of it. "Into the tunnel!" I screamed.

I heard a voice coming out of the policeman's radio. "We have the subject in a blue Ford pickup going westbound on DeKalb Avenue. In pursuit!"

The cop steered the car into the tunnel.

"Turn right!" I shrieked. Right was east. If the blue truck was going west, we needed to go the opposite way. "He switched cars!" I yelled. "He's not in the truck anymore."

The cop stopped at the end of the tunnel then sat there for a moment with his foot on the brake. He glared at me and said, "All I got to say, you better be right." Then, as though it was sinking in that he might be first cop on the bust, he got a feral smile on his face and floored the engine. He steered the car to the right and started heading east on DeKalb Avenue with a squall of tires. I watched the needle climb to ninety as he headed down a road designed for thirty five-mile-an-hour traffic. Ugly warehouses and AME churches and rusty fences were whizzing past us. There were no cars on the road at all.

"Uh. Aren't you going a little fast?" I said.

"You want him or not?" the cop said. Then he picked up his microphone and radioed the base. "221 eastbound, repeat *east*bound on DeKalb Ave in pursuit of felony suspect in green automobile. No make or model as yet. Eyewitness says the subject changed vehicles."

The speedometer was tickling one hundred. Ahead I saw a brief smear of green. Then it was lost around a curve. The cop pumped the brakes and the big car shuddered, yawed sideways with an awful broken howl of tires, then recovered. I hid my eyes.

"I loooooove this job!" the cop yelled, pounding on the steering wheel with his fist.

Then suddenly the green car was right in front of us—an old Honda puttering along at a nice safe speed.

The cop was laughing maniacally as he screeched down from nearly a hundred miles an hour to about thirty five and pulled in behind the green Honda. He radioed his position quickly, then jumped out of the car with his pistol drawn. I jumped out, too.

"Driver, take your keys out of the ignition and throw them out the window," the cop yelled. Then he went through the standard felony stop rigmarole. Yokum got out of the car, eyes wide with feigned innocence. He had a very cute face, with bright green eyes and ginger hair, and he didn't look the slightest bit frightened.

"What's this all about, officer?"

"Shut up," the cop yelled. "Get on your knees and cross your ankles."

"That's him!" I said.

By the time Yokum had gotten cuffed, Maj. Fontaine had arrived.

"Nice job, Sunny," he said. Then he read Terry Yokum his rights off the back of a small white card.

Terry answered every question with a smile. "Yes, I do," he said. "Yes, sir, I do." He turned his head, looking at the circle of cops milling around his car. "And before you ask, yes, you have my permission to search the vehicle. Do you need me to sign something to that effect?"

Somebody came out with a form which Terry Yokum initialed theatrically. Sunny assumed that meant he'd ditched the Gap bag full of money.

"Now's the moment to get straight, Mr. Yokum," Fontaine said. ''You want to tell us what you've been up to this morning?''

"Nope," the tiny red-haired man said, showing off a mouthful of small, pretty teeth. "I believe this would be more like the point where I invoke my constitutional right to counsel."

Then he turned and winked at me.

CHAPTER 17

FROM MY PERSPECTIVE everything had worked out perfectly. The police found the Gap bag full of cash on the side of the road about half a mile back down DeKalb Avenue. Apparently Yokum had ditched it as soon as he heard the sirens. And most important, the painting had been brought down from the tower undamaged.

I spent a couple of hours down at the Zone Six station on Memorial giving my statement, then dropped by the office where I found Ron's brother-in-law Sean sitting disconsolately on the hallway floor.

"I came down," he said, looking at me with a sort of wounded puppy dog face. "I waited. I didn't know if. . . ."

"Oh, God," I said. "I'm so sorry. I forgot all about you. Well, the good news is we caught Terry Yokum, and we got the painting back."

He looked at me blankly.

"You know," I said. "The guy that stole the painting. The guy that killed Leslie-Anne."

"Yeah, I was just—" He frowned thoughtfully. "So has he confessed or anything?"

I laughed. "No way. He called Daddy the second they got him to the station and Daddy hired Maurice Crane, who's probably the best criminal lawyer in Georgia."

"What a shame."

"Not necessarily. We got the painting back, that's the main thing."

"Sure, sure."

"Don't worry, I know you're disappointed, but I'll pay you for sitting here. It was my fault. This thing came up last night and we had to move so fast that I just got a little distracted. You might as well head on home."

"Okay," Sean said.

I shook his hand, then unlocked my office and called Marion Cheever at home.

She seemed surprisingly underwhelmed by the good news.

"We'll have to send an authenticator over to your office," she said.

"Actually the painting is in police custody. But I'm sure they'll let somebody take a look at it."

"Great," she said. "The sooner the better."

Amen to that, I wanted to say.

"By the way, where's Gunnar?" she said. "I had the most exciting conversation with him yesterday." Marion Cheever was one of the least gushy women I've ever met, but suddenly she was gushing with the best of them.

"He's . . . still giving his statement to the police."

"He mentioned something about quail hunting at his place in Brunswick. That just sounded like so much *fun*! Have you tried it?"

"Yup," I said noncommittally. Actually I had gone quail hunting with Gunnar once. And that was enough. You got up really really early in the morning, and then you slogged through marsh muck and brambles, waiting for a half-second opportunity to bang away at teeny birds you could barely see. And then when it was finally over, all you had to show for it was this tiny, sad, limp, bloody, pitiful little ball of fuzz in your hand, its little head lolling between your fingers. After my experience as a great white hunter down in Brunswick I didn't eat poultry for about a year.

"I would just *love* to try my hand at quail hunting." Marion Cheever said. "You tell Gunnar that I'll join him any day, any time." She lowered her voice conspiratorially. "And you can tell him I don't have any husband or children to get in the way either."

"Ah," I said.

"He just seems like the most *interesting* man!" I imagined her eyelids fluttering a little. "Is he . . . you know . . . the romantic type?"

"Above all else." I rang off and sighed. "The legend continues," I muttered.

When I got home, there was a message from Ron on the machine. He had a few spare hours this evening. Would seven-thirty be okay? I beeped him, punched in our secret code to tell him that, yes, I'd be waiting for him. But for some reason I didn't feel very enthusiastic about it.

Then I pulled off my clothes, flopped into the bed and fell sound asleep with a smile of satisfaction on my face.

CHAPTER 18

WAS BACK at the police station again. My anticipated afternoon of catch-up sleep had evaporated around three o'clock when the phone had rung. It was Fontaine asking me to get back down to the station as fast as I could.

I was sitting at a table next to an immensely fat bearded man in a tweed jacket. He wore a bow tie the color of expensive sherry and a pair of surgical gloves. Lt. Hagee and Major Fontaine were on the other side of the of the table. Propped on a cheap aluminum easel at the end of the table was the Hassam. It was the first time I'd seen it in the flesh, so to speak.

The colors were richer, more vivid than they had been in the photograph I'd seen. I couldn't see coughing up three hundred thousand for it—but still, it was more striking than I'd expected.

"So what's going on, Major?" I said.

Fontaine rubbed his face and shifted a match stick from one side of his mouth to the other. "First, got a piece of bad news. Yokum is on the street."

"What!" I said.

"That shyster Maurice Crane managed to drag Judge Hooks into her chambers for a special bond hearing. We end up with some first-year DA presenting the case to the judge. Needless to say, he fumbles the whole thing. Meanwhile

Crane's going: 'There's no physical evidence tying Yokum to the scene, he didn't have the money on him, he wasn't driving the car that the eyewitness—meaning you—put the alleged perpetrator of the ransom in, and even if he did pick up the money he just happened on it by accident, blah blah blah blah. Then he goes with the usual spiel: roots in the community, no flight risk, all that stuff. Hooks gives a big lecture to the DA, tells him he's useless and unprepared, then lets Yokum out on a hundred-thousand-dollar bond. Which Yokum's daddy coughs up in about ten seconds.''

''What about the murder?'' I said.

Major Fontaine looked at me through heavy-lidded eyes. ''We got nothing to tie him to that. Absolutely nothing. You didn't see him, we got no fingerprints, nothing.'' He shrugged. ''I hope we can make a case there eventually, but right now we're not in a position to charge him with the murder.''

I shrugged. Okay, so them's the breaks. At least I had the painting.

The detective shifted his match stick so it pointed at the fat man next to me. ''Dr. Andropoulis here is going to make a statement,'' he said. ''As a courtesy to you, since you're the one helped us out, we thought we'd let you hear it.''

I had no idea who the fat man was, or why I should be interested. Because of his gloves I assumed he was one of the Medical Examiners. The only thing I could figure is that he had just finished the autopsy of Leslie-Anne Gilmartin.

''Peter Andropoulis,'' the fat man said, nodding regally at me. He had the rich, oily voice of an announcer on a stock brokerage commercial. ''I'm an art historian and assistant curator at the High Museum. Marion Cheever has retained me to authenticate the painting you recovered.''

''Boy, she moves fast, huh?'' I said.

''Pays well, too.'' The art historian smiled broadly. Then he opened a manila folder and smoothed it out in front of him. ''What I have here is a great deal of material supporting the provenance of a painting known as 'Late Afternoon, Pont Aven, Brittany' painted by the American Impressionist Childe Hassam in 1897. Included are an original 1927 copy of a French auction catalog including a black and white photograph of the painting, a statement of authenticity dated February 12 of this year and signed by Dr. Milton George of the Frick Gallery in New York, and a great many Soviet and Ukrainian documents.''

''Look, what's the bottom line here?'' I wanted to get back in bed so I could grab another hour or two of sleep before Ron came to visit me.

Peter Andropoulis smiled patronizingly. ''If I may continue. The provenance of this painting is rather interesting. You'll note that it was purchased in 1941 by Heinrich Lundhausen, a prominent Swiss art dealer. Lundhausen is well known to have been a front man for the Nazis during their World War II art looting binge. A vast number of artworks were 'purchased' in occupied territories at ridiculously low prices by Lundhausen and others like him—with the coercive assistance of the SS, the Abwehr, the Gestapo and other arms of Nazi state terror, of course—and then laundered through Switzerland from whence they passed back into Germany. In general the dealers like Lundhausen then transferred the ownership of these works directly to the Reich. But sometimes they went to Hermann Goering personally. Goering, you see, was the head of the Nazi art acquisition effort and this allowed him great latitude in helping himself to particularly nice pieces. At any rate, the majority of these works were recovered in 1945 at Goering's famous estate Carinhall or, somewhat later, buried in a mine shaft in Alt Ausee, Austria. But some just disappeared.'' The art historian waved his small latex-gloved fingers delicately in the air. The gloves made a chirping sound as his fingers rubbed together. '' 'Late Afternoon' is one of those paintings.

''I must qualify my report here by saying that I do not read Russian or Ukrainian, but Dr. George, who does have a working knowledge of Slavic languages, outlines in his report what happened to the painting after the war. 'Late Afternoon' was recovered in the Soviet Zone of Austria in 1945 and was then sent to Kiev the following year. Why Kiev? I haven't the faintest, and neither, apparently, did Dr. George. At any rate the painting was stored in the archives of the Ukrainian State Museum of Landscape and Architectural Art, but never displayed. There were then several transfers of ownership after the break-up of the Soviet Union, all of them quite well documented according to Dr. George—but which frankly seem somewhat shady to me. That, however, is outside the scope of my charter here. My exclusive concern here is to authenticate the work.''

"And?" I said.

Andropoulis put his fingertips together, sighed faintly. ''According to the catalog the painting is a landscape executed in oil on canvas with muted greens and ochres predominating. We see that very much to be the case in this painting. 'Hooker's green' is the technical name for the pigment. Historically the painting is of interest as a departure from Hassam's usual bright palette and his focus on cityscapes and flowers. The catalog photograph, though rather muddy, shows a field, several trees, a band of sky and some sort of rustic building in the distance. Perhaps a barn? A peasant cottage? A visual comparison shows the painting to match perfectly both the description and the photograph in all particulars.'' Andropoulis heaved himself to his feet, pointed to the surface of the painting. ''The brushwork is vigorous and enthusiastic and contains many of the hallmarks of Hassam's distinctive—if somewhat derivative—impressionist style. The signature, found in the bottom left corner as per the catalog, is rendered in a dark ochre with a trace of umber. Again it is consistent with Hassam's general practice: you'll note the characteristically angular strokes and the trademark slash above the C.''

I was starting to get a little annoyed with the whole act.

Andropoulis picked up the painting with his gloved hands, turned it around. "Now, the verso."

"Verso?" Hagee said.

"The reverse side of the painting."

Hagee seemed as annoyed as I was. "Whyn't you just say so?"

The large art historian seemed unperturbed. "The canvas appears to be a heavy Ghent linen. According to a note from Buckley's catalog for the 1965 Hassam retrospective at the Corcoran, this is consistent with Hassam's European paintings. Visual examination of the fabric confirms the appearance of an age consistent with production in France during the late nineteenth century. The stretcher is in poor repair and appears to be original. Again, it appears consistent with Buckley's descriptions of the type of stretcher used by Hassam during this period."

Andropoulis took out a magnifying glass, shined it against his large thigh, peered through it at the frame. "In the bottom left corner of the stretcher—that's the wooden framework that the canvas is mounted on—we see a collector's mark. For those of you who are not familiar with them, it's common for owners of drawings and prints to stamp them with a distinctive mark identifying the work as being part of their collection. Occasionally they will mark stretchers, as is the case with this work. This red inked mark here, two concentric rings containing the letters P and S appears to be that of Pierre Stein, the collector who bought 'Pont Aven' in 1927. Would anyone like to look? I have the Lugt collectors mark listings here if you'd like to compare?" He pointed at a large book splayed out in front of him. "Anyone? Anyone?"

"Just keep going," Hagee said.

"In the interest of time, ah, we have several other marks— the Kiev museum; Goering's personal mark, that's of some historical interest; various other marks. An unusual number of marks, actually; marking the stretcher is not common practice among collectors. But they all are consistent with the provenance of 'Pont Aven'."

Andropoulis then turned the painting around. "That said, I'd like to try something entertaining here. Ms. Childs, do you have a pin with you?"

I opened my pocket book, hunted around until I found a safety pin. "Will this do?"

"Nicely, thank you," Andropoulis said. "Now, if you don't mind, let me give you a brief lecture on the materials used in oil painting."

Hagee sighed loudly and looked at his watch.

Andropoulis chuckled pleasantly. "Oil paint consists of two primary ingredients—a medium and a pigment. The pigments range from vegetable substances such as rose madder, to metallic oxides such as titanium dioxide, to natural minerals such as raw umber which when you get right down to it is basically dirt." He smiled, looked fondly up into the air. Suddenly he snapped out of his reverie. "But the medium is always the same: linseed oil.

"Now the significant thing about linseed oil, from our perspective, is its slow drying time. It take roughly a day for an oil painting to become dry to the touch and a matter of months for a painting to cure sufficiently to be handled safely. In fact, it takes literally decades for a painting to reach its final level of hardness—at which time it becomes tough enough to withstand literally centuries of exposure to air, moisture and so on. It becomes, in fact, so hard as to be almost impervious to sharp metal objects."

The art historian then picked up my safety pin from the table, brandished it in the air, then jammed it sharply into the surface of the painting.

"This, my friends," he said triumphantly, "is a fake!" The safety pin stuck out of the surface of the painting.

"Oh, man!" I said. "You're kidding!" I had an awful sinking feeling.

"Absolutely not. I estimate this little fraud was painted

within the past week," Andropoulis said. "I might add that I didn't notice it on initial examination, but after I compared it with the photographs taken by Dr. George when he authenticated the painting earlier this year I determined that it also departs from the original in several very subtle ways."

"Can somebody just shoot me in the head," I said.

"One bit of good news, though," the art historian said smiling cheerfully.

"What's that?" I said.

"Maybe it's just me, but I like the fake better than the original."

The room was silent.

"Are we done?" the fat man said.

"I believe so," Lt. Hagee said. The art historian gathered his materials and Hagee showed him out the door.

"So this guy Yokum," Fontaine said. "He spent a couple years in art school. S'pose to be a highly talented painter."

"I won't tell you how I did it," I said, "but I managed to get hold of Yokum's criminal record. The thing that struck me at the time was this shooting charge. But now I'm thinking about it again, I recall there was some sort of fraud charge, too. You didn't happen to look into what that was about did you?"

Fontaine's face was blank mask. "Happens I did. Apparently he sold a Picasso drawing to a gallery. Only it turned out not to be a Picasso at all. It was a forgery. He said he didn't know anything about it, that he'd bought it in a flea market. The charge didn't stick but the detective said everybody knew the kid did it."

"So he forged this painting, huh?"

"Here's what I'm thinking," Fontaine said. "I'm thinking his girlfriend was involved in this robbery somehow. Maybe she's got the painting at her house. He bumps into it—or maybe she tells him about it—and he figures this is a quick way to shake down the insurance company. He forges this copy—gives it enough of the right details so that even if

Gunnar had been thoroughly prepped to look for, you know, an old canvas, these little collectors marks and so on, that it would pass muster—then he ransoms it back to y'all. Boom, he's in the money.''

"All right, but what about Leslie-Anne's murder? What's your theory on how that fits in?''

"Theory? Sunny, I'm all out of theories right now.''

Fontaine took the match out of his mouth, lit it on his thumbnail then flicked it across the room. It left an arc of pale smoke in the air, bounced off the bogus painting and fell dead on the floor. The safety pin gleamed bright silver in the middle of the bogus Childe Hassam landscape, muted greens and ochres predominating.

CHAPTER 19

WHEN I GOT back to my loft there were a bunch of messages on the machine.

The first call was from Walter: "Sunny, I just made the best move in my life. Call me and I'll fill you in."

The second was from Mom: "Sunny, you've got to talk to him. He's absolutely gone off the deep end."

Then Walter again: "Sunny? Sunny? Can you pick up? I think I did something stupid."

Then Mom: "Sunny, sweetheart, I've got to . . . this is the craziest . . . it's just . . . Call me! Okay?"

Then Walter called and said—

Well, you get the idea. Situation normal: family in crisis.

I called Walter and nobody answered, then I called Mom and got her machine, then I called Marion Cheever and had an extremely unpleasant conversation. There was a lot of stuff along the lines of "Why isn't Gunnar man enough to call me?" and "I trusted Gunnar and now look what happens." I finally calmed her down and assured her the only reason she was talking to me was that the intrepid Gunnar was already out sniffing the ground for the scent of the real painting. I may have even referred to him as an "intrepid hunter" and a "peerless investigator." I know, shame on me. These things just keep popping out of my mouth.

I thought about calling Tawanda and Earl and maybe even

Sean—but I figured it was already six o'clock on Saturday night, better to let everybody get rested up and bring them in tomorrow bright and early.

I was pouring myself a glass of white burgundy when my front door buzzed. It was Walter. He came up on the noisy old elevator and I let him in.

He shuffled into the room disconsolately, went over to the kitchen area and poured a whole lot of wine into a 20-ounce plastic cup that said Atlanta Braves on the side.

"I have wine glasses, you know," I said.

"I'm punishing myself," he said taking a healthy swig of the burgundy. "God forbid I actually enjoy drinking this stuff."

Then he went over to my bed and lay down. My loft is just one big open space so you can sit on the bed and have a conversation with somebody in the kitchen or the living room area. Or anyplace else, for that matter.

I sipped my wine and waited. He didn't say anything, so I put on a Chet Baker album. I like Chet. He's probably the kind of guy I would fall in love with: romantic, smart, talented, reckless, sweet . . . oh, yeah, and a heroin addict.

"Well, I did it," Walter said finally.

Chet sang 'My Funny Valentine,' very tenderly. As a rule I don't like jazz singing—too much straining for effect—but I make an exception for Chet.

"Okay . . ." I said.

"I quit."

It took me a second. "You quit Underhill Tabb? *You* quit Underhill, Tabb, LaFollette, Gold & Pearcy, the most prestigious, white shoe firm in the southeast?"

He nodded and the bed jiggled slightly.

"That's great!" I put down my wine, pulled him up off the bed and hugged him. When I let go he had a hint of a mischievous grin on his face. He still looked like a whipped dog—but at least there was a spark of life in him. "Way to go!'' I hugged him again, shook him until his teeth rattled. ''Death to corporate stooges!'' I yelled.

Walter stared at the floor with this hint of a smile on his face, his shoulders slumped.

''Come on, say it, Walter! Death to corporate stooges!''

''Death to corporate stooges.''

''Nah, nah! Louder. More passion.''

''Death to corpor—''

''Louder!''

''DEATH TO CORPORATE GODDAMN STOOGES!'' Walter grimaced then burst out laughing.

I decided Chet Baker was a little too subdued, so I put on an old B-52s record and we pogoed around the apartment to ''Rock Lobster,'' laughing until we fell over on the bed.

''Mom must have absolutely peed her pants,'' I said.

Suddenly Walter stopped smiling. He shook his head and his eyes looked hollow. ''Oh, man. I've never seen her face like that before. She didn't say a word. Couldn't even speak. I mean, after that whole thing she did for me last night . . . I guess the timing wasn't so good, huh?''

I sighed. He was right about that. This was going to hurt her for a long time. ''Yeah, but look, Walter,'' I said. ''It's like I've always said: she can't live her life through you. You have your life, she has hers.''

''I just can't help thinking I've made a terrible mistake,'' he said.

''How? In the grand scheme of things, what does it matter if you become a partner at Underhill, Tabb? You're a bright guy, not afraid of hard work, living in the richest and most forgiving country in the world. There's no danger of your going without food or a roof over your head.''

''That's not the point.''

I knew it wasn't. But then it wasn't exactly *not* the point either.

''That night after the fund-raiser thing,'' Walter said, ''I went home and I just felt so low. So dishonest, so . . . I don't know. I just felt like a complete sham of a human being. I mean there's nothing wrong with what I'm doing with my life—it's just that I never know what's *me* and what's just some kind of silly put-on.''

I gave him another hug and then went over to my silver drawer and took out a set of keys.

"This is the key to Gunnar's place down in Brunswick.'' I jingled the keys in the air, then tossed them to my brother. "There's absolutely nothing there. A thousand acres of saw-grass and pine trees, a few million mosquitoes, and maybe a couple gators. I think you ought to go down there. Take a day, a week, a month, whatever you need. Just camp out down there by yourself. Bring your guitar, bring a bible, bring a couple dozen mystery novels—and just sit there. It doesn't matter what I think, what Mom thinks, what the managing partner at Underhill Tabb thinks.''

Walter studied the key dubiously. "You don't think Gunnar would mind?''

"Hell no. That's what it's there for.'' I went over to the CD player, played "Rock Lobster'' again, but the festive mood had drained out of the room. So I put another Chet Baker disk on. He played a long, bittersweet solo in "Polka Dots And Moonbeams.''

When the song was over, Walter put his hands on his knees and stood up sharply, as though he'd just made up his mind about something. "Yup,'' he said. "I'm going down there right this minute.''

He kissed me on the cheek, gave me a big hug and left me in tears. After he took off I felt a strange hollow feeling. Maybe I was just dreading talking to Mom. She'd accuse me of putting him up to this, of sabotaging his career, of undermining her, of these and many other sins.

But more than that I felt sad for all of us. Why do we put on these masks? Why do we try to fool each other about who we really are? Why can't we tell the truth, call it like we see it, and leave it at that? I don't like dwelling on these kinds of questions; I guess I'm not a very deep person, but it just makes me depressed. I'm happiest when I'm busy, scurrying around thoughtlessly, all worries and aspirations and philosophical concerns neatly buried beneath the shallow, plain soil of mindless activity.

Which is among the many, many reasons I was glad to hear that irritating voice when I answered my ringing phone.

CHAPTER 20

"**H**I, THERE," THE irritating voice said. "Don't hang up, okay?" It was a man with a harsh, grating tenor.

"Who is this?"

"Just don't hang up."

"Who *is* this?"

"It's Terry Yokum."

I blinked. *Here* was a surprise. I leaned over and hit the record button on a tape machine that I've got hooked up to my phone. I had this boyfriend once who took to making harassing phone calls after I dumped him; I'd hooked the machine up so I could get him on tape and turn him in to the cops. Funny thing was, by the time I had gotten it connected, I guess he had gotten tired of obsessing over me, because he never called again. It's a testimony to the perversity of my heart that I remember being strangely disappointed at the time. I guess I didn't like feeling that forgettable. At any rate I kept the tape recorder and it's come in handy a couple times since.

"So what's up, Terry?" I said. "You in a confessional mood?"

"Confessional mood." Terry laughed snidely. "Nah. I got nothing to confess to. Besides bad judgment."

"I believe that's called the Ted Bundy defense."

"The what?"

"Forget it." My mouth felt dry suddenly, so I took a sip of burgundy. "What did you want to talk about?"

"Okay, let's start with this. I'll concede I'm in like a kind of bad position. You may think I'm scamming you, but I'm all cut up about this thing with Leslie-Anne."

"Right."

"Nah, man, I'm serious. I loved her." He paused. "Okay, no, let me take another shot at that. I *liked* her. I liked her a lot. She was basically a very good kid. Not a fuck-up like me." There was a surprising hint of self-hatred in the way he said it. "Hanging out with me was kind of like a vacation for her. I mean she doesn't get along so great with her Mom, so she pierces her nipples, you know, gets some tattoos and shit. It's a phase. I'm just part of that phase. Another ten years she'll be married to some nice dentist, growing a nice crop of babies, and driving around the burbs in a minivan."

"And?"

"It's my fault that this happened to her. I didn't do it, but it's my fault it happened."

"I'm still trying to figure out why you're calling me."

"I want you to catch the person who killed her."

"Do you know who this person is?"

There was a brief pause. "Um, Sunny? How damn stupid do you think I am? You're probably recording this phone call right now."

"Who me?" There was a pause. "Okay, fine, Terry. So go to the cops."

"Let's be real here. I'm in a whole lot of trouble with the cops right now." Terry Yokum cleared his throat. "If you're even a half-assed investigator, you're taping this call. Right?"

"Possibly," I said.

"So since you got the tape rolling let me establish for the official record that I'm not making any admission of anything here. Far as this tape goes, I'm clean as the driven snow."

"Whatever."

"Let me finish. My point is, I have a problem with the cops. And—without admitting anything—let's just say it's not in my legal interest to get the cops any more involved in this thing than they already are. In terms of protecting my legal position with regard to these, uh, baseless charges, I'd have to be crazy to tell them anything about anything. You understand what I'm saying?"

"Okay."

"So let's just say I have a strong theory about who killed Leslie-Anne. I'd like to meet with you, give you some information that will help you identify this person."

"Let me ask you a question. Is this going to help me get the painting back?"

A brief pause. "That all you can think about? A girl's dead here and all you're thinking about is a few blobs of paint on a canvas?"

"It's my job to get hold of those blobs of paint."

"Hey, fine. I have some information—no, excuse me, I mean to say I have some strong theories on that issue, too."

Suddenly I was feeling more cheerful than I had all day. "When?" I said.

"Midnight," he said. "I got some shit to take care of before then. There's a coffee bar call *Beans* on North Highland just the other side of Ponce de Leon." I knew the place. It was big with the nipple ring and black T-shirt set.

After my initial burst of enthusiasm, skepticism began to set in. Why would this guy want to expose himself this way? Odds were that Terry Yokum was working me somehow. On the other hand, what did I have to lose? Time was running out and I didn't have any particularly promising leads to follow up on.

"Fair enough," I said. "Midnight."

I expected Terry to hang up at that point, but he didn't. After a few seconds he said, "So Sunny . . . did they tell you anything about me? The cops? About that thing I supposedly did to that girl a few years back?"

"Shooting her in the head, I believe is the way they described it."

"Right. Right. I just want you to understand that I'm sincere about Leslie-Anne okay? What I'm trying to tell you is that I'm not necessarily the type of guy you want to bring home to Mommy, but that doesn't mean I'm the kind of person who'd shoot a girl, either."

"Honestly, Terry? I don't care."

"Listen! Just to set the record straight, everything that girl said was crap. Her name was Rachelle Green. Her Dad hated me. I don't blame him, but hey, that's no excuse for pulling a gun on me. I mean if he'd just knocked, he wouldn't have walked in on us lying there in her bed. But no, he's got to barge in, he's got to start calling me midget this, sawed-off that, little freak and all this shit. So I punched him in the nuts. Next thing I know, he pulls out a gun, points it I me. I duck just as the gun goes off. The bullet goes over my shoulder, grazes Rachelle's head. Needless to say, I go diving out the window before he can figure out how to aim his cannon."

"Look I don't really—" I said.

But Terry kept going. "He put her up to it, see? When they show up at the hospital, the doctors have to report to the police that she's shot. So her old man gets her to tell the cops that it was me."

"This all sounds a little far-fetched."

"Well if it's so far-fetched, how come she dropped the charges?"

"What I heard is that your father bought her off."

There was a pause. "Okay. Maybe he did. I wouldn't put anything past my Dad. But just because he bought her off doesn't mean she wasn't lying to start with. Think about it."

Ron arrived ten minutes later all lathered up for a big night of passion.

Let me be blunt: I've had better sex. I was distracted, nervous about the meeting, worn out from having three hours sleep in the last two days—so that whole souls-intertwined, climbing-the-stairway-of-passion, bursts-of-cosmic-light thing was definitely not happening. To make matters worse, Ron is one of these bedroom technicians who's read too many manuals about all the different Kama Sutra positions and massage techniques and G-spots and all the rest of the hooey that goes along with the self-improvement school of sexual exercise. At his worst he seems to approach sex in roughly the same way as you'd take on cross-country running: it's up hill and down dale, and it seems to go on forever.

Don't get me wrong, that has its charm. But today I kept thinking, Just give me some of that Old School sex, baby! *Just shake things around a little and call it quits.* Instead I went along with everything he wanted and my mind was a long way away.

Afterward we took a shower and he asked me how the investigation was going. While we were washing, I told him everything.

He was concerned in a sweet sort of way, worried that I might have gotten shot or abducted during the sting we'd run on Terry Yokum this morning. I tried to downplay it. Then I told him about the meeting I had coming up with Yokum that night.

All of a sudden he got very macho and said that he was going to come with me, that I was being too reckless with this case. He went on for a while so I washed my hair and pretended I had soap in my ears and couldn't hear him very well.

After we got out of the shower Ron said, "Sunny, it's just not safe. The guy's a murderer."

"First," I said, "we don't know that. Second, it's a public place. What's he going to do, shoot me in front of fifty witnesses?"

"Okay, but put that aside. It's obvious he's manipulating you somehow."

"What, you think I didn't consider that possibility?"

I noticed Ron sneaking a peek at himself in the mirror, sucking in his stomach. He just turned forty this year and I think he has a complex about it. Then again, maybe he was always a stomach sucker.

"I just think you're getting into this too deep," Ron said.

I dried my hair, pulled on a black T-shirt and a pair of Levis.

Ron followed me around the loft buck naked. "I mean look at this whole Gunnar thing," Ron pursued. "You're lying to your clients, you're lying to the bad guys, you're lying to—"

"Enough!" I said finally.

I guess it came out a little harsher than I'd meant it to because Ron stared at me for a minute like I'd slapped him. Finally he shook his head and said, "It was so good between us a few months ago. What's going wrong?"

I sat down on the bed and put my face in my hands. I kind of expected him to come over and put his arm around and murmur to me about how everything was going to be all right, but he didn't. After a while I looked up again. "Ron," I said. "You're a married man. Your wife seems like a nice woman. You have two wonderful kids. You're at the top of your profession. Why do you need me?"

"Why do you have to turn this on me?" he said in a really condescending tone of voice. "Ever since this started, I kept hoping that you'd finally open up to me, finally let me know who you really are, what your fears are, your, Christ, your hopes and dreams and all that shit. But you never did."

"Just put your clothes on," I said softly. "We need to cool off a little before we start saying mean things to each other."

"See? That's exactly my point. Instead of getting mad, all

of a sudden you get this calm thing going, and I don't have the slightest idea what you're thinking.''

"Just go, Ron. Just . . .'' I looked down at the floor and waved vaguely at the door.

Ron dressed quickly. Sometimes there is almost nothing more depressing than the sound of a guy zipping up his fly.

When he had finished dressing, Ron picked up his wine glass, studied it as though he was about to polish off the last of his wine. Instead he tossed the liquid in the sink.

"You shouldn't go to this meeting tonight,'' Ron said. "I mean look what happened to his girlfriend. I'm telling you— it's obvious this guy's a lying scumbag and it's a really, really terrible idea letting yourself get sucked into his web.''

After he left I lay back in the bed and closed my eyes. I guess I halfway hoped I'd fall asleep and miss the meeting with Terry Yokum. But I didn't. I just felt queasy and oppressed, listening to the ticking of the clock.

CHAPTER 21

PARKED NEXT to a Dumpster in a gravel lot behind the coffee bar called Beans. On the Dumpster someone had spray-painted a graffito in bright red letters: "We fall that we may rise."

I walked up the alley beside Beans and went in the front door. Inside I sat at the bar and ordered a glass of iced decaf. After I'd been sitting there for a minute, a thin young woman came down the counter and said, "Are you Sunny Childs?"

"Afraid so," I said.

For a second she looked confused. "Terry Yokum called, wanted me to tell you he's going to be a couple minutes late."

"Thanks," I said. As she started to walk away, I said, "Wait a sec. You said his name like you know him."

She turned and looked at me without any particular expression. Her straight brown hair hung in her face and all her clothes were about size too big. She wore very dark eye make-up which gave her a sort of Weimar cabaret look. "Yeah, I know Terry."

"You got a minute?"

The girl came back and leaned against the counter in front of me. "What?"

"I was just wondering what you can tell me about him. What kind of guy he is."

She closed one eye, cocked her head. "You thinking about going out with him or something?"

I laughed.

"That's good," she said.

"You don't like him."

"I'll tell you something about Terry. Terry's not a bad guy. But don't loan him money. You see what I'm saying?"

"He's a painter, right?"

She nodded. "Really good, too. I'm a painter myself. Pisses me off: I mean I think I'm pretty good, but I mean he just blows me away." She shook her head sharply. "See that's what kills me about him. I mean aside from the fact you can't trust him further than you can throw him—he's got all this talent and he doesn't do dick with it."

"He doesn't paint anymore?"

"Oh, he paints day and night, but it's all commercial work. He's just in it for the bucks now. Pastels of guys on golf courses, oil paintings of Porsches. Total crap. But I'll give him this, it's beautifully executed crap. He does a lot of stuff for interior decorators, architects, people like that. They bring over swatches, plans, whatever and they say: 'Here paint me something with a lot of vermilion and some soft golds, like something that would go good with this couch.' And he just whips that shit out, totally cynical. You want Degas, he's Degas. You want him to rip off LeRoy Neiman, Norman Rockwell, Jackson Pollack—hell, give him a couple days, he'll do it."

"You think he killed Leslie-Anne?"

"Not the type." She laughed. "Anyway, she'd have kicked his little midget ass if he'd tried."

"Oh, yeah? I heard he already shot a girl once."

"Rachelle? No, man, that was a bunch of bullshit. Her dad shot her by accident, got her to tell the cops it was Terry."

"How do you know this?"

"She told me. Me and Rachel used to be buds."

"You know anything about Terry being into counterfeit painting?"

The girl eyed me for a minute. "If I did, I probably wouldn't tell you." She pushed a strand of lank hair out of her face. "I got to get back to work, man."

I finished my iced coffee, felt a little chilly, ordered a regular coffee loaded up with cream. After I finished my coffee, I flipped through *Creative Loafing*, the local alternative newspaper, and checked out the personals. All the entries under MAN SEEKING WOMAN sounded implausibly good or completely unappealing, so I went on to MAN SEEKING MAN, just for the entertainment value. It turned out not to be much better, though. I'd gotten to the more satisfying ALTERNATIVES section ("white pre-op transsexual seeks large black bi male who's into piercing and pain . . .") when the manager came over and said, "We're closing up now."

"Oh," I said. "Sorry." I looked around the empty coffee shop. Ten till one and no Terry.

The thin girl with the bad eye make-up was scrubbing out some dirty cups in a tiny stainless steel sink. I took out one of my cards and put it on the bar in front of her.

"I'm a private investigator," I said. "I'm trying to find out who killed Leslie-Anne. I don't suppose there's anything you could tell me that would help."

"He could probably be the next Picasso if he wanted," she said, still looking down at the dishes. Her hair was hanging down in front of her eyes. "He's *that* good. Instead he just gave up. That's the sad thing."

"Uh-huh," I said.

She looked up at me suddenly and I was surprised to see tears running down her face. "Do you know what I would give to have half the talent that little creep has? I would chop off my fucking legs, dude, I really would."

"Do you know anything about him doing a counterfeit

painting? Where he might have gotten the painting from? Who he was involved with?''

She had a funny look on her face but she didn't say anything.

"What?" I said. Two wet black streaks ran down her cheeks. I took the dish towel off her shoulder and wiped them off. She sniffled. "Tell me."

"It was sort of weird, yeah. I go into his studio a while back and he's working on this painting. Got all goofy-acting when he noticed me standing there."

"Tell me about the painting."

"It was this sort of impressionist landscape. Kind of ugly actually. Lots of Hooker's greens, a little viridian, some yellow ochres."

"When you say goofy-acting . . ."

"He covered them up with a sheet. Acting all nervous. Then when I start peeking behind the sheet, he makes up some bullshit story—"

"Wait a second. Them? There was more than one?"

"Yeah, that's what I'm saying. It was like he was practicing, trying to get it perfect. He must have had ten or fifteen of them. So after he's covered them up and I start ragging on him for acting all weird, he tells me how some architect hired him to do this landscape, like to match a room in some corporate headquarters. Said he wanted the colors perfect. It was obviously a lie."

"How so?"

"First, he would never have worked that hard on a commercial commission. Never. Normally he just tears those things off. But the other thing was that the color scheme barely changed from painting to painting. Neither did the composition. The only thing he really seemed to be fooling with was the brushstrokes. Like he was trying to match a certain painter's signature."

"You saw how he signed them?"

"That's not what I mean. Every painter has a particular

way of doing a brushstroke, just like every singer has a distinctive way of singing a note. We call that a signature."

"Oh, okay."

The manager came up behind the girl and cleared her throat. I wanted to ask more questions, but I hadn't really been prepared for this interview and nothing was on the tip of my tongue.

"What's your name?" I said. "I might want to call you again."

"Regina. Regina Flowers." She dried her hands and wrote her phone number on a dessert menu. "I hope you find out who killed Leslie-Anne. That's not right, man. It's just not right."

I thanked her, stuffed the menu in my pants pocket, and headed for the door. The manager had to unlock it to let me out.

I was surprised as I came out the door to see Ron standing on the sidewalk. He wore a leather coat, jeans, and a pair of hiking boots. He'd changed clothes since he came over to the loft.

"What are you doing here?" I said. "It's one o'clock in the morning."

"The door was locked," he said, pointing at the coffee bar.

"I meant—"

"I know what you meant." He smiled ruefully. "I got a little worried, came over to make sure you were okay."

"I'm fine," I said.

"So this guy. Terry Yokum. Did he show?"

I shook my head.

Ron looked vaguely relieved. "That's good. I don't like the idea of you hanging around with murderers."

"I don't know," I said. "I'm really not so sure he's the one."

"Of course he's the one!" Ron said. "He's the guy that had the painting. Who else could have killed her?"

I shook my head. We stood there awkwardly for a moment.

"I'm sorry about what I said this evening," he said. "I didn't mean to be a jerk."

"No," I said. "It's me. I'm just feeling . . ."

Unfortunately I'm one of those people who sometimes has a hard time identifying the exact state of my emotions. So I wasn't sure how to end the sentence.

"Where are you parked?" Ron said.

"It's okay," I said.

"Seriously. Let me walk you to your car."

I didn't want to make a thing about it. But the truth was, I didn't want to see Ron at that moment.

Ron must have seen it in my face. "Okay," he said angrily. "Okay, forget it. Forget the whole damn thing!"

He turned and walked away and I didn't say anything.

When I walked down the alley toward the parking lot, a policeman was standing at the corner. "I'm sorry," he said, "but you'll have to go around."

I pointed at my Eldorado. "That's my car," I said.

"Well, then you'll have to wait."

I started getting annoyed. "What do you mean wait? What's going on here?"

He gave me the level cop stare that told me I was supposed to mind my own business.

"I'm serious, officer. You tell me I can't get in my own car, you better have a reason!"

He grimaced, as though divulging police business to a civilian caused him intense pain. "Someone's been killed in this parking lot, ma'am."

"Who?"

"Please just stay back, ma'am. Let the detectives do their job and then you can get your car."

Suddenly something struck me. "Oh my God," I said.

"What?"

"I was supposed to meet somebody!" I said. "He didn't show up."

The cop hesitated. "What'd he look like?"

I held my hand four feet off the ground. That was all it took.

"Uh. Wait a minute," the policeman said, then he called over to a detective.

The detective, a thin black man whose name I didn't catch, said, "You up to taking a look at the victim?"

I nodded and he led me over to the Dumpster. I looked in and then said, "You better call Carl Fontaine."

Twenty minutes later Maj. Fontaine arrived looking no more or less bedraggled than he did in the middle of the day. He was dressed in white socks and black shoes, wrinkled khakis, and a silly straw hat with a plaid band like the one that Bing Crosby used to wear.

"Mm!" Carl Fontaine said, looking at the graffiti on the dumpster. He ran his finger delicately across the bright red letters. "We fall that we may rise. Amen to that."

I stared into the Dumpster at the child-sized dead man, his legs sprawled apart, his head turned to the side as though he were listening for some faint and distant sound.

We fall that we may rise. It was a nice sentiment. But things like this make you wonder about the rising part.

CHAPTER 22

I WAS DOWN at the homicide unit—which has started taking on the troubling feel of a second home lately—until almost 3:00 A.M. and when I finally got back to my loft I was so wound up I couldn't sleep. When the alarm went off at 7:30, I got up in a foul mood. Aching, exhausted, and feeling that worst of all emotional combinations: angry and defeated.

I stopped at the Krispy Kreme on Ponce de Leon Avenue and got a dozen doughnuts and four coffees at the drive-through, then headed back to the office where I mainlined some coffee, grease, and sugar, and made a few phone calls; except for Sean McNeely, my employees were less than thrilled to hear from me.

When everybody had finally arrived and was running a good caffeine and sucrose buzz, I said: "Okay. We've got twenty-seven hours to find this painting. Our two potential witnesses are dead. Our evidence is for shit." Then I smiled. "Thoughts?"

Everyone had some thoughts, but what it boiled down to was good old detective work: hitting the pavement, knocking on doors, asking questions. I had to agree, there wasn't much else we could do.

I thought I'd go back and talk to Charlie Biddle first. I sent Tawanda to talk to Roland C. Porter III, and then div-

vied up some of the other people who'd worked in or around
the gallery to Sean and Earl.

I called the gallery, but no one was there, so I tried Charlie
Biddle at home. She answered the phone after about ten
rings, sounding like she'd just climbed out of bed. She was
even less overjoyed to hear from me than my employees had
been, but I figured tough shit—if she wanted her painting
back she had to talk to me.

As I drove over I kept thinking about what the girl at the
coffee shop had told me: obviously Terry Yokum had been
working on his fakes long before the painting was stolen.
That meant that he or Leslie-Anne must have had some contact with the painting—or some pretty detailed photographs
of it—back in the late winter.

Charlie Biddle was wearing sweat pants and had her hair
up in a ponytail when I got to her house, an ugly brick ranch
in the not-especially-swank Atlanta suburb of Doraville. I'd
expected her in some charming Inman Park Victorian—but
I guess Doraville's cheaper. The inside of the house, though,
was pleasant and warm and lived-in, with books scattered
around the living room and nice paintings on the walls.

She gestured wordlessly to a chair, then flopped down on
a big white couch and lit a cigarette. "Marlboros," she said.
"Just another of the many rich blessings of this country. You
know how much I'd pay for a pack of these things back in
the Ukraine?"

"So I'm guessing Winston Percival has talked to you already?" I said.

She laughed without moving her mouth. "Yeah. Called
me up all hysterical, told me about this female cop that was
poking around trying to find out about 'Late Afternoon.' I
asked him to describe the cop. When he said she looked like
she weighed about ninety pounds, I figured it was you. I
never heard of a ninety-pound cop before."

In her own house her manner was completely different
than it had been in gallery. There was more of the Ukraine

in her accent and something heavier and sloppier in her bearing—like she didn't care how she looked or what you thought of her. She was a much more likable person in her living room than she was in her gallery. I guess she got tired of playing Charlie Biddle the ice queen all day and wanted to be plain old Ludmilla Rutskoi when she came home.

"So," I said, "do you prefer Ludmilla or Charlie when you're just knocking around the house in your sweats?"

"Makes no difference to me," she said, taking a long drag on the Marlboro, then letting it trail out her nose. "They're just words."

"So Winston Percival—or Joe Lee Nichols, Jr. or whatever his name is—he says you didn't steal your own painting for the insurance money. He says if you had, you'd have fenced it through him."

Charlie laughed. "He always did have a high opinion of himself." She closed her eyes slightly as though she was thinking about something. "He's probably right, though. If I'd stolen my own painting with the intention of selling it, I'd have fenced it through him. He's pretty much the only game in town." She stood up. "Can you hold on a second?"

She was gone for a minute or two and I could hear noises coming out of the kitchen. She came back with a bowl of Froot Loops, started eating them with relish, cigarette held in one hand, spoon in the other. "When they get Froot Loops in Kiev, I think I'll move back," she said.

"Just speaking hypothetically," I said. "If you stole your own painting, why not ransom it back to the insurance company instead of selling it through a guy like Winston Percival? That way you pocket the ransom and you still get to sell the painting."

"Speaking hypothetically, that's exactly what I'd do." She dug into the bowl of cereal. When she was done, she stubbed out her Marlboro in the film of milk in the bottom of her bowl. "But here's the thing. I'm sure you checked me out. I spent some time in prison for stuff I did with that dickhead Winston Percival and let me tell you this, being a beautiful woman in a prison is something I wouldn't wish on my worst enemy." Suddenly her face went hard. "You ever read all that shit in the papers about the two-hundred-pound lesbos, and the guards that rape you and how they sneak you out to get screwed by members of the prison commission and all that? It's all true. It's all true and worse. They'll sell your ass for cigarettes in there."

"What about it?" I said.

"What *about* it?" She looked at me wide-eyed. "I've been running a legitimate business for ten years. Haven't taken one single backward step. Not *one*! Believe me, in a business like this you've got a new opportunity to cheat and scam and steal every single day. But every day I say no. Forget it. That's not how Charlie Biddle does business. You know why? Because I'm reformed, because I've become a good person, because I've seen the error of my ways, because my heart is pure? Shit, no! It's because I have a brain. And my brain tells me that if I mess around with stealing and fraud and con games and that whole stupid Winston Percival way of living, I will end up back in prison fighting off dykes with a sharpened fork and letting guards pimp my ass to some fat old state representative at the next meeting of the prison commission. No fucking thanks, sister! No thanks!"

Her face had gone white and her hand shook slightly as she lit her next cigarette. If it was a performance, it was a pretty good one.

"Okay," I said. "Then let's backtrack. We've interviewed everybody on the list you gave us and nobody seems all that promising. Maybe you could take another look at it."

I unfolded the piece of yellow paper on which she'd listed the people who had come into contact with the painting.

She looked at it and sighed. "You know, when you run a

business, you meet a lot of people. Meter readers, salesmen, accountants, you name it.''

"First, do you know Leslie-Anne Gilmartin?''

"No.''

"Terry Yokum?''

"No.''

"Let's run through some qualifiers then. One, whoever it was, they must have come in a few times, right? This isn't a job that you'd do without scoping the place out pretty extensively. Two, they must have been fairly sophisticated— maybe not sophisticated about breaking and entering, but sophisticated about art. Otherwise they wouldn't have known which painting to take. Three, they must have had some kind of contact with Leslie-Anne Gilmartin and/or Terry Yokum. Four, ahhh . . . well, that's all I can think of offhand.''

"I talked to Roland and he mentioned this girl, this painter that he saw sneaking back into the storeroom to look as some of our inventory. Did you check her out?''

I nodded. "No good. She moved to Israel.''

"Hm.''

I decided to take a different approach. "How long has your gallery been located where it is right now?''

"Not so long. Five, six months, give or take,'' she said.

"Huh,'' I said. "So did you have movers take the paintings from your old location?''

She shook her head. "I'm too cheap and too suspicious. Roland and I moved them ourselves.''

"So what else was involved in the moving process? Think especially about anything that would have resulted in someone coming in contact with the painting.''

She lay back on the couch and looked up in the air through the cloud of smoke over her head. "We didn't do anything special. We had to fix up the new place obviously. But I had the paintings in the other location the whole time.''

"Tell me about the move.''

"What's to tell? You hire a real estate agent, you find a

place, you sign the papers, you hire an architect, you draw up plans, you hire a contractor to fix the place up, and then you move in. But like I say, that was six months ago at least.''

''What about security system installers?''

She looked up. ''If you were a security system expert, would you break into a place by knocking a hole through the wall with a sledgehammer?''

She had a point. ''Okay,'' I said. ''Let's get some names anyway.''

''The security system people were called Southeastern Security Consultants. Their sales rep was a guy named Rick McSomething. McGillis? McTavish?''

I wrote the name of the company down on my legal pad.

''My contractor for the build-out was named Maria Toricelli. One of those dyke carpenter types.''

''I see political correctness hasn't made big inroads into your life yet,'' I said, writing down the name.

''Try spending a couple years in a small room with a lesbian weightlifter who strangled her daughter with a brassiere strap,'' Charlie said expressionlessly. ''Gives you a whole new perspective on the charms of that special love betwixt woman and woman.''

''What about the architect?''

''Seriously, I think you're wasting your time here.''

''Maybe. But the insurance company pays me whether I waste my time or not.'' This wasn't strictly true. But it sounded like something your typical hard-boiled ninety-five-pound investigator would say. ''The architect?''

''Very charming guy. Attractive, too. Not unafraid of letting you know that he knows you're aware of him, if you know the kind of guy I'm talking about. I thought about it—you know? Getting a little thing going with him? At least I did till I found out he was married. Doesn't take a genius to know married men are poison, hm?''

"His name?" As soon as I said it I got this creepy feeling. What she said next only made it worse.

"Oh, yeah. Ron. Ron Widner."

"What!" Ron. *My* Ron.

"Actually I didn't meet him but a couple of times. Mostly I dealt with one of his junior people, this girl named Clarisse Jones. She must have been straight out of college."

"Did he ever go in the space? In the actual building?"

"Who—Widner? No. He was more the client relations type, a senior partner. He was recommended to me by a friend, so we got together at his office. He figured out very quickly how small the commission was going to be, so I don't think he took it too seriously. I gather his firm mostly does interiors for great big office buildings and that sort of thing." She smiled secretly. "My guess, if he hadn't wanted to screw me, he would have told me to find another firm. Then once he saw that a big fling wasn't in the cards, he shuffled me off to little Clarisse in about five seconds."

"And this was six months ago?"

"About that."

Ron and I had been going out for around eight months now. I felt like throwing up.

I took a few seconds to collect myself, pretending to write some notes on my legal pad. Finally I said, "Did you ever talk to him about the painting?"

"I don't think so." She shrugged vaguely. "Maybe. It's hard to remember."

"And you're sure you never showed him the space?"

She sat up suddenly, looked at me with a puzzled expression on her face.

"Why are you so hung up on this guy? I met him like three times. The person you want to talk to is Clarisse Jones. She's the one who drew up the plans and all that." Charlie's brow furrowed. "In fact, come to think of it, I might actually showed her the Hassam." She stubbed out her cigarette and shrugged. "Then again, I might not have. Hard to remember stuff like that."

I felt paralyzed. I had thought it was kind of strange when Ron suddenly started showing all this interest in my work. That hadn't been like him. And the fact that he never mentioned knowing Charlie Biddle, never mentioned that his firm had a commission to remodel her gallery? It was pretty hard to swallow.

The funny thing was, I don't know if I felt worse about all of those suspicious omissions or about the fact that he'd been coming on to this ridiculously beautiful woman two months after our torrid romance had started. If he was coming on to her, who else had been in his sights? And had they all given him the brush-off like Charlie had?

"Of course if you wanted I could introduce you to him," she said. "If you're looking for a good roll in the hay, he'd probably oblige."

"Ah," I said.

"He *was* good, too. I'll give him that. A little too Kama Sutra for my taste, but he knew how to romance a woman."

I stared at her. "I thought you said you didn't sleep with him," I said softly.

"I said I didn't want a relationship. I didn't say anything about *sex*." She laughed, a coarse Slavic belly rumble. "Anyway I'm kidding. You probably wouldn't like him. He's good in bed, but he's not much of a listener."

Well, that much was true. I sat there in a stupor for a while.

"So am I going to lounge around here smoking all morning while you meditate?" Charlie said after a while. I noticed she was on her third Marlboro.

"Nope," I said. "I think this will get me started."

I left her to her lounging and her Froot Loops, and walked out without saying another word.

CHAPTER 23

BACK AT THE office I checked in with my team. Nobody was turning up much of anything. I wasn't surprised after what I'd just learned. There were too many weird coincidences. Ron showing up at the coffee shop last night. Ron's sudden interest in the case. And then there was the thing the girl in the coffee shop had said last night—that the excuse Terry Yokum gave for painting all those copies of 'Late Afternoon' was that he'd been hired by an architect to match a particular painting.

I still didn't have the slightest idea how it might have fit together, though. Was Ron directly involved in stealing the painting? Or had he just been connected with Terry Yokum's counterfeiting gambit? Or was it all just a coincidence? The last possibility seemed by far the most remote.

I checked my messages. A couple from Mom (sounding infinitely wounded), a couple from Marion Cheever wanting to talk to Gunnar. Most unsettling, though, was a message from Ellen Widner. It took me a second to make the connection: Ron's wife. What in the world could she want? I couldn't imagine.

My heart was thumping away as I called Ron's wife back. The idea of having a friendly chat made me break out in a sweat, but I knew that after what I'd turned up today I needed to find out more about Ron. And who better to find it out from than his wife?

"Oh, hi Sunny!" she said. "Thanks for calling me back."

We chitchatted in the stiff way that people who don't really know each other do, and then she said, "You know I was serious the other night when I said I'd like to have lunch with you. I used to practice criminal law and now that I'm home with the kids all the time I start to go stir crazy every now and then. Sometimes I feel like one more conversation about Barbie's dresses and I'll have to shoot myself." She laughed brightly.

"Oh," I said. My gut was telling me that it would be more fun to get attacked by a gang of serial murderers than to have to spend an entire lunch with her. But I knew that I needed her.

"I know it's kind of short notice," I said, "but what about today?"

"Hold on just a minute." I heard her talking in the background, asking someone if they wanted to go to Chrissie's house. Then a little girl's voice: *Yeah! Yeah! Yeah!* She came back on the phone. "Sure, let's do it. I'm fobbing the kids off on a friend of mine."

We set a time and I hung up.

Ellen Widner had already been seated when I got to the restaurant. I'd never been able to figure out whether the place was called The Atlanta Bread Company or The Corner Cafe, because the sign over the place said both things. But regardless what it was called, they make a pretty good sandwich— if you don't mind paying eight dollars for two pieces of bread and some meat.

I sat down and we made a little conversation and all the while I was sitting there feeling vaguely like running to the bathroom and sticking my finger down my throat. Ellen Widner was a very pretty woman with blond highlights in her hair, a nice tan Ellen Tracy pantsuit, warm green eyes. Her fingernails were chewed down to the nub and she had lots of fat freckles across her nose and chest. I had the suspicion she played a fair amount of tennis and that she didn't lose much. She looked a lot like her brother. Only stronger, more fully formed, more sure of who she was.

I have to admit, I liked her immediately.

The waiter came and we ordered our sandwiches and I tried to think of a way to get around to probing her about Ron. Before I had the chance, she took a sip of white wine and smiled pleasantly and said, "So, Sunny, are you fucking my husband?"

I didn't move. I didn't say anything. For a second I imagined some sort of Fatal Attractionish scene where she came after me with a carving knife and a boiled rabbit. But all she did was study my face and smile pleasantly.

The waiter came with our soup. Ellen took a sip, set her spoon down.

"Sorry," she said. "I guess I lied. I wasn't really all that fascinated by that case of yours. I have to admit I'm the kind of person who changes the channel whenever a crime show comes on the television. That's probably why I left the law."

I was still sitting there trying to think what to say.

"If it's any consolation," Ellen Widner said, "I have a process server on the way over to visit him as we speak. I'm asking for a divorce. I thought it would be kind of kicky to have the papers served to him while he's enjoying a nice afternoon racquetball game."

"That's a big step," I said.

"I probably should have done it a long time ago." She looked at me for a minute, but I couldn't hold her gaze.

"So the answer is yes, I guess. I am . . . we're . . ."

"Having an affair."

"Right," I said. There was a brief pause. "Somehow I can't really make the words come out to say it." I sighed. "Jesus, I'm sorry. This is a terrible thing I've done."

"I wouldn't knock yourself out worrying about it," she

said drily. "It's not like you've got some kind of exclusive contract with him either."

I stared dumbly at my curry soup. It was as yellow as anything you'd find in an artist's paintbox.

"I'm curious," she said. "Has he ever talked about divorcing me? Has he ever promised marriage? Talked about the future?"

"Nope," I said. I tasted the bright yellow soup but it was too hot. Some kind of Indian spice blossomed in the back of my throat after I set the spoon down. "I wouldn't have let him."

"Smart lady."

"Is this a regular practice of yours?" I said. "Debriefing people who are having affairs with your husband."

"You're the first."

"Not to put this too nakedly, but, ah, what do you want?"

A funny look crossed Ellen's face. "When I first had the idea, I was thinking that I was going to tell you that I was going to subpoena you for a deposition in the divorce case and then I was going to gloat over the look on your face." She frowned miserably. "But I guess the truth is that mainly I wanted to torture myself."

"I don't recommend that," I said.

Ron's wife laughed very briefly. "Still, I have to say—the look on your face was pretty good."

I laughed, too. Uneasily.

"So while I'm on the subject of trying to put you on the spot and make you feel crappy," Ellen said, "I hired a private investigator to follow Ron around for a while. He followed Ron for about three weeks. You want to know how many women he was with in that time?"

I should have known something like this was coming. But even after talking with Charlie earlier in the morning, it still hurt.

"Truthfully?" I said. "Not really."

"Four," Ellen said. "He's banging this little intern in his

office, then there's you, then he picked up a girl in a bar . . ."
She wrinkled her forehead. "There was one other . . . I forget. Oh, yeah. The prostitute."

"He was with a *prostitute*?" I said. I had the same terrible
sinking feeling I'd had that morning when Charlie said she'd
slept with Ron. "Jesus Christ! Why? Why would he do
something like that?"

She shrugged. "The ineffable why. Makes you wonder
how he gets any work done, doesn't it?"

"A prostitute! No way."

Ellen smiled. "I think you're in denial, Sunny. Believe
me, I know the feeling. I was in denial for about ten years
myself." She looked at her watch. "Well, I guess he's got
the papers now. He's probably over the shock, probably on
the phone to his lawyer, figuring out how he can hide all his
assets. Move some money offshore, transfer ownership of the
BMW to his partnership. Maybe even working up some ar-
guments about how my emotional coldness, sexual frigidity,
and general lack of supportiveness drove him to find solace
in the arms of—"

"All right, all right, I'm sorry," I said finally. "But this
is a little too uncomfortable. Why don't I just leave, and you
can sit here and eat your soup and be bitter at your husband
by yourself."

She reached across the table and put her hand on mine.
"Wait," she said. "Not yet. I promise, no more of that.
Sometimes I just can't help it."

I studied her face.

"What I'm curious to know," she said, "is why *you* came
here. Knowing what you knew about me, I just have a hard
time seeing how you could show up here in good conscience.
I mean you seem like a nice enough person."

"You want to know the truth?"

She shrugged. "I guess by now I can take it."

"I needed to know where Ron was last Monday night
around one fifteen in the morning."

"Last Monday?" For a second she looked at me blankly, then her eyebrows went up sharply. "You're asking if I know where he was the night that painting was stolen!"

"I know this sounds crazy, Ellen. But listen." And then I told her some things that had been going through my mind since I talked to Charlie Biddle: "Ron's firm designed the space for the gallery where the painting was stolen. I talked to the gallery owner this morning, and she admits she might have told him about the painting. No big deal, right? But then last night I'm supposed to meet this guy Terry Yokum who forged a copy of 'Late Afternoon' and tried to sell it back to the insurance company. Well, the guy never shows up. But while I was waiting for him, a friend of his told him that Terry Yokum was working on what sounds like a forgery of this painting months ago. And when she asked what he was doing, he told her he was painting it for 'an architect.' Then as I'm leaving the coffee shop where I was supposed to meet Yokum, guess who walks up to me?"

Ellen Widner's face looked pale beneath the tennis player freckles.

"Uh-huh," I said. "There's Ron. And for some reason he's changed clothes in the three or four hours since I last saw him. Anyway, we have a mild argument, he walks away, and I go around to my car. Imagine my surprise when I find a bunch of cops back there. And ten feet away from my cat there's a body lying in a Dumpster. Terry Yokum."

Ellen kept staring at me. "No," she said finally. "My husband is an incredible asshole. It's taken me a long time to face that. But he's not a murderer."

"Why would a guy change his clothes at midnight? Maybe because he got blood on them?"

Ellen just kept shaking her head.

"Who's in denial now?" I said. I touched her hand. "I'm sorry, that was a mean thing to say. Look, I was thinking about it this morning and my first reaction was, come on, get real. It just didn't seem plausible, knowing what I know about him. But then I started thinking: how well *do* I know him? And what I realized is, I don't know how well I know him. He's a guy who cheats on his wife, who cheats on the woman he's cheating on his wife with . . ." I spread my hands in front of me. "I mean I don't have the slightest idea what he is or isn't capable of."

"No." Ellen whispered it. Her eyes were opaque and unfocused. "No. I do know him. There are some things that even he's not capable of."

"He's a guy who screws prostitutes, Ellen."

"That's not the same thing as killing somebody." She looked wounded now, no longer in control.

"Ellen, I only told one person where and when I was going to meet Terry Yokum. That person was Ron."

"No. No. No." She just kept shaking her head, looking at me with her wide green eyes.

"Okay, imagine a scenario," I said. "Imagine you're Ron. You start dating a private investigator. One day she tells him that sometimes her firm gets hired by insurance companies to ransom stolen property. A few days later he meets a woman who runs a gallery. After screwing this woman, he finds out that she's just acquired a very valuable new painting. Because he's involved in the design of the new gallery, he's in a position to learn all about the security system, the layout, the way the paintings are displayed, the whole bit. And a stray thought occurs to him: *hey, I'm in a great position to steal this painting!* He doesn't really take it seriously: it's just whimsy. But then he gets intrigued by the idea. He thinks about it a while and finally he realizes that not only could he could steal it, ransom it and walk away with around a hundred grand . . . but the cool thing is, he could do it all and nobody gets hurt."

Ellen was shaking her head the whole time. "That's just not his kind of thing," she said.

"I'm not so sure. I mean, why would he have sex with four women including a prostitute in a three-week space of time? Because he's a horny guy? Of course not. It's because he likes the sneaking around, he likes the subterfuge, he likes the lies, he likes the secret life and the secret beeper codes and the secret women.''

"Besides, he doesn't need the money.'' A tear leaked out of her eye and she wiped fiercely at it.

"That's exactly my point. It's the rush, you see, Ellen? It's the hidden life!'' Suddenly I realized that in a strange way I was describing myself too. I had a brief flash of anger at myself, a realization that maybe *I* had some things I needed to think about once this was all over. But there was no time to dwell on it right now.

"Okay, just for the sake of argument,'' Ellen said. "Supposing he really did steal that painting. That's still a hell of a long leap to murder.''

"Ron's a clever guy. We can agree on that much, right? Being a clever guy, he doesn't want to put *his* ass on the line. While he's planning the theft, he realizes that things can go wrong; he says to himself, 'What if some cops just happens to show up in the alleyway behind the gallery during the theft?' Maybe he's not into taking on that level of risk. Besides, let's say his plan for stealing the painting involves bashing a hole in a wall. The smaller the hole, the less time it takes. The less time, the less risk of discovery. Who better to hire to crawl through a small hole than a four-foot-tall guy with a police record? So Ron comes up with a name: Terry Yokum.

"Problem is, Terry's the kind of guy who's always working an angle. Terry—who's a very talented painter—decides he's going to forge a copy of the painting and screw Ron over. Instead of ransoming the real painting back and taking a small cut of whatever Ron makes, Terry figures he'll switch the fake for the real one. Sure, the insurance company will quickly realize they've been had . . . but by then it'll be too late. Once it comes out that the insurance company's been scammed, Terry can then fence the real painting.

"Now let's suppose that somewhere along the way, Ron

realizes that he's being screwed. So then he comes after Terry who's supposedly ransoming the painting. Probably Ron isn't coming after Terry with the idea of killing him, but he's got a gun just to spook him or something. So Ron shows up where the ransom meeting is supposed to happen. Only when he gets there, he finds that Terry has gotten his girlfriend Leslie-Anne Gilmartin to do the ransom in his stead. Now Leslie-Anne, she's a stubborn kid. Contrary. She refuses to give up the fake painting. There's a struggle or something and Ron ends up shooting Leslie-Anne. Maybe the gun went off by accident—who knows? Ron grabs the painting out of the trunk of the car, climbs over the fence with it, drives away. When he gets home he destroys the bogus Childe Hassam.

"Only, guess what? Ron doesn't realize that Terry has painted a *bunch* of fakes.

"So Terry just grabs a more recent fake off the shelf and he's back in business with his plan to ransom a forgery. Problem is, he gets busted. So at this point, Ron's freaking out. He knows that Terry knows who killed Leslie-Anne. And if Terry knows, he might eventually roll over on Ron for the murder in order to make a deal in his fraud case. So yesterday when I mention to Ron that I'm meeting Terry at midnight and that Terry is going to tell me who killed Leslie-Anne, Ron panics. First he tries to dissuade me from meeting Terry. Then, when that doesn't work, he pumps me to find out where the meeting is going to be. From there it's a simple matter of waiting around in this dark little parking lot behind the coffee shop. When Terry arrives, Ron pops out from behind a car, *bam bam bam* with a hammer or something, then Ron tosses him in the dumpster. It wouldn't take five seconds if you did it right. I mean Terry's the size of a child, there's no way he could have defended himself."

When I finished Ellen was looking out the window at the cars tearing by on Piedmont. "Doesn't make sense," she said. "Doesn't make sense."

"He's backed into a corner, you see?" I said. "Once the die is cast, he realizes that if Terry gives him up, he could go to jail. Can you see Ron letting that happen?"

Ellen just sat there for a while, stirring her spoon around in her soup. Finally she leaned over and took a white, letter-sized envelope out of a briefcase that was leaned up against the leg of her chair. She pulled a thin sheaf of papers out of the envelope and set them next to the basket of bread on the table. I recognized the papers as an investigator's surveillance report. There were photographs underneath. Two of them showed me and Ron embracing. The rest showed him with other women, kissing them, smiling so the laugh lines showed around his eyes. All of the women were very attractive. I couldn't tell from looking which one was the prostitute.

"Not those," she said. "I was thinking you might learn something from looking at the surveillance thing. I had this guy following him until last Tuesday."

I raised my eyebrows, flipped to the page dated for the previous Monday, the day the Hassam was stolen. Here were the entries for Monday night.

10:05 P.M.   Subject arrives at Unit 211, Village Creek
               Apts, Dunwoody, GA.
10:21 P.M.   Subject leaves Unit 211 Village Creek Apts
               with Virginia Reeves.
10:37 P.M.   Subject arrives at Stein Club (nightclub).
12:05 A.M.   Subject leaves Stein Club accompanied by
               V. Reeves. Proceeds back to V. Reeves'
               apartment at Unit 211 Village Creek.
1:18 A.M.   Subject leaves Unit 211 Village Creek.
               Proceeds home to his residence.

"Okay," I said. "The theft was called in at 1:12 A.M."
Ellen looked terribly relieved.

"So he wasn't at the robbery," I said. "But remember

my clever new theory here is that he hired Terry to do it.''

Ellen lifted the spoon to her lips, then set it back in the bowl without tasting the soup. ''I've never even heard him mention this Yokum person before,'' she said. ''I don't think he even knew him.''

I skimmed the surveillance report until I saw something that caught my eye. ''This entry was two weeks ago Thursday,'' I said. Then I read the entry out loud. '' '5:36 P.M. Subject arrives at 449 Ottley Drive, enters.' ''

''So?'' Ellen said.

''449 Ottley Drive is where Terry Yokum had his studio.''

Ellen seemed frozen for a moment. Then she jumped up suddenly, knocking her soup over on the surveillance report and the photographs, and rushed toward the door. The waiter scurried over and started swabbing at the electric yellow soup with a white towel.

''I think we better get the check,'' I said.

CHAPTER 24

WHEN I GOT back to the office I asked Sean McNeely to run a Dun & Bradstreet and an Equifax on his brother-in-law.

"Do you mind my asking what this's about?" Sean said, looking slightly puzzled. "I don't . . . I mean he *is* my brother-in-law. I feel a little uncomfortable . . ."

"Oh, no, it's nothing serious," I said. "He's in the process of making some changes in his firm's banking relationships and so he wanted to take a peek at his credit reports before he starts the negotiations."

"Oh," Sean said. "I see."

After Sean had left, I sent Tawanda and Earl out to talk to some friends of Terry and Leslie-Anne, to see if I could establish anything about the nature of their relationships to Ron. After they left, I sat there for a while staring out the window. I had worked up an intellectual argument that showed how Ron seemed to be involved in this thing—but I couldn't get my heart around it.

Maybe Ron was not the greatest guy in the world, the most trustworthy, the most thoughtful—but still . . . An art thief? A killer? Every time my mind would tip-toe up to the idea again, I'd start to get the shakes. And anyway, I still didn't really have motive. I'd glibly said to Ellen that he was just doing it for kicks—but I wasn't sure I bought that argument.

After a few minutes Sean came back, handed me the reports. I glanced over them while he was standing there with his usual eager-beaver look on his face. He was like a puppy that wanted to be petted. "Great work," I said—though truthfully any moron can pull a credit bureau.

The credit reports were an unpleasant surprise. The Equifax, his personal credit report, was a lot worse than I'd expected. He'd gone thirty days overdue on a couple of notes recently—no big thing, but not really excusable for a guy who was reporting a hundred and fifty grand a year in income. But the thing that really surprised me was how big his debt load was. He was carrying nearly sixty thousand dollars on his credit cards, plus two car leases and a fat mortgage note. His finances hadn't quite reached meltdown— but barring a miracle, he'd be there soon: it was clear Ron was living way beyond his means. He had put a second mortgage on his house, too, sucking off all his equity to keep on top of his bills. That would be a shocker for Ellen when she started working on the divorce settlement.

Then I took a look at the D&B for his firm. Another bombshell: his business had expanded over the past couple of years, and—while that was theoretically a good thing—it was obvious that expenses had shot up too fast to keep pace with revenues. His firm was slow-paying every single creditor on the report, and they were in dutch to the bank for around a million dollars.

Kind of like Peachtree Investigations when you got right down to it. Only the numbers were a lot bigger.

The bottom line was that he had a good income and a good business. But he needed breathing room, time to get outflow back in line with inflow.

And a hundred grand buys a pretty fair amount of breathing room.

When I looked up, I was in for another shock: Ron was standing in the doorway with a strange, hangdog look on his face. My face probably went a little pale as I slid the credit reports off the desk and into a drawer.

"Ron, how are you?" I said. Then I looked over at Sean McNeely who was still standing in front of my desk. "Could you give us a couple minutes, Sean?"

Sean looked mildly startled. "Oh, gosh. Yeah! Sure." Then he scuttled out of the room.

After he left, Ron closed the door. My heart started beating as he crossed the room and slumped down in a chair. I was relieved that he didn't seem to want to kiss me.

"I can't believe it," he said. "She finally did it."

"Who?" I said innocently. "Did what?"

"Ellen! She served me the papers! I'm right in the middle of a racquetball game with a client and some fat little troll in a windbreaker that says Sheriff's Office on the back barges in and hands me the letter. Can you believe that?"

I decided to play dumb. "I'm sorry, what papers?"

Ron blinked. "The *divorce* papers!"

"Gosh." I sat there for a minute feeling acutely self-conscious. How was I supposed to act? I felt like I was watching myself in a movie, operating my own body by remote control. "I, uh . . . well, how do you feel about that?"

"How do I *feel*?" His mouth opened and he looked at me as though I had something wrong with my mental wiring.

Normally a conversation like this would make me pretty emotional. But with everything that was going on, I was feeling this weird distance from myself and everything that was going on in the room. "It doesn't take a genius to figure out that you've had affairs before, Ron. Right? Probably a bunch of them. So . . . if you were really committed to your marriage, it would move me to wonder, like, well why are you screwing around on your wife all the time if you want to stay married?"

He kept staring at me. "I can't believe you're taking her side in this."

For my part, I couldn't believe I'd just wasted six months

of my life on this self-centered jerk. I smiled pleasantly. "It's not a matter of taking sides. I'm just trying to be objective here."

"Well, it's not helping," he said irritably.

"Okay, what do you need me to do? Give you a big kiss and a big hug, pat you on the head? Tell you it's going to be all right?"

He stared down at his hands for a minute, rubbing his thumbs together. "Maybe if I promise to go to counseling or something . . ."

"I'm not trying to be unsupportive here, but does it occur to you that asking your, ah, mistress for tips on how to save your marriage is maybe not the most tactful thing in the world?" I was finally starting to get a little steamed, just on principle. I was also beginning to suspect that Ron had a near pathological lack of ability to see things from someone else's perspective. *How* pathological, though: that was the question.

"You're right, you're right," Ron said, shaking his head. "God, I'm sorry."

"Hey . . ." I shrugged.

"Christ, it's probably a lost cause anyway. I probably just need to start with a clean sheet of paper, you know? A whole new thing." Ron looked up at me suddenly, a look of boyish hope on his face. "So, after it's over . . . maybe we could . . . I mean, what do you think about the idea of us getting married?"

I couldn't believe the guy. What do you say to something like that? After a few seconds a nasty-sounding laugh came out of my throat. "Ron!" I said. "Listen to yourself!"

He looked surprised for a second—as though it had never occurred to him a mere Sunny Childs might not leap wildly at the opportunity to marry an exalted specimen such as himself. But then his face composed itself. "No, no, you're right. I'm a little shaken up. I'm not thinking. I'm not thinking. I'm not . . ." He banged on the side of his head a couple of times with the heels of his hands. I had the feeling I was watching a man fall apart right in front of me.

All of which was making me very nervous.

Suddenly something came to me—a plan of sorts. A test. What I needed to do was give him some sort of information that would only be of interest to him if he was actually behind the robbery. If he reacted, then I'd know it was really him. If not . . .

How to pull it off, though? The first step was to bait the hook. And the second was to get him out of my office as fast as possible. I took a deep breath.

"Look, I know it's a bad time for you," I said, "but things are going kind of nuts around here right now." I paused. "See, I heard from Gunnar a few minutes ago."

"Huh?" he said distractedly.

"Yeah, Gunnar called. You know how he's been MIA all week? Turns out he's actually been operating undercover this whole time." I lowered my voice dramatically. "And guess what?"

Ron just looked at me.

"He's turned up an informant!"

"What are you talking about?" Ron said.

"That's what I'm saying. The reason I'm so busy is the case just took a new turn. This informant who contacted Gunnar knows all about the stolen painting. They know who killed Leslie-Anne Gilmartin, who killed Terry Yokum, who stole the painting. Gunnar's meeting the informant tonight, face-to-face!"

Ron's eyes seemed somewhat unfocused. "Where?" he said finally.

"The informant is showing up at nine-fifteen," I said. "Nine-fifteen at Terry Yokum's loft."

"Nine-fifteen." Ron kept looking at me with that blank expression on his pretty face. There was a long pause and finally he stood up. "I don't even know why I came here, Sunny. I have so much stuff to work out and I'm trying to dump it on everybody else. No wonder she wants to leave me.''

"All I'm saying is that I'm under a huge amount of pressure," I said. "This thing should be over by tomorrow evening. Then I can get together with you and we can have a talk. I think we've needed to have a good talk for a while."

"Maybe so, maybe so," Ron muttered vaguely. Then he opened the door and was gone.

If Ron was really a thief and a killer, he'd show up tonight at Terry Yokum's loft to find out who the "informant" I'd just invented was—presumably to kill them. If not . . . well, then I'd be out of a job as of tomorrow at noon. But I guess, all in all, I'd be pretty relieved. Losing your livelihood is no picnic. But falling in love with a psychopath—that's a whole different ballgame.

CHAPTER 25

DON'T KNOW much about what drives a person to become an artist. Or a criminal either for that matter. But I think it has something in common with the reasons I lie.

When I was in college I read this Dylan Thomas poem that seemed so true that I memorized the entire thing. Here's part of it:

> The force that through the green fuse drives the flower
> Drives my green age; that blasts the roots of trees
> Is my destroyer.
> And I am dumb to tell the crooked rose
> My youth is bent by the same wintry fever.
>
> The hand that whirls the water in the pool
> Stirs the quicksand; that ropes the blowing wind
> Hauls my shroud sail.
> And I am dumb to tell the hanging man
> How of my clay is made the hangman's lime.

As I stepped into Terry Yokum's studio, I was reminded of that poem. Sometimes the mysterious force that underlies everything in our world grabs hold of you, and after it does the things that happen are too powerful and strange to be imprisoned in neat little boxes with names like ''life'' or "death" or "good" or "bad" or "art" or "forgery" or "crime."

Terry's studio was on the second floor of an old warehouse, the floor made of worn wood, the ceiling grimy and black with age. There were a couple of paint-splotched tarps hanging from easels in one corner of the room. I'd used a pick gun to open the lock downstairs, and once I was inside, I just took the elevator up.

There was nothing special about the studio—nothing, that is, except what was in it: the bare brick walls of the big space were lined on all sides with copies of *Late Afternoon, Pont Aven, Brittany.* There must have been thirty or forty of them—an extraordinary amount of work. And I suspect that these were only half of the paintings he did because the floor was covered with curlicues of Hooker's green and ochre: after practicing the painting on modern canvases he'd probably painted the picture over and over on an antique canvas, then—finding each copy lacking after a couple day's viewing—had scraped off all the paint and started over. The floor was so thick with the paint scrapings that in some places it looked almost like moss or patchy grass had begun to reclaim the old wooden floor.

To stand in that room was to understand something about the indistinct line between artistic impulse and obsession, between art and crime: I was completely overwhelmed by those paintings. Some of them had meandered away from the original idea, turned abstract or more crisply realistic—but it was clear that they were all in *pursuit* of something, that after a few paintings Terry had stopped being interested in mere fakery.

I don't know if Terry had turned into a madman or a saint there at the end. But on some level this had obviously stopped being about money: all he'd wanted to do finally was to perfect this idea, to turn paint not just into a perfect fake but a perfect work of art. For a guy who'd abandoned art for commerce, truth for lies, pressed his talent into the service of crime, he'd found in this painting some sort of tunnel back from the darkness and out toward the light. A lie to lead him out of dishonesty, a crime to free him from his sins.

Oh, hell, I don't know.

Maybe I'm just trying to romanticize a lying, cheating, worthless shitheel. But it seems a shame to me that he never got the chance to go wherever it was that *Late Afternoon* seemed to be leading him.

I had been waiting for an hour or so when the freight elevator finally wheezed up to the floor and opened.

"Ron?" I said.

No answer. I saw a something glint in the darkness of the unlit elevator.

"Ron?"

But it was not Ron Widner: it was Charlie Biddle who stepped out into the brightly lit room. She had a small silver automatic pistol in her hand. "Where's Gunnar?" she said.

I cocked my head, feeling suddenly very confused. "I have no idea. Where's Ron?"

"Ron?" she said.

"Ron Widner."

She squinted at me. "Why are we talking about Ron Widner?"

"The painting. He hired Terry to do the painting."

She looked at me impatiently, then stalked across the room, threw a drape off an easel and then opened the door of a closet. She seemed to be looking for somebody. "Where is he, dammit? Where's Gunnar?"

"I just told you," I said. "I don't have any idea."

She pointed the gun at my face.

"It was a ruse," I said. "There's no information. I just wanted to get Ron to come here."

"Why do you keep talking about Ron?" She seemed irritated.

I guess I'm a little slow on the uptake, but I had been so

sure it was Ron that it wasn't until that very moment that it
occurred to me that maybe I'd been wrong all along. I don't
know what sequence of coincidences had been involved—
but it was obvious that Ron had nothing to do with this
whole business. It was Charlie. Only . . . how had she found
out that Gunnar was supposed to be showing up here? The
only other person I'd told was Ellen Widner. So how had
Charlie known that Gunnar was supposed to be here?

"There's no Gunnar," I said. "No information. It was just
a lie."

"So who *is* here? SWAT's outside? Yes? The cops?
Who?" Her Slavic lilt had gotten very strong.

"Yes," I said.

"Yes *what*? SWAT? Cops? FBI?"

"All of the above." It was a lie, of course. I'd come here
alone, told no one. And I'd done it because I'm a romantic
fool. I don't know what I'd expected from Ron, but I had
wanted to give him a chance to come clean. Not of the crime
so much as of his philandering, his lies, his selling out of his
wife and children. And I don't know—maybe I also wanted
to put myself at risk as some sort of penance for the shameful
part I'd played in destroying his marriage.

Maybe in my own stupid way, I still loved Ron—or at
least the idea of Ron that I had once constructed in my
mind—and I wanted to hear him confess his sins, beg forgiveness, make some thin promise to change his life. And if
he'd done it, maybe I'd have said, "Okay, Ron. Go back to
your wife, promise to take care of her and love her and never
stray again. If you do that, my dear, I'll never tell anyone."

Remember what I said a long way back, that I'm an idiot
when it comes to men? Case closed, huh?

But of course it wasn't Ron who was behind this thing
after all. He was just a garden variety jerk, a garden variety
cheat, a garden variety man of weak principle. And when I
finally recognized that, I'd been willing to believe anything
of him.

"So I guess we have a problem here," Charlie said.

"That's fair to say."

Charlie walked around the room for a while, looking at the paintings. I started to get up, but she pointed the pistol at me and I sat back down. I had the impression she was the sort of person who could hit what she was aiming at.

"I had no idea," she said after she'd made a circuit of the room.

"What?"

"Terry. I had no idea he was such an extraordinary painter." She pointed at the wall near the door. "You see where he started? Right there. They go in order, I believe. See? How they developed, changed as he went."

As soon as she said it, I could see the progression.

"The early ones—they're just facile crap," she said. "They're just brush strokes. But then right in here they start to become kind of nice." She pointed around at the second wall. "See how the colors are bolder, the modeling of the land is more refined. They're fakes, but they're lovely." She turned and studied the last paintings in the progression. Suddenly a tear came out of one eye. "But these. My God! It stops being a counterfeit, and it starts to turn into something else. Something much better than that awful Hassam."

"Yeah," I said.

Suddenly she turned to me. "So I guess you're wearing a wire."

I nodded.

"This isn't such a good place for a trap," she said. "The SWAT team has to come up in the elevator. As soon as the elevator starts to move, I'll know they're coming."

I shrugged. "Your best bet is just to give me your weapon, come out peacefully, keep your mouth closed and hire a good lawyer. If I'm correct, you haven't made any admissions yet. Maybe you could get off scot-free."

She seemed to think about it, but then her face wrinkled

up in a look of profound disgust. "No. No, I don't think that will work."

"Why not?"

"You know my record. They'll trace everything back. It's all over." She slumped down in a chair. But the gun, I noticed, didn't waver. I tried to think of a way out, but there was nothing I could do. The only way out was the elevator and it was on the far side of the room.

I sat there in a sort of stupor, trying to think of something clever to get me out of this.

"You know," Charlie said after a while. "It's funny how you never escape your upbringing."

"Hmmm," I said. "I'm agnostic on that one."

"No, no. No, no." She waved her hand dismissively. "It's true."

"So tell me . . ." I said. Get her talking, that was my first thought. Maybe she'd talk herself out of doing something stupid.

"My father was an artist in the Soviet Union. He was a Ukrainian nationalist, though, so he couldn't become a member of the Academy. Back in those days, the Academy of Arts was the big gravy train. I went to a special school when I was a kid, and a lot of the girls in my school, their fathers were big party assholes or members of the Academy or nuclear scientists—people like that. These were . . . I guess you would say they were the provincial elite. And so these girls had all the arrogance and the perks of that social position. Blue jeans, Walkmen, Led Zeppelin albums, family dachas, vacations to the Caucasus—that whole bit. They used to make fun of me because my clothes were cheap and ugly, because my father was always getting in trouble with the Party."

She stared at one of Terry's first paintings, one of the frauds.

"You can't imagine how angry I was at my father. You know? I mean all he had to do was sell out, join the Party, paint pictures of shiny tractors and noble factory workers and that kind of shit and I could have had everything the other girls had. But he wouldn't do it.''

"Look—" I said.

But she ignored me. "So one day I heard him talking to this guy who was in town visiting from Moscow. He was a sort of dissident type, had served some time in the gulags for painting stuff that wasn't on the approved subject list or whatever. They were drunk, bullshitting, letting off steam. I forget why, but I'd borrowed this Japanese tape recorder that one of my girlfriends' fathers had brought back from an overseas assignment. And for some reason, I just hit the record button and walked away. The next morning I got up and I had this tape, this tape of them saying all these silly, drunken subversive things.

"Well, I don't know why I kept it, but I did. It gave me a feeling of power, I think—and that was a scarce commodity back in those days. Anyway, I kept it for a while, and one day before school I got in an argument with my father— you know how these things happen between fourteen-years-olds and their parents—and I was so mad! So mad! So on the way to class, I took the tape to this building on vulitsya Zhovtenevoi Revolyutsii. There was no sign on the building or anything like that, but these two guys with black leather jackets were always standing around outside smoking and everybody knew it was the KGB. So I just walked in the front door and there was a man sitting at a desk behind a counter, and I gave him the tape, and I walked out.''

"Jesus Christ," I said softly.

"Yeah."

The room was silent for a long time.

"So what happened, Charlie?"

"Oh, he spent a couple of months in the gulag. It could have been worse, I guess. I don't think they tortured him or anything. But after he got back, he lost his job as a commercial artist. None of the magazines or publishers or ministries in Kiev would take his work anymore. So he had to get a job in a factory.'' She looked terribly angry now. ''He was a sweet, gentle guy. Soft. Not cut out for hard labor, or for that kind of drudgery. We lost our apartment, the few little things we had, ended up living in this horrible, depressing working class slum. My father felt that he'd betrayed us. After that he spent maybe four or five years trying to get into good graces with the authorities, to get into the Party, to slime his way into the Academy so that he could get me blue jeans and vacations and maybe a Japanese tape recorder.

''There was an application process, lots of bureaucracy. He filled out the forms, he bribed officials, he kissed ass, he humiliated himself and sold out his beliefs in a hundred ways. And so finally the Academy put him on the nomination list. He got his hopes up, I think. But then the day came where they announced the final acceptances for the Academy and his name had disappeared. I don't know why, but it was gone.''

She smiled with a grim, sad fondness. ''He had treated me so tenderly after I betrayed him. So decently. I can't imagine how he ever forgave me for what I did. But anyway, his name wasn't on the list and so it was finally a closed book. He had gone through all that debasement and it had amounted to nothing. That day he knew for certain that he was going to end up spending the rest of his life assembling reading lamps at this factory. It was the end of the road for him.''

Charlie shook her head as though trying to get rid of the memory.

''After that it was never the same. I hated the Soviet Union, hated the Ukraine, hated myself. All I could think about was escape. I thought that if I just got out of the Soviet Union I'd be a new person. Clean, you know? When I was nineteen I went on this college exchange program to Bulgaria and managed to sneak out of the country. A friend hid me in this packing crate at the Sofia train station. I stayed inside that box with nothing but a litre of water for over forty-eight hours. After a while, I went unconscious from heat and fear and dehydration. When I finally woke up, I was in a hospital in Istanbul.

"Eventually I got asylum in the States. But when I got here I had no skills, couldn't speak English. So I ended up doing some bad things, hooking up with some bad people."

I chipped in: "Like Winston Percival?"

She laughed. "Are you kidding me? Winston was my savior! He was the best thing that happened to me . . . which shows you how bad it was before. Before that, I didn't care. I'd do anything to degrade myself. Trying to make up for what I did to my father maybe. I don't know. But Winston showed me that at least there was an opportunity to do something better with myself. He taught me how to act, how to dress, how to talk. He even came up with this silly name of mine!" She laughed. "But what I realized after a while was that if you faked it for long enough, who was to say what was fake and what was real? You see? If I could *pretend* to be a decent person, a reputable art dealer's assistant—the whole fraud that Winston wanted me to engage in   then why not simply *be* that person?"

She shrugged. "So when the chance came, when Winston sold me to the cops, I decided it was an opportunity—a clean break, absolution for my sins. And then it would be the straight and narrow path forever."

"I don't understand," I said. "Then why this business with the Hassam?"

She laughed sardonically. "I spent a little too much money expanding the business, buying new stuff, building the new gallery. I was overextended, scared, afraid of falling back into that pit I used to be in. So when the opportunity presented itself, I fell back into old habits. I told myself that *just this once* I could get away with it. And then everything would be fine."

"But Terry scammed you. He made the fake and tried to

sell it back to Reliance. Which would have shot down your scheme to get the painting back.''

She looked at me pityingly. ''Don't be silly. There was never a painting to start with.''

''Huh?''

''Here's how it worked. I did some research looking for paintings that had disappeared during the second world war. Something relatively obscure . . . but not so obscure that it hadn't been documented before the war. I needed a provenance to make it plausible. And it had to be in the right price range—the kind of thing that's just below the radar, but still worth some money.''

''*Late Afternoon.*''

''Right. It had been owned by a Jew, stolen by the *Nazis*, and then disappeared. Perfect. So I gave Terry that blurry little picture from the old French auction catalog and said, 'Here. Paint this.' ''

''I get it. So the plan was to 'steal' it, file an insurance claim, walk away with three hundred thousand dollars.''

''Right. The key was authentication. I took care of that by hiring this guy up in New York who I knew about. He had some big gambling debts and I figured that with suitable cash incentives, he'd be game to help out.''

''Then what? Terry decided to double-cross you and ransom it back to Reliance?''

''No. That was Leslie-Anne's bright idea. Terry thought she was such a little goody-goody but she wasn't. She was a snake.''

''So you got wind of it and caught her in the act. And you killed her.''

''I'm tired of talking about this,'' she said wearily. She got up and looked out the window. ''Where are they? Where are the cops? In that van over there?''

''Okay, then why did Terry try to ransom the painting after Leslie-Anne got killed?''

Charlie pulled a heavy black curtain across the window,

then stared at one of the last paintings. "How the hell should I know?" she snapped. "Maybe Leslie-Anne gave him the idea: once he realized he could make a lot more money with the ransom scheme than I could afford to pay him, he just gave into the temptation. Or maybe it was hubris. Maybe he wanted to find out if he could do a painting that the authenticator would say was as good as the original. I don't know."

"I don't know if it's much consolation," I said, "but the authenticator liked it better."

"Me, too." Charlie laughed bitterly. "But then I was never that crazy about Childe Hassam anyway."

We sat in silence for a long time.

"You need to give me the gun," I said finally.

She glanced at me, shook her head. "What's the point? It's like I told you the other day: I'm never going back to prison again. Never."

"You might beat this thing."

"What—after I just admitted to everything on tape? Get real."

"There's nobody out there," I said.

She looked at me with flat, skeptical eyes.

"I made it all up," I said. "I was just bullshitting you about the SWAT team. There's no microphone, there's no tape, there's no team of cops hidden out there in a van."

For a second she seemed to believe me, but then she snorted derisively. "Yeah right! You set a trap for somebody with no backup? Nobody would be *that* dumb."

"If only that were true."

But she just shook her head, dismissing me. "Nope. It's done. You start something and it plays itself out." She smiled coolly. "We Ukrainians are fatalists, you know."

And I knew that she wasn't talking about the painting. "You were fourteen years old. How could you know?"

Charlie's lip curled scornfully. "In the Soviet Union we came out of the womb knowing. I knew *exactly* what I was doing. There comes a time when the thread runs out. Then you have to pay.''

She rubbed the gun against the side of her face, and suddenly I thought I understood what she meant. ''Wait!'' I said. ''What about redemption? What about forgiveness?''

Charlie didn't even bother looking at me as she put the gun to the side of her face.

''What about your father?'' I said. ''Maybe if you talked to him? Maybe he could help you understand . . .''

She looked at me then. And as soon as she did, I knew I'd screwed up. ''You child,'' she said.

''Walk away,'' I pleaded. ''There's no one out there. You know why you brought the gun into this room: self preservation. Listen to that instinct! Put the gun down and walk out. Make your peace! Walk away, Charlie!''

She pointed the gun at me, her hand trembling. ''My name is Ludmilla.''

''*Walk away!*''

''Say my name.''

''There's still time, Charlie. This doesn't have to be who you are.''

''The day after the Academy turned him down I came home from school and there he was. In the bathroom, hanging from the ceiling. *That* is who I am.''

''Charlie . . .''

''That's not my name.'' She kept pointing the gun at me. ''Say my real name.''

I put my hand over my eyes.

''My name is Ludmilla Rutskoi,'' she said again. I tried to take my hand away from my eyes but I couldn't do it. It was only a second or two before I heard the shot.

CHAPTER 26

BY THE TIME the cops came and I had given my statement to Carl Fontaine and called Marion Cheever, it was almost midnight. Lucky for me—I guess—my mother is a night owl. So when I parked in front of the garish pseudo-Mediterranean villa in which she and Husband Number Five live, the lights were still on.

She opened the door and when she first saw me I could tell that she was ready to lambaste me for not returning her calls, for ruining Walter's life, for sabotaging her motherly efforts and so on. But I'll say this for Mom: when the chips are down, she comes through. She saw the look on my face and the anger went out of her; she just put her arms around me and gave me a hug and let me cry right there on the front porch.

After I calmed down we went inside and I told her the whole story. The paintings, the insurance, the false trails, the impending collapse of Peachtree Investigations, the horrible and saddening deaths—all of it. Like I say, give her credit: she didn't mention Walter quitting Underhill Tabb once. Or the party, or the phone calls I didn't return, or any of that. She just listened and held my hand.

When I was finished, I felt emptied out, stripped of human feeling. She held my hand for a while and somewhere in the distance I could hear a grandfather clock ticking and the

occasional distant snore of her husband. Finally she stood up
and led me into the bathroom. It was the first time I'd looked
in the mirror since Charlie Biddle pulled the trigger of her
gun and killed herself. There were flecks of dried blood on
my blouse and in my hair and on my cheek.

I started shuddering when I saw it, then Mom said, "No,
no. Close your eyes, sweetie." Water chortled in the bath,
and a soft tongue of steam brushed against my hand. I kept
my eyes squeezed shut. "Up, sweetie," she said when the
bath water had started making a deeper, richer, fuller sound.
"Up."

I stood up and my mother took off all my clothes. Then
she guided my leg over the lip of the bath. The water was
very hot, but I sank into it with relief. And still I didn't open
my eyes. Mom washed my hair and then cleaned off my face
and my body with a washcloth. I think it was the most comforting sensation I've felt in my adult life. I guess I haven't
let someone take that kind of control of my body since I was
four or five years old, and it brought back some very sharp
and powerful memories. I could remember the feel of the
washcloth on my face from when I was a child, the slightly
abrasive quality of the warm, wet fabric as she rubbed my
face. She'd always washed a little too hard—and she still
did—not wanting anything unclean to cling to her daughter.

I remembered the smell of Dial soap and Johnson's baby
shampoo and her perfume. And then I remembered a pungent
tobacco odor. It took me a moment to realize it was not the
smell of my mother but of my father, who had died in Vietnam when I was nine years old.

I have no idea how long she washed me. In fact I have
no memory of anything else that night. I hadn't slept more
than a few hours in the past three days. Somewhere along
the way the gentle abrasion of the washcloth and the smells,
real and remembered—soap and perfume and tobacco
smoke—faded into dreamless dark.

CHAPTER 27

MARION CHEEVER MADE a big deal about giving Peach-tree Investigations five grand for the work we'd done—despite the fact that the contract only required that she pay us in the event we recovered the original painting. Since the "original" *Late Afternoon* had been a fake, her contract with the gallery was voided and Reliance wasn't out a thin dime. For Marion, it was the best news possible.

For me, it was the worst: no painting, no hundred grand. And no hundred grand equalled bankruptcy at high noon.

I'm not entirely sure why I bothered to show up for work at all. I don't know when to quit, I guess, is the answer.

So I sat there all morning, staring out the window at the parking lot across the street. What I found, from my careful observation, is that not much goes on in a parking lot: people park their cars and then they walk down the street. Not exactly a revelatory experience—but then I'd about had my fill of revelation for a while.

Around ten a courier showed up with an envelope marked URGENT!!! I recognized the handwriting as my mother's. There was no question in my mind what was in the envelope. I'd told Mom about the missing hundred grand the night before, about the impending demise of Peachtree Investiga-tions, so there was no question at all: she'd whipped out her checkbook and written me a check for a hundred thousand dollars. Mom to the rescue.

Only this was a rescue I couldn't accept. I could let her bathe me, console me, even buy me a silver lamé dress. But I couldn't take a hundred-thousand-dollar loan from her.

I love my mother, but I'm thirty-four years old and I will not, can not, *must* not let her run my life.

Every so often I'd get up and have another cup of coffee, then I'd go sit down again and stare out the window. A couple of times I would make a move to pick up the envelope, but then I would stop. I couldn't even bring myself to touch it.

It was a strange feeling. Ten years I'd been working at Peachtree Investigations—going from junior to senior investigator and finally to a part owner and de facto head of the firm. Ten years of busting my ass in here and now it was all going to slide into the drink.

Every few minutes I'd look at my watch, waiting for the magic moment when we would be officially broke.

I didn't feel sad or desperate. Something would turn up. I could go work for one of these huge international outfits like Pinkerton's—an experience that would probably be as deadening as being an associate at Underhill, Tabb, LaFollette, Gold & Pearcy. Or I could hang out my shingle and scrape along for a while on my own doing domestic cases, car wreck investigations and process serving for down-market lawyers. It wouldn't be much fun, but it would be all right. Whatever happened, I would be okay.

I looked at my watch. Eleven fifty-three.

"Aw screw it," I said finally. Then I picked up the cardboard envelope, tore it open, felt around for the check that I knew would be there. A piece of paper rustled around and I tweezered it in between two fingers. Just feeling it made me depressed. After fighting it all these years, I was finally going to give in to my fate and let Mom rule my life like she did Walter's.

I hesitated, settled into the chair. Then went ahead and pulled the check out.

Only it wasn't a check at all but a letter, a handwritten note on Mom's cold-pressed French stationery.

The message said:

My lovely girl,

I would offer you all my financial resources in a heartbeat, but I know you would never accept my money. You're too proud to take my help. And I understand that. So I just want you to know how proud I am of you and how much I believe in you. Whatever happens to your business, just remember that I love you.
Love, Mom.

I started to cry. I don't know whether I was more disappointed in myself for underestimating my mother, or in *her* for not sending me the goddamn money. Before more than a couple of tears leaked out, I heard someone pushing the door open and I looked up, wiping hastily at my face.

Imagine my surprise. Gunnar Brushwood, in the legendary flesh!

The Legend ambled into my office. Well, ambled is not the right word. Hobbled is more like it. But he hobbled in an ambling sort of way. He was wearing his legendary bush jacket and his legendary Aussie hat, and there was a huge bruise on the side of his legendarily rugged face. His right arm was in a cast and his left ankle was taped up inside his sneaker.

"I'm sure it doesn't interest you in the slightest," Gunnar said in his genially hectoring low-country accent, "but the ordeal is over and I am entirely safe."

I sighed.

Gunnar smiled coyly and lowered himself slowly into the chair on the other side of my desk. I knew I was in for a very long story.

"Before you say another word," I said, "you better haul your butt out of that chair and get me the money."

"Money?"

"The hundred grand you walked off with."

"Oh," he said, raising his eyebrows dismissively. "*That*." And he slid an envelope out of the breast pocket of his bush jacket.

I made the call to my account rep over at NationsBank, and once he relayed to his boss the fact that I had a cashier's check for $100,000 sitting on my desk, everything seemed just a hair less urgent. We set a time for me to come over to his office—3:15 that afternoon. Evidently that was soon enough to stave off the wolves in the NationsBank legal department.

CHAPTER 28

I T WAS ABOUT an hour later when Carl Fontaine's partner walked into my office.

"Lieutenant Hagee," I said. "What's up?"

"Let me ask you a simple question," the detective said.

"Sure."

"Do I look like a horse's ass?"

I suppose I probably blinked. You could practically smell the anger coming off this guy. And I didn't have the slightest idea why.

"You want to explain?" he said. "You want to take even the feeblest little stab at explaining what in hell's going on?"

I scratched my head. "Did Major Fontaine forget to put your leash on this morning?" I said. "Or is this some kind of good-cop/bad-cop thing."

"Fuck Carl Fontaine!" he said.

"I'm sorry," I said. "But I really don't know what you're talking about. I've had kind of a stressful weekend, and unless you plan to be a little more coherent—not to mention pleasant—I'm going to ask you to leave."

He strode across the room and threw a color photograph on my desk. "Look at that!" he said. "Tell me what you see."

It was a picture of Charlie Biddle lying on the floor with a small hole in her temple. Her right eye was swollen slightly, like somebody had punched her, and there was some blood on the side of her neck. She was lying just as I'd seen her when I opened my eyes this morning. Just as the police had found her.

I pushed the picture away. It made me sick.

"What's wrong with you?" I said.

"I'm sure being a private investigator and everything, you've made some study of basic forensics. Look at it, Sunny!" Then he threw down another picture, a close-up of the wound. It was just a small, red-rimmed pucker mark bordered on one side by a half moon of very white flesh and on the other by an arc of hair. I glanced at the picture, then turned them face down.

"If you're trying to make me feel nauseated," I said, "it's working."

"Stand up!" Lt. Hagee said.

"Huh?" I just looked at him.

Hagee charged around the desk, yanked me out of my chair, spun me around roughly, and started putting cuffs on my wrists.

"Ow!" I said. "That hurts!"

"You have the right to remain silent," Lt. Hagee said. "Do you understand this? Anything you say can and will be used against you in a court of law . . ." He went through the whole Miranda litany.

"What are you charging me with?" I said.

"For now? Obstruction of justice. Later, who knows, maybe murder."

While Hagee was busy pushing me toward the door, holding onto me by the chain between my handcuffs, Sean McNeely poked his head around the corner. "Uh . . ." Sean said, "I guess now's not a good time to ask when I can pick up my paycheck, huh?"

I sat by myself handcuffed to a chair for about an hour in a small interview room down at the homicide unit, before Maj.

Fontaine came in and set a cup of coffee in front of me.

"Whew!" he said. "What a *day*, what a *day*."

I glared at him.

"Coffee?" he said. "I can get sugar, cream, whatever you want? Or maybe herbal tea? Juice? Coke?"

I just looked at him.

He unlocked my cuffs.

"First thing," Fontaine said. "I want to apologize for my partner. I don't know what goes through that boy's mind sometimes." Then he started talking about a boat he wanted to buy when he retired, how he wanted to move down to the coast, do some deep sea fishing.

"Look, I'm sure on any other day, I'd be very interested in your retirement plans," I said. "But today? No, forget it."

Fontaine looked at the floor as though I'd embarrassed him. "I'm sorry. I'm sorry." All part of his shtick. "Look, about this obstruction of justice thing, Sunny, that's gone. There's no paperwork done, you haven't been booked in or anything, so we can just forget about that."

"Okay . . ." I said.

"And Lieutenant Hagee, I don't know, the kid just pops off sometimes, I don't know what gets into him."

He was still looking at the floor, shaking his head wearily. Suddenly he looked up and all the vacant-old-guy stuff had evaporated. His black eyes were hard as stone. "But, sweetheart, you gonna have to come clean. You really gonna have to tell me the truth about what happened this morning."

I studied the detective's face for a moment or two, trying to figure out what he was talking about.

"Look, I'm being straight with you, Sunny. No more Uncle Tom Fontaine. No more playing around. So I need you to be straight with me."

"I don't—"

"No, no, sugar. That's the wrong approach. See, we in the position right now where we got to re-evaluate everything—*everything*—that you've told us so far. All this stuff, all these strange little loose ends, all these places you coincidentally been showing up when people start getting dead? Nah, sugar, it don't add up. Now Lieutenant Hagee, he tends to rush to judgment on these matters.'' He winked at me. "But I'm sure you got a good explanation for everything."

I rubbed my wrist where the cuffs had chafed me and tried to figure out what he was talking about.

"I thought he showed you the photographs, Sunny."

"Of Charlie Biddle? Yeah."

"Well, of *her*, yes, but more specifically of the *wound* in her head."

"To be honest with you I didn't look at it very carefully."

Maj. Fontaine made a show of searching around in the pockets of his miserable coat till he found the evidence photographs, then he put them on the table. "Why don't you take another look?"

I pushed them back across the table. "No," I said. "If there's something significant about them, you tell me what it is."

Lt. Fontaine stood up, came around the table and pointed his index finger at my temple, moving it closer and closer until it touched my skin. I could see his reflection in the two-way mirror. He had his thumb up in the air like kids do when they're making a gun with their hand.

"When a weapon discharges," he said, "extremely hot gases are expelled from the barrel. From a distance in the range of here to here—" He pulled his finger back from my temple until it was four or five inches from my head. "—those gases are so hot that they burn the flesh right around the bullet's entry point."

Then I understood what he was getting at. Only . . . it didn't make any sense.

"From here . . ." He pulled his finger back farther until he was a couple of feet from my head. ". . . to here, small pieces of burning gunpowder are expelled from the barrel in a cone-shaped pattern. They tend to tattoo the skin with little black dots which we call stippling. The further back the gun, the wider the pattern of the stippling. But then obviously after a certain point the gunpowder burns out in the air or eventually doesn't even hit you at all. Outside three feet or so, no stippling. Nothing but a nice clean hole.''

Fontaine backed up until he was leaning against the two-way mirror. He was still pointing his finger-gun at my head. There was a lazy smile on his face.

"There was no burn mark on the entry wound," I said wonderingly. "No stippling either."

"Ergo, somebody else shot her."

I shook my head. It didn't make sense.

"Now you told us that there was one shot, right?"

I nodded dumbly.

"But the thing is, Sunny, there were two bullet holes in the room. One in the floor and one in the wall. Based on the blood spatter evidence, the bullet that went into the wall was the one that killed Miz Charlie Ludmilla Biddle Rutskoi Whatever-Her-Name-Was."

"There was one shot," I said firmly. "One shot killed her."

"The bullet that killed her hit a brick wall, flattened right into the brick. All I had to do was peel it off and put it in a bag." He held up a plastic evidence bag with some writing and an evidence tag on it. Inside was a lump of splintered, mushroomed, flattened, deformed metal—part lead and part copper. "On visual inspection, this appears to be what's known as a jacketed hollow-point. Now, Sunny, I weighed this bullet on a very accurate scale. Came out to about nine point five two grams. As you know the measuring system generally used for bullet weight is something called avoir-dupois, the unit of measure for which is called a grain. Nine point five two grams converts out to a hundred and forty-seven grains."

"I'm not—"

"Listen!" The detective glared urgently at me, his finger still pointed at my head. "A hundred and forty-seven grains is about the size of a standard police-issue nine-millimeter bullet. The weapon that was found in Charlie Biddle's hand was a twenty-five caliber. A standard twenty-five cal round goes about forty grains."

It took me a second. Maybe more than a second. Because the whole thing failed to add up.

"You're saying it wasn't her gun that killed her," I said. He nodded.

"Impossible," I said. "I was standing right there. She had the gun in her hand and I closed my eyes and the gun went off and I opened my eyes and she was dead."

"Try again," he said.

"Impossible."

"Maybe it was an accident," he said. "She made a move for you and you had a gun in your—"

"It's not *possible*!"

"Okay then, maybe there was somebody else in that room with y'all. Somebody you're trying to keep out of trouble."

"That's not *possible*! I was there!" I heard myself getting shrill, verging on the hysterical.

"Let's don't get too committed to words like possible, impossible, none of that. Hm? Let's go with *mysterious*!" Maj. Fontaine widened his eyes, and waggled a long finger at me. "Mysterious, now that's a word that gives you a little leeway."

Suddenly I had a cold, sinking feeling in my gut. "Could you stop pointing your finger at me," I burst out. "It's making me nervous."

"And what you need, Sunny, is a whole bunch of leeway right now. Otherwise?" He brought his thumb down like a hammer falling on a gun. Then he lowered his hand.

"I'm just as mystified as you."

"That's fine. I'm comfortable with mysterious." He walked across the room, thumped on the mirrored glass with his knuckles. "Lieutenant Hagee, he's standing behind this here window—the Lieutenant, he's not in his comfort zone with a mystery and so he gets all bent out of shape. Not me. I *love* a mystery. Makes me feel alive!" His eyes were bright.

I stared at him bleakly.

"All I'm saying, Sunny, tell me exactly what happened. Let's get all mysterious together." A brief smile touched his lips.

I started telling the whole thing again, everything that I could remember about what Charlie had said, what she had done. Finally I got to the part about the end of our conversation, the part where she shot herself—or that's what I thought had happened. "I guess . . . she was talking about how it didn't matter what happened now, that it was all over or something like that. And at that point she lifted up the gun." My skin crawled as I thought back on that moment. It all seemed very slow in my mind. "I guess I wasn't completely sure whether she was going to shoot me or shoot herself—I just knew something bad was going to happen. So I just closed my eyes."

The interview room was completely silent for a while. After a minute I realized that I had closed my eyes again, trying to somehow shut out everything that had happened. Everything that was *happening*.

When I finally opened my eyes, Maj. Fontaine was sitting across the table from me, studying me like a laboratory specimen. As soon as he saw that I was looking at him, his face changed into one of sympathy. But it was too late: I'd already seen what he was really thinking. "Sunny," he said softly. "Sunny, sugar, that just don't make a lick of sense."

"There was somebody else in the room," I said. "There had to be. Somebody else shot her."

It sounded so lame, so ridiculous. I had a sudden odd slithering feeling in my chest, like I had an hourglass inside of me and the sand was running out, emptying, sliding away.

"Who?"

"I don't *know*!"

His eyes were utterly impassive now, trying to cover up how ridiculous that sounded.

"Look," I said. "Ron Widner must have told somebody who then told Charlie that Gunner was supposed to be meeting this informant. Otherwise, how would Charlie have known to be there in the first place?"

"Go on," Fontaine said.

"So whoever Ron told, they must have told Charlie. But for some reason, they wanted Charlie dead. So they showed up at the loft before I did. They waited until Charlie showed up, and then they shot her. They must have been in a closet or something. And since I had my eyes closed, I didn't see them." Suddenly I was excited by my theory. "There's no phone in the loft, right? So I had to leave to call 911. As soon as I was gone, they fire Charlie's pistol into the ceiling so that forensics will show the gun's been fired. Then they take off."

Fontaine said, "Uh-huh. I could see how that might happen." But of course he was just playing along with me. It didn't sound even vaguely plausible. Unless you'd been there.

So we went around and around and around for a while. But each time we'd end up back in the same place: my eyes closing, the startling crack of the gun, my eyes opening again to find Charlie Biddle slumped on the ground in a widening puddle of crimson.

In other words, we got nowhere.

Then he started asking me about Leslie-Anne Gilmartin's murder and then Terry Yokum's and then Leslie-Anne's and then back to Charlie Biddle again. All I could do was tell him the truth. But it didn't seem to be enough.

Somewhere along the way I looked at my watch and suddenly I realized how late it had gotten. We'd been in here for a couple of hours: it was getting close to three o'clock.

I was due over at the bank with my $100,000 check in exactly seventeen minutes.

"Oh, my God!" I said. "I've got to go right now!"

Maj. Fontaine looked at me curiously. "Sunny, no offense, but you're gonna have to kind of keep the calendar clear here until we get this whole business resolved."

I shook my head. "This is a total emergency. I can come back in an hour, but I *have* to go."

"Sunny . . ."

"Am I under arrest?"

Fontaine shrugged. "Not at this precise moment."

"Then I'm leaving." I grabbed my purse with the check in it, stood up.

"Ah," the detective said. "Well! In *that* case I guess I will have to place you under arrest."

"Oh for godsake." I tried to shoulder by him, but he grabbed me by the elbows and pushed me up against the wall.

"Sunny Childs, I'm placing you under arrest for the murder of Ludmilla Rutskoi, also known as Charlie Biddle. Please place your hands behind your back."

"Wait!" I screamed. "Wait! I have to go to the *bank*!"

From the other side of the glass I could hear someone's muffled laughter.

CHAPTER 29

THEY BOOKED ME, they fingerprinted me, they strip-searched me and gave me an orange jumpsuit with the words *Fulton County Jail* stenciled on the back, and then they put my purse and my clothes and my watch and my earrings in a red plastic hamper with a number on it.

I don't remember a lot about the next couple of hours. There was a jail cell; there were some other women in orange jumpsuits, some of them sullen, some crying inconsolably, some angry; there was a smell of White Diamonds perfume and disinfectant; there was that slithering feeling again: like sand was running out of my chest.

I lay down for a while on a wooden bench. My body had become leaden and flaccid.

Eventually a large female cop with a mole above her eyebrow and a clipboard in her hand came out and called my name in a loud voice. When I came to the cell door, she checked the wrist band with my name on it against the paper on her clipboard, then put me in leg shackles and a pair of handcuffs—both of them attached by a jingling stainless steel chain to a leather belt that she cinched tight around my waist.

"Don't you think this is overkill?" I said.

"You don't shut your smart little mouth, I'll hogtie your skinny ass," the cop with the mole said.

I shut my smart little mouth.

CHAPTER 30

THE FEMALE COP with the mole over her eye took me down a hallway to the back of the building and out into a room that looked like a loading dock only it was completely enclosed by windowless concrete walls. A brown van that said FULTON COUNTY SHERIFF'S DEPARTMENT on the side was idling in front of a steel door big enough to drive a truck through.

The cop took me over to the van, handed a clipboard to a thin sheriff's deputy with glossy black hair, a mustache, and dark sunglasses. He and the female cop had a brief conversation, then he handed her some keys and walked off.

"Silly-ass sheriff," the cop muttered as she opened the door of the van. "Ain't *my* goddamn job, put you in here. Ain't *my* goddamn job, put your stuff in here. Sheriff feel like going to the baffroom, next time better do it on his own goddamn time."

She pushed me roughly into the back of the van, slammed the door shut, locked it with a key. The whole back of the van was a cage: the floor was heavy steel, and the grimy windows were covered with a steel mesh that was spotted here and there with rust. I watched the female cop open the back door of the van and stow the red plastic hamper with my belongings in it on a rack behind the holding cage. After a while the thin deputy with the mustache came back and hopped in.

The big steel door opened slowly, and the van rolled out into the sunshine.

I don't think I have ever felt so hopeless and wrung out as at the moment that van began to move. As an investigator I had been in contact with the criminal justice world, of course, but to feel it from the inside is a whole different thing. My entire sense of self had always been predicated on keeping control of my life; now suddenly I was thrown into a huge machine the sole purpose of which was to control *me*, to eliminate all freedom, all choice, all latitude from my life. And it was not a benign machine. It was a machine that held me in contempt, a machine in which might was right, in which people could shout at you, belittle you, physically attack you—and there was very little you could do about it.

I'd heard the first thing that happens in prison is that other women try to steal your shoes. I looked down at my feet, wondered if I'd have the strength and will to hold on the scuffed pair of suede ankle boots I was wearing. Suddenly they seemed a lot more important to me than any pair of shoes I'd ever had. They seemed like the most important things in my life—almost worth dying for.

How quickly the mind adapts to repression and confinement.

We drove for a while, and I stared listlessly out the window. The leather belt around my waist squeezed me so tightly that it was hard to breathe, and the shackles were biting into my ankles. The van meandered through town, then cut down Edgewood and got onto the ramp that took us northbound on the I-75/85 Connector. We had been driving for a couple of minutes when something struck me.

"I thought the jail was down on the south side of town," I said.

"First time in prison?" the deputy said cheerfully. There was something about his voice that seemed familiar.

"Yes," I said.

"Well, then lesson number one is you don't ask questions of a law enforcement officer. Lesson number two, you do exactly what we tell you."

"Yeah, well I still think you're going the wrong way," I said.

The deputy took off his hat, set it on the seat next to him. Then he took off his glossy black hair and peeled off his black mustache, tossed them to the side. He turned around and smiled.

"*Sean?*" I said.

"I don't know if you remember looking at my résumé," he said, "but I was a Fulton County Sheriff's Deputy for a while."

The slithery feeling was getting really strong, and the belt was tight around my waist and I could barely breathe at all.

"Yeah, the Sheriff's department, boy, what a bunch of numbnuts. They're dumber than security guards. Driving prisoners around, guarding courtrooms, all they understand is paperwork."

"I don't get it," I said.

"I come in with my old uniform, a couple of the right pieces of paper, they just let me drive right off with a van. Tell 'em, yeah, buddy, just got transferred over from bailiff duty at Magistrate Court. They say, 'Sign here,' I put Deputy Ron Widner down on the form, they don't even notice it doesn't match my ID. 'Here's the keys, ta-ta, have a nice drive.' "

Sean laughed.

"So it was you?" I said, not quite believing it even as I said it.

"Then you show up at the jail, flash some more paperwork, tell them you got a special transport, taking this lady prisoner down to Superior Court for a bond hearing, sign here, initial there, thanks a million, y'all take care now. All you got to do is know the procedure."

"That's why you went to the bathroom and made that female office put me in the van: so I wouldn't see your face clearly."

"You think I didn't know procedure? I *always* knew procedure." I got the scary feeling that Sean was way far gone, having an argument with somebody about something I didn't have much to do with. "I knew more procedure than everybody in the entire sheriff's department. Makes me sick just thinking about it. Procedure, procedure, procedure. How about some daggum police work!"

Suddenly his voice softened. "Yeah, I got mixed emotions about law enforcement," he said. "I could have been a great cop. But these jerks, it's the Peter Principle all over again. The people that rise, they're all bureaucrats, paper-pushering, brown-nosing yes-men. A guy gets in there wants to kick butt and take names, do some *real* policework, lock up some *real* bad guys—hey, does he get any recognition? Shoot no! He gets all the crud work, all the duty assignments nobody else wants, the fat desk clerk paper pusher bureaucrat cops babbling at you all the time about some *form* you didn't fill out . . ."

"Why don't you just take me back to the homicide lockup?" I asked.

Sean laughed harshly. "I mean a prisoner tries to escape, what are you supposed to do? 'Stop or I'll fill out some forms on you!' No, you have to lay down the law. Thin blue line, man. Nobody understands this anymore. A prisoner escapes, you got to shoot him. That's just the way it is. And then the FOP won't even back you up when they put you on suspension! Your own brothers in blue won't stand by you when they take away your badge. Any wonder that the crackheads and the dope dealers are taking over America?"

"Is that why they fired you from the sheriff's department? You shot a prisoner?"

"He was *escaping*, Sunny!"

"Yeah, well."

"The only cops that can survive today are little homosexual bureaucrats driving around in their little office on wheels, filled out paperwork every time they turn on the daggum siren. Here's a form for responding to a cat-in-a-tree call! Here's a form for undoing the daggum snap on your holster! You think I'm joking? Here's a form . . ." Sean looked in the mirror. "But, hey, are my problems boring you?"

"Sean. Before you get in more trouble . . ."

"More trouble. Uh, Sunny, I just killed three people this weekend. How much more trouble could I get into?" A harsh noise came out of his throat that might or might not have been a laugh.

"I don't understand what you're doing," I said.

When the interstate divided on the north side of downtown in front of the big red neon sign on the Equifax building, Sean took the I-85 North fork then turned off onto the Piedmont exit. "Well, here's my dilemma," Sean said. "I could take you way out into the dingleberries and shoot you someplace—but I'd have to drive forever in this extremely conspicuous vehicle. So I'm thinking I'll just find an unused industrial building and take care of you there. Nice big space, not many people around. Someplace like, oh, an artist's studio. It ought to be as safe a place as any."

"Why?" I said again. My mouth had gotten dry and my tongue felt like a piece of rough, crumbly limestone.

"Those guys down at homicide, they're not geniuses. But they're not morons either. They'll eventually figure out that it wasn't you that whacked all those people. Once they get to that point, it wouldn't take them too long to sniff me out. They'd find that I worked as a security guard at Charlie Biddle's gallery six or eight months ago. They'll find that I asked my jerkoff brother-in-law Ron a suspicious number of questions about this private investigator who was a quote unquote good friend of his. They'll find that I was working for you during part of this thing. They might find phone records showing that Charlie Biddle and I have talked on the phone an awful lot over the past six months. They start look-ing, eventually things'll pile up.''

I sat there sliding back and forth on the black vinyl seat each time the van took a corner until we reached the rundown industrial building where Terry Yokum had his studio. Sean pulled the truck around the back of the building next to an abandoned loading dock where we couldn't be seen from the road.

Sean parked the car, put on a pair of surgical gloves, wiped the steering wheel and the door handle of the van, then jumped out with his pistol drawn and unlocked my door. "If you scream," he said. "I'll shoot you."

He prodded me with the gun and I shuffled up the concrete steps next to the loading dock. It was bad enough with the shackles on, but I was so scared that my vision was going gray. I could barely keep my feet under me. Sean used a pick gun—just like I had—to get us in the door on the ground floor. A pick gun is a device that looks like an electric screw-driver, and opens the average lock as quickly as a key. Sean put the pick gun back in his pocket, shoved me into the big, dark freight elevator, and pressed the button that took us up to the second floor.

When the elevator stopped, he pulled open the telescoping metal gate, ripped the crime scene tape down and herded me into the big studio. There was still blood splashed across the green and ochre paint shavings on the floor. But now the blood had turned a brownish black. There were no chalk marks where the body had been. I guess they only do that in movies.

"I still don't get what I'm doing here."

"Well," Sean said. "I guess it could be anywhere. But I don't want them to lose the significance of this whole thing." He looked at his watch. "Ron should be here any time now."

"Ron?" I said.

"Ron." Sean yawned, stretched. "He would be what we call 'the fall guy.' The homicide guys go down to that big colored gal in the lockup—the one with the mole?—and they say, 'Who picked up Sunny Childs?' She flips through her stack of paperwork, says, 'Right here's his signature. Looks like Deputy Ron Widner.' They show her a picture of a white guy with black hair and a mustache, and say, 'Is this him?' She goes, 'Yeah, that looks about right.' "

"You don't look anything like Ron. Even with the mustache."

"Don't kid yourself, Sunny. They've done studies on this. Facial identification is notoriously unreliable." He smiled. "Especially across racial lines."

"This is really stupid, Sean. You'll never pull it off."

Sean looked out the window. "Daggummit!" he said. "Have you ever noticed Ron is never on time for anything?"

"Yeah," I said.

The room was silent for a while, but Sean kept glancing at me as though expecting me to say something. Then I realized: he wanted an audience, somebody he could tell what he'd done, somebody he could gloat to.

"Go ahead," I said. "Explain to me what a sinister genius you are."

He lifted his chin slightly, studying me. He was dying to talk.

"Seriously," I said. "We're just sitting here. You're going to kill me. What's the harm in telling me how you put this whole scheme together?"

"Okay," he said finally, pretending to be grudging about it. "Here's what happened. Six months ago, I was talking to Ron. He's tells me about this fascinating woman he's met. Private investigator, so on so forth. Any time he uses the word 'fascinating' to describe a woman I know he's screwing them. Anyway, he tells me about how this fascinating private investigator does a lot of work for insurance companies, how sometimes they ransom back things that have been stolen from them. Interesting, I think. And I file it away.

"Couple weeks later he helps me get a job as a security

guard for another fascinating woman he's met. Ron meets a whole lot of fascinating woman, I've noticed. Don't know why my sister ever put up with that guy. Anyway, this second fascinating woman owns an art gallery. So I work for her, guarding some stuff when she's moving a bunch of expensive paintings from her old art gallery to her new store. We chit-chat about this and that, and I bounce this idea off her. What if you bought a really expensive painting, stole it from yourself, then ransomed it back? Just a hypothetical conversation, right? And she says, yeah, but the problem is coming up with enough money to buy a painting that would get you enough ransom to justify the risk. So I said, well, what if you just had some kind of forgery? See? It was all my idea. All *mine*!''

He sounded insistent as though I might have thought he wasn't up to the task of inventing a scam.

I shrugged. "Hey, I believe you.''

Sean was still staring out the window.

"Let's go, Ron,'' he said. "Jeez.''

"You were saying,'' I said.

"Oh, yeah. Well, anyway I didn't think about it too much, until like a month later Charlie Biddle calls me up and hypothetically wants to know if I could help her stage a bogus break-in to her gallery. I said hypothetically, yeah, if the money was right. Bottom line, we get together, we sketch out a deal. I'm gonna get ten grand to bust the wall down, go in, take this painting. She, meanwhile, has hired this guy—also for ten grand—to forge this painting *Late Afternoon, Pont Aven* or whatever the heck it was called. And she hires some old poot from New York to give it a bogus authentication, and she goes to Eastern Europe to trump up a bunch of fake documentation and all this junk.'' He pointed at his chest with the pistol. "*I* drove it, though. Once the idea came, *I'm* the one who made sure everything stayed on track. She just happened to be the one who knew about the art stuff.''

"Fine," I said.

"Now here's the key thing: my original idea was to steal the painting and ransom it. But once you throw in the forgery angle, why bother to ransom it? There's more money in the deal if you just take the insurance. If it was a real painting, you'd want to collect the ransom and then sell it. But since it's a fake—and you didn't pay but a fraction of the 'real' value for it, there's no need to go through the risk and hassle of the ransom.

"So anyway, the appointed evening arrives, Charlie turns off the alarm, I steal the painting, turn the system back on, drive off as the alarm bell starts to ring. So far so good. I figure I've done my part, get my cut, walk away, right?

"Only the next morning I'm in for a shock. Charlie calls me up and says that somebody's called up Reliance Insurance saying they've got the painting and they're willing to ransom it back. We figure obviously it's got to be that daggum midget Terry Yokum. He's the only person who could have another copy of the painting. Problem is, it's not like we can tell the people at Reliance, 'Hey, the guy you're dealing with is trying to pawn off a fake on you.'

"So I tell Charlie that once we find out where the meeting is going to be, I'm going to have to show up and figure out a way to, shall we say, dissuade Terry Yokum from going through with the ransom. So what I do is I follow you to the place you're supposed to do the ransom. I pull up and park the car while you're sitting in that shed and I climb over the fence, start looking around for Terry. Only—big surprise—instead of Terry, I find his girlfriend. I get the drop on her, tell her she and Terry are gonna have to give up on this brilliant little idea they had. But, no, she's got to be little miss potty-mouth, telling me that I can go, uh, F myself." Sean pursed his lips disapprovingly. "So next thing you know, it's F you, F this, F that. Well . . . it wasn't what I meant to have happen." Sean's gaze drifted for a moment. "It just . . . I kind of lost it. Made me mad—you know?—

the way she's carrying on and everything? So it was her fault really. If she'd just been a little more polite, hadn't used all that bad language, everything would have worked out."

There was a long silence.

"Goshdang it, Ron! Where *is* he?" Sean started pacing up and down.

"So you found the painting in her car and took it?"

"Right. Burned it. But then after that, Terry beats us to the punch again. We didn't know he'd painted like ninety of these durn things." He waved his hand around the room at all the green-and-ocher landscapes. "But this time he gets busted and they figure out it's a fake. So I tell Charlie, hey, look we got a problem here . . . but we also got an opportunity. The problem is that Terry is the only person that's been busted. And Terry knows he didn't kill Leslie-Anne. So when the DA starts pushing the fraud charges along, he's gonna try to plead out by giving up me and Charlie and hanging Leslie-Anne's, ah, demise on us. The opportunity, on the other hand, is that we still have a chance to get the claim paid off for the painting.

"But obviously the key to fixing our problem is the same thing as the key to seizing our opportunity: Terry Yokum has got to get dead. By this point, I've managed to con my high-and-mighty brother-in-law into getting you to give me a job, so I'm working from the inside. So my problem at this point is getting rid of Terry before he tells anybody what's going on. So as soon as I hear you say that you're meeting Terry that night, I know that I've got to beat you to the punch. I show up there, take out the midget."

I thought about it. Listening to his story had started to calm me down a little, getting my mind back in the groove of trying to put all the pieces together. "Something puzzles me, though," I said. "I didn't tell you about this alleged meeting. I told Ron. How did Charlie find out about it?"

"I was standing there in your office when Ron showed up. Remember? I'd just run his credit bureau on the computer. So you asked me to give you and Ron a couple minutes together. All I had to do was stand there outside the door and listen in on the conversation.''

''So as far as you knew at that point, there really was an informant?''

''Right.''

''Then why send Charlie? Why didn't you go there yourself?''

Sean wrinkled up one side of his face thoughtfully. ''Well, by this point I'm realizing that I'm in this thing pretty deep. But my part of the action was really not a sufficient amount of money for the amount of risk I've undertaken. I mean, I come up with the plan. I do the break-in. I take care of Terry and Leslie-Anne. I'm doing all the work, but she's only paying me ten grand. I'm way out on a limb here, Sunny, and I'm not getting paid what I deserve!''

He seemed to be appealing to me so I just nodded my head like, yeah sure, anybody would feel the same way if they had walked a mile in your shoes.

''So by this point I'm telling Charlie that ten grand ain't gonna hack it. I want half of the three fifty from the insurance. But she won't give me any more. So when I hear about Gunnar supposedly having this informant, I tell Charlie: okay, you want the whole nut for yourself, you can take care of this informant yourself. And she kind of hesitates—but then finally she realizes she's got no choice.

''So then I sneak in here ahead of time and hide behind a big tarp over in the corner. My plan is, I'll take out everybody. Take out Gunnar, take out the informant, take out Charlie, burn the place down. Then I'll ransom one of these other paintings back to the insurance company. It doesn't matter if Charlie's dead or not—the insurance company's still thinks there's a real painting out there somewhere and they still have to pay the claim if they don't get the painting back.'' He squinted at me. ''Why are you looking at me like that? I mean, I did all the work, I deserve everything I can get. It's only fair.''

There was a sudden angry noise from the other side of the room and we both jumped. But it was just the door buzzer. Sean went over and pressed the button that unlocked the door downstairs.

After a few seconds we heard the old motor start grinding, sending the elevator down to pick Ron up.

"So what happened?" I said.

"Well, I wasn't expecting *you* there," Sean said. He looked momentarily shame-faced. "I mean . . . Well, I guess, what happened is I kind of like you, Sunny. You're a nice person and . . ." His voice petered out, and his face colored.

"You couldn't do it," I said. "You couldn't shoot me."

"Well, not for a second. I mean, I shot Charlie and then I'm sitting there looking at you and I just can't seem to pull the trigger. And watching you I realized that the way the noise was reverberating around in there, you thought it was *her* gun that went off, that she'd killed *herself*. So I'm just hesitating there, trying to make myself do what I need to do and then I think, hey, what if everybody thinks she shot herself? And you go hauling butt out the door. So once you're out of earshot I fire Charlie's gun into the ceiling and take off."

I said, "You know there's no way you'll be able to pull off the ransom now. I told the cops that the painting was a fake from day one. Reliance knows. It's all over with."

Sean shook his head sadly. "Shoot. A hundred thousand bucks down the toilet. What a daggum shame." He shrugged. "But I still can't have you wandering around knowing what I did."

The elevator started clanking and grinding again.

"So what happens next?" I said.

"Oh, the usual. I dictate a murder-suicide note to Ron. He takes responsibility for killing Terry and Leslie-Anne, he's distraught, his wife's leaving him, he and his mistress have botched this ransom thing they planned together, everything's falling apart, blah blah blah, now it's time to end it all!'' Sean laughed, then opened his mouth and put his index finger inside. ''Good-bye cruel world.'' He looked over as the elevator door clattered open. ''Ah! Here's Mr. High-and-Mighty himself!''

Ron stood in the doorway of the elevator looking at Sean with a puzzled expression on his face. Then he looked at me. I don't think he noticed the gun yet.

''What the hell is going on, you moron?'' Ron said to Sean.

Sean pointed the gun at Ron's face. ''You know some thing, Ron,'' he said. ''Your patronizing attitude really bugs me. You never took me seriously.''

''That's because you're a fucking idiot,'' Ron said.

Sean turned to me. ''See what I mean? This is what I have to put up with.''

Which is when something struck me.

''Hey, Sean,'' I said. ''You still want the hundred grand?''

Sean looked at me suspiciously.

''This is crazy!'' Ron said.

''Shut up, Ron.'' Sean and I both said it at the same time.

''What are you talking about, Sunny?'' Sean said.

I looked at him and smiled. I don't know if it was much of a smile, but it was the best I had. ''Let me tell you a story . . .''

CHAPTER 31

I SAID, "YOU take a woman like Marlene Getty and you think: why would anybody stand by her? A stumbling drunk, a liar, a cheat? That's how Gunnar said she was—even when he first knew her. Well, I'll tell you why: because a long, long time ago—back when she was young and beautiful and rich and helping somebody out cost her nothing she did something really decent (I don't even know what) for Gunnar Brushwood. And Gunnar does not forget these things."

Sean said, "Who in the heck is Marlene Getty?"

"Wait! Listen!" I said, holding up both hands toward him, palms out. "See when Gunnar went down to Venice, Florida last week, Marlene Getty was living in a single-wide trailer subsisting on Mr. Boston vodka and store brand neapolitan ice cream. Looking at her, he told me, you would have thought she'd been born old and ugly and drunk and poor. She got a $637 Social Security check every month for some sort of dubious disability which allowed her to pay the trailer hook-up, the cable TV bill, the lights, and precious little else. A phone, for instance, was out of the question. She had had to call Gunnar from her neighbor's mobile home . . ."

Before I could go any further, Sean stuck the gun in my face and said, "Wait a minute wait a minute wait a minute. This is a bunch of baloney. You're just stalling."

I turned my head so my temple was snugged up against the barrel of his gun. "Right here, Sean. Squeeze one off. Right in the temple, okay?" I could feel a muscle trembling in my thigh. It must have been only a second that I paused, but it seemed like forever. "But remember this, Sean: after the TV news tells about how Sunny Child's killer missed out on a hundred thousand dollar jackpot that was right under his nose, it's not going to be me that has to get up every morning and look in the mirror and say: 'Hi, there. Aren't you the dumbass that threw away a hundred grand?' "

After a minute Sean backed up, lowered the gun slightly, "This better not be some kind of Scheherazade act."

"Just let me tell the story, you'll see what my point is." Of course one reason for telling the story *was* to slow him down so I could figure a way out of this thing. But that was only half the point.

"Anyway," I said, "Gunnar told me that Marlene Getty had called from the neighbor's place last Monday saying something about a stained glass window, impending death, a murderous Cuban guy. Very confusing. Saying that she needed Gunnar's help, that Gunnar was her last hope. Gunnar, Gunnar, oh Christ please Gunnar. He could tell that she was drunk and very possibly insane. But not so drunk that she forgot to mention: oh yes, and when you come to save me, could you bring along a hundred thousand dollars?

"It would all be repaid, she had said. It would all be repaid.

"Now Gunnar *knew* Marlene. Gunnar *knew* she was a liar. He knew that if he brought a hundred thousand dollars down there to Venice Florida that the odds of her trying to run some kind of scam on him were pretty damn good.

"But that evening he got on the first plane to Florida anyway. He owed her, you see, for her kindness—whatever kindness it had been, this kindness he never exactly described to me. And in the breast pocket of his bush jacket he had a cashier's check for a hundred thousand dollars.

"That is why—despite his unreliability, his ego, his bush jacket, and all his self-aggrandizing bullshit—I am proud to call Gunnar Brushwood my friend. He's a rare man.

"Anyway when he got down there to Venice, he found Marlene in her trailer, drunk, selling herself to some Haitian truck driver. She claimed she didn't recognize Gunnar, that she didn't even remember making the call the night before.

"But leaned against the back wall of her tiny bedroom Gunnar found a very old and grimy stained glass window that had obviously been removed intact from a church. It was a picture of St. What's-his-name—the one who got all the arrows shot into him?—and some happy little green demons looking up from the ground."

"St. Sebastian," Ron said.

"Right. St. Sebastian. So anyway Gunnar took Marlene by the arm and dragged her back to the room and pointed at St. Sebastian and said, 'What is this?' And she started trembling and saying, Oh Gunnar, Gunnar, Gunnar!'

"It took her a while to get sobered up and coherent, but he finally got the story out of her: turned out she was doing a modest amount of whoring to pick up where her Social Security left off. Semi-pro, you might say. Somehow, while engaged in that trade, she'd met this guy, a writer she said, who wrote books in Cuban that nobody read."

"Cuban isn't a language," Sean said.

"Thank you for that sharing that nugget of wisdom," Ron said sarcastically.

I continued. "I'm just telling the story the way Gunnar told me. Anyway, this Cuban writer had come to Marlene one day and asked if he could store something in her house. She figured, you know, drugs or something, so she made him pay her some money upfront—which he was ready enough to do. But then he drives up with a U-Haul and he and a couple of his Cuban buddies unload, not drugs, but this great big heavy church window.

"Next day she sees on the TV that her Cuban writer and

two of his buddies have been murdered. The cops speculate that it's drug related—but then in Miami that's what the cops always say if nobody rushes up to them and confesses within five minutes.

"Now, Marlene Getty, she's absolutely sure this is about the stained glass window, so she's petrified. But she's weak from years of living on a diet of ice cream and Mr. Boston vodka, and it's possible there's some physical disability, and besides she has no car and no money and no friends. So how's she gonna drag this four-hundred-pound window out of her trailer—much less haul it off to a dump or someplace where she can ditch it? Needless to say, calling the cops is out of the question.

"So what course of action is left for her to take? Only one: she gets stinking drunk and falls asleep in front of the television.

"When she wakes up, there's a bunch of Cuban guys in her trailer. And get this, she claims they're dressed like a SWAT team: black fatigues, submachine guns, lace-up boots, all kinds of straps and belts and grenades hanging off their clothes. But not cops. Definitely not cops. Gunnar asks her how she knows. She says: 'Because they're all speaking Cuban.'

"So these Cuban SWAT guys find the window and then they speak Spanish into a radio and after a minute or two the door opens and this blond guy in a trench coat comes in. Blond hair, ice-blue eyes—like a Nazi colonel she says—but speaking Spanish. Then he turns to her and he says: 'Congratulations, Miss Getty. You get to be our bait. If you leave this trailer, we'll kill you.'

"Then he starts speaking Spanish again, ordering the SWAT guys out. Five minutes later, boom, everybody's gone. And that stained glass window with St. Sebastian and all the arrows sticking out of him is still there in her bedroom.

"Well, she waits for a couple of days and nothing happens. She runs out of neapolitan ice cream. Still she waits because she doesn't want this blond guy to kill her. She waits another day. Nothing happens. She runs out of Mr. Boston. *Now* she's got a problem. She weighs her situation: stay in the trailer and dry out . . . or go out for vodka and get killed.

"Naturally, being a worthless drunk, she goes out for vodka. Only—to her mild surprise—she doesn't get killed.

"So at this point Gunnar says, 'Where does the hundred grand come into the story?'

"Marlene says: 'What hundred grand?'

" 'You told me on the phone I needed to bring a hundred grand.'

"She shrugs. 'Well, what can I say, I was drunk. Maybe the Cubans said something about a hundred grand. I don't remember too good.'

" 'So you don't need the hundred grand?'

"She gets this look in her eyes and says, "Wait a sec, are you telling me you brought a hundred thousand bucks down here? For me? Just because I asked?'

" 'Sure,' he says. 'Not to give you permanently, but . . . '

"Before she gets a chance to start thinking of a way to scam the money off him, the door bangs open and in come a bunch of little dark-skinned guys in guayabera shirts, pointing guns everywhere. One of the guys goes: 'Where's the fucking window?'

"Gunnar points back into the bedroom and says, 'We have nothing to do with any of this, okay. Take the window and go. We never saw you.'

"So the guayabera shirt guys start wrestling the window out of the trailer. Only just as they're about to get it out the door somebody throws a smoke bomb through the door, there's a bunch of shooting, guys in black looming out of the smoke. Gunnar tries to draw a pistol he's got holstered under his bush jacket, but before he gets the chance someone jumps on him. In the smoke he can't tell if it's a guayabera shirt guy or a SWAT guy. All he can tell is that that the guy's fists are very fast and very hard. Next thing Gunnar knows his face is bleeding and his arm is broken and these guayabera shirt guys are all lying around dead and these Cuban SWAT people—or whatever they were, maybe they're Mexicans, maybe they're Argentines, who know?— but whatever they are, they're hauling him into a van with no windows.

"They put a mask over his head and off they drive. After a while, they stop somewhere and hustle him out of the van. He can't see anything, but he can tell from the smell that they're somewhere near the ocean. He figures he's dead, right?

"Only they just take him inside a house and lock him in a room. After a while he takes the mask off, finds that Marlene is lying on the other side of this bare room. No windows, no beds, no furniture at all. He's in a lot of pain from his broken arm and his hand is swelling up, turning purple.

"A few hours later a man comes in wearing a black executioner's mask over his head. Gunnar figures now finally he's dead, but instead the man sets his broken arm. They lie there in the room for days. On the second day Marlene gets the DTs. Every once in a while someone in a mask comes in and feeds them. Marlene gets better. But when she's finally sobered up, she just nags and complains all day. Turns out she's a lot nicer when she's drunk. Terrible combination—the fear, the boredom, the waiting, the nagging. Poor old Gunnar's about to go nuts.

"So one day they're waiting for the food guy to show up and they wait and wait and wait and they're getting really hungry. So Gunnar finally bangs on the door. Nobody comes. He tries the handle. Miracle of miracles, the door swings open.

"They walk out and they're in this empty house. It's like a beachfront rental property—lots of cheap plaid furniture, crummy knives in the kitchen, gas grill on the deck. And the place is stone empty.

"So they walk out the door, hike down the street and call the cops."

At that point I stopped talking and looked around the room at all the paintings.

Sean looked at me, waited for a while. "Go on," he said expectantly.

I looked at him and shrugged. "That's it. That's the end of the story."

His brow knit up and he stared at me. "Well, what was up with this stained glass window?"

"Beats me," I said.

"Gunnar never found out? Who were the SWAT people? Was it like a CIA thing or something?"

"I have no idea," I said.

"Well . . ." He looked angry suddenly. "Then what in holy heck is the point of the story? What happened to the woman? Did she sober up, change her life or something?"

"No. Last time Gunnar saw her, she was sitting there in her living room spooning neapolitan ice cream and Mr. Boston out of a dogfood bowl."

"Well, what about the cops? Did they figure out what was going on?"

"Nope."

"And the hundred thousand dollars? She asked Gunnar to bring all that money down there for nothing?"

"Apparently."

"Well, then who were the guys in the guayabera shirts?"

I shrugged. "The cops took a wild flying guess, said it was probably drug-related."

"That's the dumbest story I ever heard in my life!" Sean narrowed his eyes and scrunched up his forehead. "Why did you waste my time? Where's the punch line? Where's the pay off?"

"Oh, right," I said. "The point is, these SWAT people frisked Gunnar to find if he had weapons, but they never noticed this envelope stuck in a pocket of his bush jacket."

"*What* envelope?"

"The envelope with the hundred thousand dollar cashier's check in it," I said.

"I'm still missing the point," Sean said.

"Okay, you're the expert on law enforcement procedure," I said. "When a prisoner gets booked downtown, their effects get taken away and put in this red plastic hamper. When they get transferred from the booking center to the County Jail, what happens to their effects?"

Sean studied at me. "They get transferred with the prisoner."

I nodded. "So that means my purse is in a red plastic hamper in the back of the van down there."

Sean said, "Gosh dang it, quit beating around the bush!"

"That check I was telling you about? The one for a hundred thousand dollars? Gunnar gave it to me. I put it in my purse. My purse is out there in the van."

Sean's eyes widened. "A hundred grand?"

"Here's your dilemma, Sean," I said. "It's a cashier's check made out to Gunnar and then signed over to me. From your perspective the only problem is that *I've* got to be the person who cashes it. So if you kill me, that check is just a worthless piece of paper. You want to get the money, you better keep me alive until I can cash that check. Now either we can work out a deal for the hundred grand, or we can't. But if you kill me now, you lose the whole thing."

It may sound like I had some kind of brilliant plan cooked up—but I didn't. Truth is, Sean's Scheherazade comment was pretty much on the mark: I figured the longer I stalled, the more hoops I could get Sean to jump through, the more chance we'd have to get away.

"Okay," Sean said. "First I need to get Mr. Brilliant Architect locked up." He threw a pair of handcuffs to Ron and said: "Cuff yourself to that drainpipe." He pointed to a stained washbowl on the other side of the room.

Ron did as he was told. "You're going to regret this, you

idiot," he said once he'd secured himself to the pipe.

"If I hear you yell or bang on the floor or anything like that, I'll shoot you the second I get back up here," Sean said. "Let's go, Sunny."

We went down to the van and got the red hamper and came back up.

"It's in my purse," I said. Sean eagerly ripped open the red hamper and my purse fell out, skittered across the floor a few feet from the sink where Ron was crouched.

I leaned over and picked it up. Sean hurried toward me, reached for my purse. "Give me that," he said.

I guess Ron must have loosened the drain trap under the sink somehow and gotten his cuffs freed from the pipe, because at that moment he sprang forward, tackling Sean and grabbing hold of the gun.

Sean stumbled backward jerking on the gun, trying to get it free. He was taller and slightly heavier, but Ron had the edge in adrenaline and momentum. They slammed against the wall, pushing and pulling on each other, then fell over and rolled on the floor. Bits of Hooker's green and pale ochre paint scrapings stuck to their hair and their clothes, and I could see Ron's hands grabbing for the gun and then there were a couple of loud bangs and Ron jumped up and said, "Hey, now! This is not right!"

Sean was still lying on the floor looking up at him with this funny vacant look in his eyes and for a second I thought Sean must have been the one who got shot. But then Ron's knees buckled and he fell over backward and I could see a red stain spreading across his belly.

For a minute nobody moved. Then, without giving it any particular thought, I grabbed a paint bucket full of gunky-looking liquid which I assumed was turpentine and hurled it into Sean's eyes. He start howling and pawing at his face. From the smell of the liquid, I realized it was not turpentine but gasoline. Terry must have been using it as a paint solvent.

Sean fired a couple of blind shots in my direction, both of which missed me.

The flash from the gun apparently set off the gasoline, though, because suddenly he was covered with a wobbly, smoky veil of fire. The gun went off again.

I ran into the freight elevator, slammed the door and the steel accordion gate and pressed the down button. The elevator seemed to take forever, but finally it started moving. I could still hear Sean screaming in agony when it stopped. I yanked open the gate and started running out the front door of the building. Well, running is not exactly the word to describe moving at maximum speed while your feet are attached to each other by a foot and a half long piece of chain. But whatever it was that I was doing, a ridiculous shuffling hopping sort of thing—I kept doing it all the way down the road, down past the row of old brick warehouses, past a Citgo station, under the interstate and up onto Monroe Street. Finally, gasping for breath, I slowed down, my ankles bleeding painfully from slamming against the shackles.

I looked behind me. There was no Sean back there, nobody following me at all.

I realized I had to find someplace to call the police and to get an ambulance for Ron. I ran toward the closet building, a goofy round brick building that looked like a squashed grain silo but which was actually a bank. I threw open the front door and ran into the bank yelling, "Call nine one one! Call nine one one!" Everyone in the room was staring at me. I guess it's not everyday you see a woman running into a bank wearing prison shackles and an orange jumpsuit with *Fulton County Jail* stencilled on the back.

Nobody moved. The room went utterly silent.

I hustled up to the counter, my shackles jingling, where a teller stared at me, frozen, eyes wide. "Nine one one, for godsake!" I said. "Someone's been murdered!" Everyone was still staring. The teller hesitantly picked up her phone, made the call, set the phone back on the hook.

On the back wall of the bank I noticed there was a big digital clock with the NationsBank logo on it. The red letters said 4:57 PM. Three minutes till closing time.

At which point I realized that I still had my purse clutched in my hand. The purse with the hundred thousand dollar check in it.

"Oh . . ." I said, picking up a pen off the counter and signing the check, ". . . and could I have a deposit slip?"

CHAPTER 32

A COUPLE OF days later I had lunch with Walter.

"I don't know," he was saying. "I just got down there to the coast and I'm out there by myself in Gunnar's hunting cabin in the middle of this endless, smelly marsh and I've got nothing but my guitar and a couple of paperback books and all of Gunnar's fancy Italian shotguns, and I start thinking: What the hell am I doing here?"

"Uh-huh," I said.

"Really. I mean in the grand scheme of things, what the hell am I doing on this planet?"

"Maybe you should have bitten off something a little less ambitious."

"No," he said. "It was the right question. So I try to write some songs. I sing a couple of James Taylor tunes. I drink some of Gunnar's booze. I swat mosquitoes. I watch the sun go down. But what I realize is that I feel like a big blank. Like a book with no words in it. I don't have any songs I'm dying to write. I don't have any deep things I'm burning to express. You know? And after like a day of this I realize, hey, I'm just a lawyer who likes to sing and play a little guitar in his spare time."

"Oh, man," I said. "I feel sick to my stomach. I'm worse than Mom. I made you lose your job and everything . . ."

"No, no," he said gently. "Absolutely not. It was absolutely the right thing for me to do. All these years I've been moping around, feeling like I gave up music in order to do something really boring and tedious and adult. But realistically, music was just a youthful thing. I had fun singing and playing guitar in little bars, but it never would have lasted. I'm not tough enough to live that life for very long. So it wasn't really all that horrible to face the fact of who I really am, to realize I was going to have to come back here and beg to have my job back, to kiss ass and plead and prostrate myself and tell them I'd made a huge mistake, that I'd even take a pay cut and give up my partnership track if they'd just give me my job back.'' My brother smiled brightly at me. ''I'm serious. It wasn't that painful at all.''

I covered one eye with my hand. All these years I'd been pushing him to go back to singing and writing songs, and it wasn't even what he really wanted to do. I just felt so embarrassed and ashamed.

''God, Walter. I ruined it all for you. I screwed up everything.''

''Uh, actually, no. As it turned out, Mom trumped up this rumor through a couple of her rich lady friends. She told them that the reason I quit Underhill Tabb was that I had this mammoth offer from Alston & Bird. Immediate partnership, corner office, huge bonus plan. She even insinuated they were going to give me a Bentley as signing bonus. Can you imagine that? A *Bentley*? I mean give me a break, it was the most preposterous thing in the world. Anyway, Mom was sure that by spreading this bullshit to these judiciously chosen friends of hers, the word would filter back to the partners at Underhill Tabb. See?''

I gaped at him. ''She's unbelievable. Surely they didn't fall for it.''

Walter just laughed. ''Listen to this! I get home, there're like six messages from Gordon Maloof. Not Gordon, Junior, *Big* Gordon, the managing partner, whom I've barely even *met* before! I call him back, he wants to have lunch with me at the freaking Capital Club. That day! So I put on my Hickey Freeman suit, go down to the Capital Club and damned if they don't have a whole parade lined up for me: all ten litigation partners, plus Gordon Maloof. My God, they even dragged old Royce Gold in there, this ancient goat who's been in retirement for like fifty years. I sit down, there's scotch, there's steak, there's creamed spinach, there's another scotch, there's pecan pie, there's brandy. And not a word of shop talk. It's all quail hunting and trips to Italy and breaking in the new Porsche. We're all best chums, right? Just hanging with the old boys. Then they hand me an envelope. I open the envelope. I look around. I smile. They smile. Chums till our dying day."

I just shook my head in wonderment.

"It's a preemptive partnership offer, Sunny—I mean, so much money you wouldn't even believe it. Car lease allowance, my own private paralegal, bonus plan, the whole schmear. I look up, I smile. I say, 'Gosh, thanks.' Then, get this . . ." Walter raised his eyebrows. "They stand up and they applaud."

"So you took the offer."

"Damn straight."

"Well," I said. "Mom must be pleased as punch."

His shoulders sagged. "You're disappointed."

"No," I said, smiling feebly. "If it's what you wanted, I'm really happy." Then I gave him a big hug. I guess I was happy for him. I don't know. I'd invested a lot of emotion in poor old Walter, trying to make him out to be some sort of romantic artist whose big dreams were being crushed by a heartless and conformist world. When the reality of his life—isn't reality always this way?—was actually a lot more complicated.

As it turned out, Ron was okay. Apparently the bullet hadn't hit anything vital and he'd fallen down out of shock or fear. But when then the room caught on fire, he managed to stum-

ble up, smash out a window and jump down to safety. He
tore the anterior cruciate ligament in his knee, and lost a foot
of bowel to the bullet wound. But he made it.

Sean, however, didn't. There was a lot of flammable material in the studio and it went up fast, consuming Sean in
the blaze—along with all evidence of Terry Yokum's last
obsession. The fire station was only three blocks away—but
by the time they got to the studio, it was too late.

Ron confirmed my story to the police, told them that Sean
was behind the whole business, that he'd confessed to being
the mastermind of the scheme and the murderer of Terry and
Leslie-Anne and Charlie as well.

"No hard feelings?" Maj. Fontaine had said as he officially released me from custody.

"No hard feelings," I had said.

I'm such a liar. Truth is, I could have throttled the guy.

I called Ron's hospital room a couple of days later, just to
make sure he was okay, but his wife answered and so I hung
up without saying a word. I didn't see him again for at least
six months.

Then one day I ran into him at Oxford Books. Actually
he ran into me. I was poking around in the art section—after
this thing was over, I'd developed a mild preoccupation with
American Impressionism—when Ron came hustling around
the corner from the children's book room and banged right
into me.

"Oops!" he said.

"Sorry!" I said.

And then we stood there awkwardly for a few seconds. "I
guess I should have called you," Ron said.

"No," I said. "There was no point. It was already over
between us. We both knew it."

Ron nodded silently.

"Doing okay out on your own?" I said.

Ron gaze flicked over my shoulder for a moment. "Ellen

and I got back together," he said. "That whole experience made me do some very serious navel gazing."

"That's . . . good I guess."

"Yeah. I realized that I'd stepped over some lines a long time ago and that after a while I kept stepping one line further and one line further until my whole life had gone out of control."

I nodded. "I know what you mean."

"I'm not sure you do," he said.

I shrugged. "Your wife told me that she'd had you tailed. You slept with four women in three weeks. I'd call that out of control."

Ron's gaze flickered over my shoulder again. "Yeah. But that's not what I'm talking about," he said. His voice was almost a whisper.

I frowned, puzzled.

"How long did you know Sean?" he said.

"What, four or five days maybe."

"Did he seem like a real effectual guy?" he said. "A real go-getter?"

I studied Ron's face. That's when something occurred to me, something that had nagged me vaguely for a while. Ron had told the police that Sean had confessed to everything. But Ron hadn't been there when he confessed. So how had he known?

"Sean could kill a man," Ron said. "He could do what he was told. But he was never exactly anybody's archetype of the criminal mastermind."

I felt a cold breeze blow across my neck.

"I mean Charlie gave him ten grand. Do you think if he was the guy behind this whole plan, the guy who worked out all the details, who executed the whole thing—that he would have agreed to do it for a piddly little ten grand? Doesn't it seem likely that someone else was involved, someone who was more focused and deliberate, someone who had contacts in the art community, someone who would have been in a position to put Terry in touch with Charlie and Charlie in touch with Sean, someone who was in a position to influence you to hire Sean so there'd be an inside guy to keep an eye on your investigation?''

With a sense of queasy recognition I thought back to the resentment that Sean had showed Ron in the studio, the way Sean had seemed strangely eager to take credit for the entire plan. He kept calling Ron ''Mr. High-and-Mighty'' . . . as though he was used to Ron ordering him around. At the time something about the whole scene hadn't seemed plumb and level—but I hadn't been able to put my finger on what it was.

''Why are you telling me this?''

Ron had a strange look on his face, like a drunk who has woken up to find himself cold sober with terrible memories from the night before. ''I want you to understand that I've changed my life, utterly changed it. I've stepped back behind the line and that's where I'm going to stay. Forever.'' He paused. ''That's all I'm going to say. I've got *her* to think about now. Her and the children.''

I stood there with the picture book I'd been looking at still clutched in my hand, trembling.

''Anyway,'' he said. ''Nothing can be proven.''

He turned and walked back into the children's book room. I watched, wondering why he had told me this.

It was possible that he was worried I would put everything together and develop suspicions about his role in the forgery and the killings. In which case, was his carefully framed speech something he had come up with in a Machiavellian attempt to head me off at the pass, to dissuade me from going to the police? Or had he—as he claimed—actually hit a wall in his life that had sparked a genuine metamorphosis in his character?

Lie or truth?

Sometimes these things are hard to know.

And maybe there was no final, unambiguous answer.

Maybe two men moved inside him: one a virtuous ideal, the other a liar and a cheat and a killer. Maybe Ron didn't even know for certain whether he spoke the truth, the two halves of his soul twisting and struggling within him until it was impossible to tell them apart.

After the case was closed and the insurance issues straightened out, I managed to get hold of Terry's only surviving forgery. It's hanging from a rusty hook on my wall, unframed, a mute testimonial to my belief that every so often it's not the truth but the lies that set us free.

So maybe I'm a dumbass and an easy mark and a self-deluded fool. But I choose to believe the best of Ron. I choose to believe that we can change, that we can become finer, that we can shed the worst parts of ourselves like old skin. Like the graffiti said on the Dumpster where Terry Yokum's body was found: we fall that we may rise.

I mean if we don't have faith in that, then what *do* we have?